The Hor

The second in the Sword of Cartimandua series
By
Griff Hosker

Published by Sword Books Ltd., 2013
Copyright © Third Edition

A CIP catalogue record for this title is available from the British Library.

Contents

Chapter 1

Fainch

The closer she was to Mona the more uplifted and confident she became; she felt as though the spirits of her dead sisters were protecting her from the eyes of the Romans. She and her sisters worshipped Mother Earth. She had spent many years, as a child and as a young woman, on the island of Mona where she studied and worshipped with the Druids. She had been there when the Romans had first desecrated the holy places and slaughtered the Druids. As she had hidden and watched she had seen the ruthless Romans slaughtering the priests and priestesses, killing those that she thought of as family. She swore an oath then on the holy places that she would have revenge and drive these Romans from her land she would create an alliance which would defeat these Romans who had disembowelled and crucified the only man she had ever loved; Vosius son of Lugotrix a king killed himself by the Romans. They had killed the only chance she would have of happiness; she would ensure that they had none. In this part of the world, the Romans had a habit of killing before questioning; they had learned the hard way that even the women of this wild land could be as ruthless as the men. Fainch did not find it difficult to travel at night time, in many ways she preferred it and she relished the deep dark cloak it afforded her. The most dangerous time was when she came to the shore of the mainland and she could see the sacred island of Mona rising above the fierce, raging white tops. She would need to find a way across the wild waters.

She watched the Roman patrols from a rocky crag and she quickly realised that their regular patrols were her salvation. They would not deviate from their routine. She smiled to herself. This was the Roman weakness, their predictability. This would be their downfall. She would need to persuade the warrior leaders that they could defeat the Romans but first she had to get across the straits of Menaii. The journey from her home had been difficult as she avoided the Roman patrols. On the second night, she had rested enough and she left the safety of her cave and made her way down to the shore. The winds had abated somewhat and she knew that this was her best chance to get across the short stretch of water. She headed purposefully towards a wooded beach. She had remembered the place from the time she had spent growing up in this area and training to be a priestess. The coracle was invisible unless you knew where it was; the straggly undergrowth masked it completely. Fainch quickly checked that it was without holes and then she launched it into the waters. She made sure that the prevailing current worked in her favour and her strong strokes, which belied her size and sex, took her swiftly to the opposing beach. It was the work of moments to hide the boat and then she prostrated herself on the sands of the sacred shoreline. "Mother I have returned. Sisters I have returned. Vosius we will have revenge."

It was a day later that she arrived at the sacred grove of Porthdafarch on the tiny island off the westernmost tip of Mona. It was wild and windswept with cliffs filled with screaming gulls. The beautiful trees which had covered the grove were long gone, ruthlessly ripped out by the Romans who feared the priests more than any warrior. The bones of the priests still littered the valley floor and Fainch was careful to avoid them.

By the time she had found the sheltered dell it was becoming dark and the rocks and crags took on sinister shapes. To Fainch they were reassuring for they were of the land and of the island and as such, they would protect her. She lit a small fire with the dried wood she had carried for just such a purpose. She filled her water skin from the bubbling stream which erupted from the valley side and drank her first draught of this elixir of life. As soon as she tasted it she felt whole again. She half-filled the small cauldron and then began the potion and incantation which would help her to see her sisters. Removing her clothes she knelt in front of the cauldron wafting its powerful smell into her face. The pungent, acrid aroma rose in tendrils of smoke barely visible in the purple cloak of the night but they acted as a magnet. Even with her eyes closed, she knew that her sisters had arrived. Without opening her eyes she murmured, "Welcome sisters, join me in the invocation."

Her hands were taken in the hands of the priestess on each side of her and she slowly opened her eyes. There were six priestesses joined in this circle of power and like Fainch they were all naked. Some were old with leathery skin hanging off skeletal bones whilst two of them were barely more than children with tiny breasts and pale skin. Even though most did not know each other their chants joined and unified them into a single being. The following morning saw all seven of them lying exhausted in the dell by a dead fire.

When they had awoken and dressed they sat in a circle nibbling on dried hare meat. One of the older ones recognised Fainch. "It is many years since I saw you, child. The years have been as kind to you as they have been cruel to me."

Fainch shook her head. "Do not think like a man Maelwyn. We of the sisterhood know that beauty is inside as the true beauty of our Mother Earth is hidden from others."

The others nodded at the wisdom of the statement. Already she was acknowledged as the leader. "Is this all that remains?"

Maelwyn coughed and spoke for them all. "There are a couple of others on the main island but it is hard to move around for the Romans hunt us still. The people hide us but still, we are found. Your coming is the first hopeful sign that the Mother has not forgotten us."

"You should know that the Mother never forgets as the Romans will discover. Are you ready to defeat them?"

Their eyes, no longer tired, lit up and they all nodded eagerly. "I came here to find the survivors and to worship for one last time at this holiest of places. You are right; the Romans will hunt us until we are dead so we must move away from their eyes. We are the last; we seven sisters have one last duty to perform before we join with Mother Earth." They leaned forward ready to devour Fainch's words as manna to a beggar. "The Romans can be beaten. Caractacus had the right idea. Join all the tribes together. Too many kings and queens," she spat the last word out as an insult, "looked to themselves and what they could gain. We will each travel to a different part of the land. I will go to the North, you to the Trinovantes, you to the Iceni, you to the Atrebate, you to the Silures and you two shall travel to the far south. We must persuade all the leaders of the tribes that they should all rise as one. We shall use the feast of Eostre as the day we attack. Use all your power and magic to aid these kings and princes for doubt it not, the Romans are still a mighty army but we can defeat them."

Without speaking they joined in a circle and held hands. Their last chant was much shorter but of such power that at the end they stood silently. Fainch kissed each of them hard and full on the lips as they left. Maelwyn had tears in her eyes for she knew that Fainch was the chosen one spoken of by the old ones and she was honoured to be part of the campaign that would throw the invaders back into the sea and give the land back to the people and the priests.

Cresens

Gaius Cresens, the ex-quartermaster of the auxiliary cavalry, felt lucky. He could have been captured and crucified for the murder of Cartimandua and the attempted murder of Ulpius Felix. He had been lucky because he had managed to turn his ill-gotten gains into jewels that were more portable. He had had the luck to avoid capture and secure a berth on a small sailing ship heading for Gaul. The luck he had had in escaping Eboracum deserted Gaius Cresens almost as soon as they reached the mouth of the estuary and the sea. As the small boat headed southeast towards Gaul, a fierce storm began to blow from the east. Hail and snow mixed with winds which threatened to tear the tiny sail from the stick of a mast. The captain and sailors quickly tore it down lest they be driven onto the shore which was littered with the sharp teeth of submerged rocks just waiting for the opportunity to rip out the bottom of any boat foundering there. Cresens huddled near to the stern with his possessions gripped in his white-knuckled hands. He had worked and plotted a long time to acquire his riches and he had no intention of letting the sea have them. The sailors cursed the overweight Roman as they tried to control the doomed ship.

6

"Release all three anchors!" screamed the captain as he tried desperately to slow down their inexorable slide towards the shore. The helmsman, a mighty young man, clung on to the rudder for his very life, seemingly fighting the ocean on his own. The anchors slowed them for a time and the captain issued oars so that they could try to control the direction of the ship's slide. Cresens was beginning to think they might just survive when disaster struck. One of the stern anchors was torn away by a particularly fierce gust and the ship began to cant and tip at an alarming angle. The captain's dilemma was that to stop the cant of the ship he would have to cut the remaining anchors and if he did that then they would be wrecked upon the shore. It was one decision that the doomed sailor did not have to make as the frayed ropes of both anchors gave way and the ship was hurled onto the rocks beneath the towering cliffs.

Cresens found himself in the water, still clutching his bag of possessions. Looking back later he realised that this had, in fact, saved his life for it contained enough trapped air to support him. He could hear the cries of his fellows as they hit the rocks or were dragged beneath the waves. He could see that the shoreline was quite close and, fortunately for him, he was approaching a sandy spit at the foot of a cliff. As he dragged himself onto the sandy shore he could see the ship being driven and dragged over the rocks to a small inlet. He suddenly realised that the reason he could see so well was that there were lights on the shore. He could see men and women with flaming faggots of wood. It looked as though the few sailors who had survived would be rescued. He saw the people with the lights reach into the water and drag the unfortunate sailors to safety. Just as he was about to reveal himself to these erstwhile rescuers he was horrified to see them slitting the throats of the men. They had been cruelly pulled from the sea and then slaughtered like seals on the beach. A sandy charnel house which soon became littered with not only the flotsam and jetsam of the wreck but the mutilated bodies of the Roman sailors.

Lying as flat as he could, he watched as the pirates plundered the bodies and the wreck taking everything of value. As callous as he was even Cresens found the savagery of these predators hard to stomach. It was dawn before they had stripped the shore of all that could be salvaged. His eyes followed them as they trudged up the valley to their roundhouses on the cliff tops. He began to see how they were so successful for they could see far out to sea and they were totally isolated in their cliff top eyrie. He began to plot and scheme; he would control these savages and become their leader. As he raised himself from the sand he saw a shape lying on its back half in the surf. It looked like a survivor who had missed the culling. He crept slowly towards the recumbent shape. It was a sailor from the ship. It looked to be the young helmsman whom he had seen and he recognised the immensely strong helmsman who had obviously been powerful enough to defeat the sea.

Cresens grabbed the arm which was lying in the sand and dragged the youth back into the shelter of the cliff overhang. He could feel the pulse throbbing in the boy's arm, he was still alive. Cresens took out his wine flask and poured a few drops down the sailor's throat. This was not an act of kindness nor even charity for Cresens intended to use the survivor as the first of his gang.

The youth coughed and spluttered, opening his eyes to view the person he thought had saved him. "Thank you, sir, I owe you my life. Are there others?"

Gaius realised the error made by the sailor but did nothing to correct it. "No. I am afraid you were the only one I could save."

"I will serve you until I have repaid my debt. "The smile which danced on Cresens lips was a cruel smile but the boy took it to be kindness. "My name is Atticus sir."

"And I am," Cresens paused. He had the chance for a new start in life and a new identity, Gaius Cresens died in the sea off this savage coast. "Just call me Master, it will serve."

"That I will sir. What now?"

"First we need to get away from here for I fear the natives are savages. "He gestured to the body ridden beach. "They slaughtered the rest of the crew. We are all that is left. There looks to be a path going south. North is uncharted territory but at least to the south it should be more peaceful."

The shocked look on Atticus' face bonded him even closer to Cresens. Together they headed south away from the valley, following the beach that Cresens hoped would lead to safety.

Streonshal

Gaius Cresens and Atticus peered over the boulder-strewn cliff. Below them was a small cluster of huts. They had travelled for many hours to avoid the murderous inhabitants of the settlement to the north. As they looked down they could see that there were few men.

"Should I go down sir? We need shelter tonight there is a storm coming."

Gaius shivered; he hated the discomfort of the wild. He preferred all the trappings of civilisation; it looked like he would have to wait for that. "No lad, whatever is down there we will face it together." Cresens was gratified to see a look of almost hero worship on the young man's face. In reality, he could not have cared less about what happened to the boy but he needed protection and if that meant playing a hero then he would do so. Patting him in a paternal fashion on his shoulder he added, "You keep your sword handy."

As soon as they were an arrow flight from the village the dogs started barking. Within moments the huts emptied and a swarm of people appeared. They were both pleased that none of the boys who faced them looked older than twelve summers and there were no men. Gaius Cresens held up his hand in the universal sign of peace. "We come in peace."

An old man said something in the local dialect, the boys looked relieved and the panic from their faces was replaced by relief. The old man said," I am the only one who speaks your language." Cresens looked at him quizzically. "I tended the horses at the fort at Derventio when the Romans had the fort."

The implication was not lost on Cresens for it meant that there were no Romans to see through his subterfuge. "Where are your men? And why do you all look so lean and hungry? The sea is close by you should be able to harvest the sea."

"Come into my humble dwelling sir and I will tell you the tale while we get you what little we have to offer." He spoke to the boys who raced off.

They entered a small roundhouse. The two Romans were pleased to see a small fire burning. As they sat down two boys came in with bowls filled with a warm liquid. Cresens looked at it suspiciously but Atticus began lapping it quickly. He grinned. "Soup! Tasty sir."

Gratefully Gaius Cresens drank the soup. In truth, it was not the best he had even drunk but half-starved as he was it tasted like ambrosia. As they drank the old man told his tale. "I am Jared. I am the headman of this settlement. We call it Streonshal. Until a few months ago we were a thriving community of six families. The men were fishermen and they provided good food for us all. Then came the night of the storm. None of them returned. Some of the boys went north to see if they had foundered on the rocks. They found them. They had wrecked on the beach at Stagh-herts." Cresens looked up questioningly. "The settlement in the next bay."

Atticus and Cresens exchanged looks. "Master?" Cresens held up his hand for silence.

"Continue Jared."

"They had been slaughtered by the animals that live there. The boys wanted to go there for revenge but I told them they would not survive."

"It is a sad story. Why do the boys not fish as their fathers did?"

"The savages took their nets and boats. We are poor as you can see; we have not the skills to make the boats for we lack tools and we grow weaker by the day."

Cresens nodded and an idea began to form in his mind. He had seen the effect an act of apparent kindness had had on Atticus. If he befriended the village in the same way then he would become the headman. Once he was in control he could expand. All it would take was a few denari. "It grieves me to see people treated this way. I will send my servant to Derventio to buy the tools you need."

The look on Atticus' face showed Cresens that he had gone even higher in the young man's estimation and he thought that Jared would burst into tears. "But sir why would you do that?"

"A simple kind act for I empathise with you and in truth, I feel I owe the gods for saving me and enabling me to save my friend here but if you felt the need to repay me then perhaps we could build me a house here and when the young men produce boats and then catch fish perhaps we could look to sell some and repay me."

"I will tell the people. Thank you." He grasped Cresens in a hug. The smell was so bad it nearly made him vomit but he managed to grimace his way through it and assure Jared it was nothing. They knew from the cheers that he had told the villagers of his idea.

"You truly are kind, master."

"We will be kind to these people Atticus but to those savages who murdered our shipmates and the good men of this village we will be ruthless."

Atticus face hardened. "Aye sir and you can count on me."

"I intend to, do not worry, I intend to." He had used and taken advantage of young men for twenty years in the auxiliary; he would continue to do so and to milk this community for all that they were worth.

Chapter 2

The New Governor 70 AD

Quintus Petilius Cerialis had spent most of the long journey from Rome still smarting from his briefing from Vespasian and his inner circle. He smashed his hand down angrily on the stern of the ship. Damn that Bolanus! How could he have been appointed as Governor when he managed not only to lose a valuable ally and client queen in Cartimandua but also nearly a whole legion. But for the fortuitous and timely intervention of an ala of cavalry then Rome's tenuous grip on their northernmost province would have been loosened not to say lost. His instructions had been quite clear; bring order to the province by whatever means. There was also an implied message of 'or else.' The Emperor knew the province well having served here in the early days of the invasion. Although preoccupied in the east if he had to come to Britannia to pacify it then Quintus Petilius Cerialis would suffer and his military career would be over.

He looked down again at the tablet in front of him which gave the numbers and dispositions of his forces. They were thinly spread. The second Augusta was still dealing with the insurgents in the southwest. The powerful fourteenth legion was already on its way back to take part in the wars in the east. The twentieth legion was with his most successful general, Agricola, subduing the west and the troublesome island of Mona. The Second Adiutrix was a newly formed legion and he could not rely on it yet. He had decided to base it at Lindum. The Ninth was Cerialis' own legion and he had been prefect during the Boudiccan uprising. He knew them better than any legion and, more importantly, he trusted them and their officers. He had two reliable, though committed legions, one new to the country and one brand new legion untried in any action. He had auxiliary units but he knew that any campaign would be won by the legions. The auxiliaries were only there, as far as he was concerned, to stop the legions from taking casualties before they could attack.

The sun was setting but the white cliffs to the north looked almost red. Cerialis hoped it was not a bad omen. In his experience, a good soldier needed good fortune almost as much as he needed brave soldiers and the right battlefield. He would have little time to spend at Camulodunum which was still in the throes of being rebuilt following the savage slaughter unleashed years earlier by Boudicca. He would have to race up to Lindum, the northernmost fortress before finally taking the Ninth to the new fortress at Eboracum. The new fortress was still being built and he needed to make sure he had a secure base from which to attack. At least his deputy, Sextus Julius Frontinus would be able to mop up the west and remove that headache. He would have to leave the second Adiutrix at Lindum, which was least settled.

They would be his reserve and he would have to test the mettle of the Ninth in the coming months. Bolanus had been given two years but Quintus knew that he needed success in less than a year for this new Emperor, who was familiar with the province, would not be patient. The Brigantes were about to learn a savage lesson at the hands of the new ruthless Governor.

North of the Dunum Fluvius

Marcus Aurelius Maximunius half turned in the saddle as his two turmae struggled to climb the steep banks of the river. They had left the newly built fort at Morbium before dawn and it was now nearly noon. The rest of the much depleted ala was some way behind awaiting a report from Marcus' two turmae. The first part had been easy for they had travelled across the new Roman bridge and up the partially paved Roman road which one day would become Dere Street but which was now an easier way of travelling in this road less land. They were deep in enemy territory now and Marcus was well aware that he had some fresh recruits with him. His old decurion, the fabled Ulpius Felix, would have trained them for at least another three months before going on such a hazardous patrol but there were so few experienced men that he had had no choice. He threw a leg over his horse's hindquarters and slid to the ground. "Rest the horses. Gaius put out two sentries."

Leaving his chosen man to manage the troopers the decurion climbed the slope and peered over the top, careful to avoid being silhouetted against the skyline. They were on the borders of Brigante territory and he knew little of the tribes who lived this close to the coast. He suspected they were allies of the rebel Brigante but he had no way of knowing. The Carvetii, the tribe which the dead Venutius had led also lived close to here. There were no allies. The best he could hope for was neutrals. They had seen no one since leaving their fort and this worried Marcus. It was almost a year since the battle of Brocavum when his great friend and mentor Ulpius Felix had died killing Venutius, the king who had ordered the death of Cartimandua Queen of the Brigantes. Just thinking about Ulpius made Marcus slide his hand down to the mighty sword he carried, the sword of Cartimandua. If the Brigante rebels knew that he wielded their most holy weapon then they would not rest until he was dead and it was returned to them. That was the main reason he carried it with him at all times; that way anyone who saw it would be on its receiving end and could tell no one.

Thinking back to the dark times after the battle Marcus remembered counting up the four hundred auxiliaries who had survived. Almost as distressing was the number of dead mounts. The result was that even after the vexillation returned from the abandoned Glanibanta fort they only had four hundred and thirty men and one hundred and fifty mounts. Even now they only had five hundred men and less than half were mounted, although the prefect, Flavius Bellatoris had promised them replacements of both men and mounts. Even the prefect had had to take on the role of Decurion Princeps as all the senior decurions had died in the mighty battle. He glanced back to the troopers. There was only Gaius and Lentius that he knew well. He had grown and changed dramatically from the eager callow youth of two summers ago. Now he was a battle-hardened veteran and Marcus knew it was only a matter of time before he would have to put him forward as decurion. He always missed Ulpius but at times like this, he missed his friends Drusus who was with Decius, Metellus and especially the irascible Decius Flavius now a decurion with the rest of the ala.

He turned back to view the distant woods and scanned them from east to west. He saw nothing. There was no movement and, surprisingly no birds. He was about to rejoin his men when he noticed a movement from the corner of his eye. He fixed his attention on the centre of the wood and he saw the warrior low down on his pony's back; it was the enemy. Which enemy he did not know but it was an enemy. He slid down the bank. "Mount!" He gestured to Gaelwyn their Brigante scout. "Belly up the rise and identify the warrior near the woods." The Brigante scampered up like a squirrel up a tree. "Gaius, take half the men and head east. If this warrior sees us I don't want him heading back in that direction. The rest of you we will head west. I want this warrior alive. You," he pointed to a young warrior," Er Flavius have your bow ready and take down his mount. Not the man. Got it?" He nodded a nervous reply and Marcus wondered about the wisdom of taking over forty untrained men as the main scouting party.

Gaelwyn quickly mounted his pony. "It is a Novantae." The way he said it implied that it was so obvious that Marcus should have known. He still could not distinguish between the tribes. Impishly he added, "From the west. They are close allies of the Carvetii."

"Thank you, you wise old, "He paused, "man. Right Gaius you take your men down the valley and we will head straight across. Ride!"

As the best horseman in the ala Marcus soon found himself ahead of his men and he had to rein in his mount Moon Child. In time his troopers would become more proficient but the battlefield was not a good classroom. The enemy scout saw them and turned, as Marcus had expected, east. Suddenly the file of riders following Gaius appeared and he whipped his pony around with a dexterity that impressed Marcus. He headed back towards the wood which worried the decurion as he would soon lose the heavy cavalry mounts in that tangled mass. "Flavius!" He shouted over his shoulder. He hoped the recruit would realise what was wanted. The boy galloped past unslinging his bow as he did so. His riding impressed Marcus who saw that he controlled his horse with his knees; all troopers were supposed to be able to do so but the decurion had found that many could not. The grain-fed mount quickly gained on the warrior who kept glancing back. Flavius first arrow overshot as the Novantae jinked right. The manoeuvre cost the fleeing horseman distance and the next arrow plunged into the horse's rear. Although not a fatal wound it made the mount more difficult to control and Flavius notched his next arrow confident that he could lame the horse. Marcus realised with dismay that the edge of the woods was a mere ten horse lengths away. The last arrow flew true and would have hit the pony on the right rear had the tribesman not repeated his jinking manoeuvre and the arrow struck the side of its head. It was killed instantly and pitched forward. The rider flew through the air to crash into the bole of a tree. The troopers raced forward in case he ran off but when they arrived he was still recumbent, he was dead.

"I am sorry sir. I did not mean to kill the beast."

"And yet you did." As soon as he said the words he regretted them. The boy had done all that could be asked of him. "Do not worry Flavius it was good shooting but the fates were not with us. Gaelwyn, search the body. I want a volunteer to find the ala." The words were barely out of his mouth when the thought rushed into his head. 'I should have detailed a man' for he knew who would volunteer.

He heard the voice cry, "Me sir, I volunteer."

He turned and looked; he was correct. It was Macro so keen he made Gaius, once the most energetic and keen member of the turma, looked like a dormouse about to hibernate. The truth was he was a very likeable young man. He was powerfully built, in fact, some said he would have made the perfect legionary for he would have been as a rock in line of battle and very hard working but he insisted on volunteering for everything. He was also so full of self-confidence that had Marcus asked for a volunteer to take on the whole of the Brigante he would have jumped at the chance. "Macro! Why I am not surprised? Do you think you can find the ala?" Gaius smiled for he knew as all the rest of the turma did that Macro would reply yes. "Forget that, stupid question. You could find the end of a rainbow, couldn't you? Don't answer that you moron! Find the ala and tell them that we have found a Novantae scout. "He looked at Gaelwyn for confirmation and the Brigante nodded. "That means that the main force may be nearby. And don't flog your mount into the ground." The young man grinned, saluted and rode off south whooping loudly. "And don't be so noisy about it!"

Gaelwyn searched the body and the men began hacking chunks of meat from the dead pony. "Don't cook that yet;" ordered Gaius anticipating Marcus' next command, "the rest may be close enough to smell the smoke. At least we will eat well tonight."

"Find anything?"

"He is a Novantae scout and he has not ridden far. He has no provisions so I assume that he would be eating with the main party which means they are, "the scout looked up at the sun "within camping distance. He is lightly

14

armed," he held up a dagger and sling. "I would think that he is young and he has yet to fight in a battle." He gestured at the bare arms; there were neither tattoos nor trophy torcs."

"Ride back along his line of march and see if you can see the main party. Don't get spotted!"

Gaelwyn snorted in a derisory manner. "Had I have been him you would still be lying in the valley awaiting food." In one movement he mounted his pony and sped off back towards the valley. Marcus knew that the wily little warrior would not be spotted. He was the best scout since poor Osgar had met his end defending Cartimandua when she fled Stanwyck.

"Rest your horses. Let them eat the grass. Gaius, detail two sentries. I will be, "he looked around and pointed to a large oak, "under that tree asleep." The young troopers looked at each other with amazement. Their leader the infamous Marcus was sleeping with the enemy close by. To the young men, he was all they would ever want to be.

The sun was beginning to set by the time Gaelwyn returned. He sniffed contemptuously at the butchered carcass; the look told the recruits that he would have done it better. Gaius nodded to him and they went over to the dormant decurion. "I can hear you both. Well, "he said raising himself onto one elbow, "where are they?"

The Brigantes did not use time as the Romans did; instead, they used instead the time it took to get to places. "Half a Roman march."

"Good that means they won't smell the smoke and they won't surprise us. Gaius get that meat cooked I am starved. How many men are there?"

The Brigante shrugged, "A couple of war bands. Twice your number of cavalrymen."

"So over a thousand and they are Novantae?"

"Yes, mainly on foot with some ponies. Some have armour," he added meaningfully.

Just then they heard the hooves of the rest of the ala approaching. Marcus noticed with pleasure that the decurion of the lead turma was his old friend Decius. "I knew the minute we started cooking you would be here."

"Well, as long as you are not cooking I will eat. And what are we eating?"

"Pony."

"Excellent."

The look of horror on the faces of the men of Marcus' turma was universal. They had counted on eating the pony themselves not sharing it with the voracious Decius. "Spoils of war, Decius spoils of war, although I may invite you to our fire." He looked around. "Where is the prefect?"

Decius grinned, "I think he finds the saddle a little harder than he used to. He has stopped a couple of time to," he grinned conspiratorially, "consult the map. He will be along later." He looked over to his turma. "Lucius picket the horses and put out some sentries." He looked up as he saw Gaius. "Well young Gaius how is it being a chosen man?"

Before he could answer there was a cough from behind the decurion who turned to reveal Macro. "I found them sir and I brought them," he added lamely," as fast as I could."

The three of them looked at him, then each other and burst out laughing. "Marcus I see you have a new Gaius to replace this sober young leader I see here."

"Well done Macro, rub down your mount and rejoin your comrades, you have done well."

Macro strode off as though he had completed the labours of Hercules. Gaius shook his head. "He will now regale the rest of them with the details of the whole journey from beginning to end. There will be warriors he had to avoid, rivers to swim,"

"Carrying his horse of course," added Marcus.

"And all without a wound," finished Decius.

"Ah, I see my young recruit has ridden with you today then?"

"Is he always so keen?"

"Always but to be fair he is a good trooper and would do anything for our decurion here," smiled Gaius. "He hero-worships him a little."

"Before you get too big for your own boots young Gaius I would look at myself first." Decius was delighted when Gaius blushed like a virgin and scampered off to the roasting meat.

Just then another familiar voice sounded. "Well done Gaius I love roast pony."

"Drusus there might be a little for Decius but a man of your appetite…"

"Think yourself lucky Lentius is with the rear guard or you would be eating mane and tail stew."

As they laughed and slapped each other about the shoulders Flavius Bellatoris rode up and gingerly dismounted. "I am glad that my decurions are so happy it makes an old man happy. How in Hades name do you do this every day?"

"I seem to remember Ulpius Felix told us tales of the two of you doing so yourselves."

"Aye," the prefect cackled, "but we were younger and fitter. This is a young man's game." He pulled Marcus over to one side and spoke quietly. "This will be my last campaign. When we return I will recommend you for Decurion Princeps that way I will get to sleep in a soft cot until my retirement." Marcus looked up in surprise. "Oh, you are ready. Old Ulpius knew that and we need experienced men with these, "he waved his arm vaguely around the camp, "boys. And now let me sit down and you can give me your report. I assume you have wine to go with the pony I smell?"

16

Marcus smiled wryly, "Would an old campaigner like me fail to anticipate his leader's comforts? This way. Gaius, food and wine. Come, Decius."

Later that evening when they had eaten sufficiently and drunk enough so that the prefect could sleep on the hard ground the three of them discussed the course of action for the following day.

"Why don't we just wait for the bastards here and ambush them?" The very blunt Decius always followed the line of least resistance.

The prefect smiled as Marcus gave the intuitive answer he knew he would. "This is their line of march; true for it is where we saw the scout. But the scout did not return, nor did his pony..."

"So they will wonder where he is."

"They will wonder where he is and be suspicious. If I was their leader I would travel west as they planned but further north. Remember they cannot be heading for the bridge as we have the fort there. Their only route is through one of the fords further west. We know where they are going. I would also have scouts beginning to infiltrate those woods." Decius looked in mock alarm at the woods which suddenly seemed threatening and dangerous. "They will not worry until he fails to return."

"Probably about now." Interjected the prefect happy to hear the clear analysis from the man he intended, one day, to lead the ala.

"Right about now. They will spend some time debating and then send his scouts out so that they will arrive just before dawn."

Decius' grin was from ear to ear. "By which time our lads will already be there and we'll gut the bastards."

The prefect nodded. "Bluntly put but correct. We will leave here within the next couple of hours. Our most experienced men under you, decurion. Decius will be in the woods ready to despatch those that come that way. The rest of the ala will split into two and await them north of the woods. You will wait, decurion, until you hear two blasts on the buccina and then flank them."

"Sounds good. I suppose I had better pick my men then." Saluting, the newly promoted decurion strode off to pick the best men. The first one he found was, of course, Gaius.

"We need men like the Decurion Decius Flavius, Marcus, but we need leaders like you more. Ulpius chose well all those years ago when he identified you as someone who stood out from the crowd. He saw in you, as I do someone who has vision and understands, even more than Ulpius did how to motivate and inspire the men of the ala. Tomorrow it is your battle. I will be there in the front line with you but you must lead. They will follow you I know but tomorrow we forge anew the sword that is this ala."

The next day the two wings of the ala were strung out below the crest of a hill. A small party, the bait in the trap, was camped a thousand strides from the northern edge of the wood. In the woods, Decius and the rest of the turma were cleaning their weapons from the dead Novantae scouts who had been slaughtered as they crept through the woods in the early hours of the morning. Their heads were already on stakes although they were hidden in the woods. When the battle was over they would be displayed as a reminder of the power of Rome, after the battle. They now waited under the eaves of the trees.

"I don't envy those poor sods," said Decius to Gaius. "There's nothing worse than being the bait in the trap. Sometimes the rat is a bit quick and takes some of the bait before he gets it. That's why I never volunteer.

"It's a dangerous place alright." Gaius suddenly stiffened. "I don't believe it. He's volunteered again."

"Who does he think he is, bleeding Achilles?"

There in the small camp was Macro leaning against the hindquarters of his horse as though he were the decurion. Gaius shook his head. "No not Achilles, he is Hercules and he won't stop until he completes all twelve labours. He's either going to have a glorious death and short career or we are looking at the next hero of Rome."

Their conversation was cut short by the roar as a thousand tribesmen erupted from the foggy dell to the east. Both men were pleased that Macro had been prepared for they saw that all ten were in their saddles in an instant. Pausing only to loose a hopeful volley of arrows they fled west.

"Right lads this is it. Wait for it. On two buccina calls, we take them in the flank. Loosen your swords. We attack silently. I don't want them to know we are there until it is too late. When they see us then you shout and scream all you like."

All the men loosened their swords for it had been a cold night and they didn't want them sticking. The half a dozen archers put three arrows in their mouths ready for a volley whilst the rest hefted their javelins.

Marcus could hear the thunder of the hooves even though he could not see them. He looked to where Gaelwyn waited with arm raised, watching the approach. Suddenly he dropped his arm and Marcus lowered his sword. The two lines began to move forward. On his left, he could see the prefect at the head of his one hundred and fifty men performing the same manoeuvre. He raised his sword again and they began to trot, their javelins held in their right hands low, next to their horse's heads. As they rose over the top they could see, a thousand paces away the ten members of the 'Macro volunteer club', as they had been nicknamed. Riding as though they were riding for their lives but in fact riding slowly enough so that the men on foot could catch them. Behind then, less than four hundred paces in the rear were the eighty Novantae horsemen and two hundred paces behind them the rest of the warband. It would be a close-run thing. He turned to the Cornicen." Be ready when I command. Two blasts right?" The man nodded his mouth around the mouthpiece ready to give the signal.

He lowered his sword again, the gleaming sword of Cartimandua which sparkled even on such a dull morning and they thundered into the charge. The Novantae suddenly realised their dilemma but they were northern warriors and they believed they could win for these Romans were a new enemy to them. They too surged forward and began loosing arrows. Marcus grimaced as two of the volunteers fell from their mounts. He shouted. "Now!" The two blasts encouraged the Romans to ride faster as Decius and his men erupted silently from the right flank. As Macro and his men wheeled through the Roman front line. Those troopers hurled their javelins and then charged almost before the javelins had struck. They tore through the enemy cavalry like water through a sieve. With their heavy mounts and armour, those horsemen who were not impaled on javelins were hacked and thrown to the ground by cavalry who were much better trained and equipped.

The warband saw that their cavalry was gone and the chief halted his men and formed them into a shield wall. This was the most protective formation the tribes had and was very effective, each warrior protected the man on his left with his shield. The problem was it took some time to get every man in position and the cavalry was closer than the chief would have liked. Marcus wasn't certain, later, if Decius had been lucky or just chosen his moment well for his turma suddenly roared their shout and the left flank of the shield wall faltered. It was only a momentary lapse but it was enough to create gaps for they lost their cohesion and a shield wall without cohesion is useless. The fifty troopers bundled the hapless left flank into their companions just as Marcus and the prefect hit the front of the line. The best warriors were in the front line of the shield wall and they all perished in the initial onslaught as the horses and mailed auxiliaries bowled into them. The ones who remained had not expected to be in the front line so quickly and the slashing spathae soon demolished all sense of order and planning. Every Novontae just fought for survival. Many ran which was the worst thing to do when facing cavalry for an unprotected back is an easy target. Soon the only ones not dead, dying or fled were the bodyguards of the two war chiefs who remained.

The prefect held up his hand and the Romans, as well disciplined as ever halted. Riding forward with Gaelwyn he shouted over to the remaining Novantae. "You are defeated. We could kill you now for I have more than enough arrows and I see little armour. I would rather you lay your arms down and march back to your own lands."

Gaelwyn translated. One of the chiefs stepped forwards and spoke in halting Latin. "Do you think we are fools? When we lay down our weapons you will kill us."

"If I wanted you dead, "the prefect raised his arm and fifty arrows were strung into fifty taut bows, "you would be dead. If I give the command my men will pour arrows into you and you will all die for nothing." The two chiefs looked at each other as Gaelwyn translated. They had been told that the Romans did not take prisoners. "Listen to me. Go home; raise crops and children, hunt animals and promise me that you will not make war on Rome again and you will survive."

The chief returned to the shield wall. An argument ensued which lasted some minutes but eventually the Roman auxiliaries could see the weapons being thrown into the ground. The prefect lowered his arm and the bows were relaxed. All of the Novantae began walking north led by the two chiefs except for one warrior who suddenly ran forwards screaming. His tattooed body had trophy torques and amulets and his eyes were wild with the hot blood within him. He hurled his mighty war axe at the prefect. Even before it was in the air the rebel was pieced by a dozen arrows and two javelins but the blade struck home and found its mark. It had hit the horse's head and carried on, hitting the prefect on the knee. Even though the dying horse took most of the force the axe was heavy and sliced through the prefect's flesh to the bone. It had struck him on the kneecap. By the time Marcus reached the old warrior his men had tied a tourniquet to stop further bleeding but Marcus and the rest could see that the prefect was crippled. They could see the bone of his kneecap and there was a jagged crack across it. He would soldier no more. He would have the soft bed he had desired but he would be in pain every time he climbed into it.

"Well, decurion, it seems I have fought my last battle. This is how old soldiers end their days; dead like Ulpius or crippled like me. Take command for you are now their leader."

Stanwyck

The two half-sisters of Cartimandua, Lenta and Macha had insisted that Marcus Bolanus allow them to refortify Stanwyck. They were now quite concerned that, as he had left his successor might not approve. Lenta was becoming quite outspoken about the Romans and blamed them for not protecting Stanwyck when Venutius had assaulted it and killed her family. Since Macha had borne a child to the Roman decurion, Marcus, she had become far more placid and supportive of them. In their increasingly frequent arguments, Lenta had been loud and angry. Macha usually backed down and spent more and more time with her child, the young Ulpius. He had been named after the centurion who had been the lover of Cartimandua and had perished at the battle of Brocavum. She just wished that Marcus, the boy's father, could be with her. Damn the Romans and their rules. They could live together, unofficially, but not marry. Worse he was stationed away to the north and rarely had time to visit. She ached for him and she knew that he missed both of them as his messages and occasional visits constantly reminded her. She yearned for peace so that they could have stability.

Lenta, for her part, had taken to a powerful Brigante warrior called Aed. Aed was the nephew of the ex-king Venutius. He was a well built and athletic warrior. More importantly, he had taken many of the Roman attributes and methods of war. He adapted the Brigante style of warfare. Many of the younger Brigante looked to him as the future; King Maeve was seen as too old and not the face that would make the Brigante world better. He had helped the Romans at the battle of Brocavum and he now led the loyal Brigante. He had shown both the Romans and Lenta a hope that the Brigante tribe could join in the Roman world and he might be able to increase the number of loyal Brigante. Lenta worried that this number was becoming fewer and fewer. There were weekly desertions and without someone like Alerix or Ulpius to inspire them they would not stay. Too many Brigante leaders had died in the bloodbath that followed the murder of Cartimandua and Lenta knew that she would have to replace her dead sister as a force for good and the identity of the tribe; Macha was too domesticated and overly concerned with her son and Marcus; Lenta had nothing else in her life. She began to feel hopeful again that with Aed at her side she would have some purpose in her life.

She began her morning as she always did walking the ramparts and speaking with the people. She had deduced that her informal chats revealed much about the undercurrents in the fortress. She had encouraged the pottery makers and tanners to work within the secure walls. She had used her contacts with the Romans to develop markets for the Roman soldiers were well paid and just looking for places to spend their money. The year she had spent with the auxilia had taught her much. She had begun to increase the production of fine weapons. Her people were masters of metal working and Romans liked good blades and strong metals. Whilst some of the warriors might have deserted Stanwyck she was pleased that they had increased the metal workers and begun to attract those workers who would make Stanwyck strong again.

She smiled as she saw the young men cheerfully clearing the ditch of the debris which had been thrown there during the last battle. Empty ditches made them more secure and she was sure that the new, self-proclaimed king, Maeve would soon be heading over the mountains to raid. She had insisted that Aed regularly send his warriors out on patrol. They had barely two hundred warriors who were loyal to the Romans but they were all well-armed and mounted. Lenta had seen the advantage the Romans had had over the Brigante and Carvetii rebels and their arms and armour had resulted in victory over a numerically superior force. Her warriors might not be as well trained as the Romans but they were at least as well protected. Every warrior had a mail shirt, helmet, sword and shield. The shields were based on the Roman design with metal built into a wooden framework to make them stronger. Yes, the Brigante under Lenta and Aed were well on their way to creating an army strong enough to fight alongside the Romans almost as equals and who knew perhaps in the future they would be indeed their equals. Satisfied she headed back towards the new hall built especially for them by the Romans; as she approached it she eyed the newly built bath house perhaps later she would take advantage of the Roman's love of luxury and enjoy the freshly finished building.

At that moment some twenty-five miles away, there was a meeting in a thickly wooded valley. She would have shivered, despite the warm bath she was about to take had she known what was to transpire but she was blissfully unaware of the events which were about to unfold. Maeve, or as he styled himself, King Maeve of the Carvetii and Brigante was alone apart from a single, muscular bodyguard. The man on his knees was his spy; himself well-armed and muscled though younger than both the king and his bodyguard.

"You say that the ramparts are all finished?" The spy nodded. "And the men armed as you are?"

"Yes my lord."

"We will not be ready for at least a moon." He looked keenly at the young man. "You have done well, the deserters you send are making my army even stronger."

"Thank you, my lord."

"But you must be careful. You must avoid discovery at all costs. Our other men can die, they are expendable but without you, the plan fails. Do you understand me?"

"I am careful my lord. No one suspects me at all." He smiled grimly. "They are just pleased that I have not joined the other deserters. You need have no fear I will be there when you need me."

"Good. The signal has not changed it will be some time after the next moon rises. I am hoping that some of the Novantae will join us and then we will have sufficient men."

"I will be ready."

They clasped arms in a soldier's salute and then the young man rode east, back to Stanwyck, back to the Brigante and back to his treacherous, traitorous work.

Chapter 3

The prefect did not complain during the whole journey back to the fort at the Dunum Fluvius. They had built a sick bay at Morbium and he knew he would be well looked after. The medical orderlies had made sure that the wound did not become diseased but it was obvious that his knee was shattered beyond repair. As soon as they arrived at the fort the doctor confirmed what all knew, the prefect would be retiring and Marcus would be in charge of the ala. Soldiers all knew that this could happen, a blade that could not be deflected, the accidental slip, any of a thousand events could end your life as a soldier and then you would face a world away from the one you had known for twenty-five years.

No one had much time to rest for, since they had been out on patrol more recruits and mounts had arrived. While Flavius completed the reports and paperwork Marcus set to work organising the ala for training purposes. Decius might not have been the greatest strategist but Marcus recognised that he was a first-rate training sergeant. The first decision the acting Decurion Princeps made was to appoint Decius as officer in charge of training. The normally bluff decurion was touched by the promotion and confirmed in the prefect's eyes that Marcus was the right man to lead the ala. Whilst Decius chased and chivvied the men to build the training circle, the gyrus, Marcus sat with the clerks and Gaius assigning the new recruits to their turmae. Because they were now short of decurions, after discussion with the prefect, Drusus and Lentius were both confirmed as decurions. That took some of the pressure off the Decurion Princeps for he had four turmae that could organise themselves. He took the opportunity to spread out the more experienced men. Gaius was given a turma to manage until a decurion could be appointed. Much as he would have liked to promote his acolyte he knew that it might be seen as nepotism and in his own mind, he knew that Gaius had much to learn. Gaius, for his part, did not mind. He had not expected a promotion. The only part of the situation which did not please Gaius was that Marcus gave him the 'volunteer' Macro. "Sir of all the men you could have given me why him?"

"When I look at young Macro I see a younger, albeit heavier, version of you. If he models himself on you Gaius then I shall be happy."

Mollified Gaius went off to assign some organisational tasks to Macro who took to them like an eager puppy chasing a ball. When he left Marcus looked at the list and then asked the clerk. "Have we a quartermaster yet?"

The clerk consulted his list. "The decurion, Lucius Demetrius, who was wounded at Glanibanta. The prefect asked him to take on the role when he arrived back at the fort last month but he is due to be retired soon."

Another problem for him to deal with; he would have to find a suitable replacement. Marcus rubbed the side of his head which had begun to ache suddenly. There was so much to do. It was not like a battle where you could focus on two simple things, killing the enemy and staying alive. Of course, now he remembered that the prefect had asked the brave Lucius to take on the role and it delighted Marcus. He just worried why he had forgotten it.

"Thank you." He smiled at the clerk who was the oldest man in the fort. "I am glad that you have a memory for I have none. Now refresh my failing memory for other details. How many mounts have we? How many new recruits? How many need uniforms and arms and when will the new decurions be arriving?" If he thought he had asked too much of the old man he was mistaken, Aurelius reeled off the answers like someone who has learned them for a test.

"We have eight hundred mounts; one hundred and ten need schooling." Marcus nodded that was another task, who would school the horses? One hundred and twenty-eight fresh recruits plus the one hundred and twenty who went on patrol," he paused as though admonishing Marcus, "without the proper training." Marcus grinned, Aurelius was correct but that had been the prefect's decision. "We have enough uniforms and arms for a thousand troopers. There will be six decurions arriving within the week."

"Well done Aurelius. Until I can find someone else to do it I will take over the schooling of the horses. Just find out who has experience of schooling horses." When the clerk raised his eyebrows in an unspoken question Marcus replied irritably, "I haven't got time to tittle-tattle and find out such minutiae. Just do it, man."

"Yes sir well if you will allow me I will go and," he looked up with a cheeky grin his faded blue eyes, "tittle-tattle."

Laughing at the man's cheek he took out his wax tablet. They had five hundred and two troopers. With the five decurions he had plus the six he was going to get he could reorganise into twelve turma. He could leave Gaius in acting command until they could appoint another. He suddenly realised that, if he were to continue as Decurion Princeps he would need two more. At least that meant the turma would be up to full strength with forty-two men; that was a much better number. Marcus had always felt that the under strength thirty-two man turma was not an effective number for it was too small to use apart from in a scouting role. He decided to go and look at the new mounts. He did not intend to begin schooling them yet but he wanted to see the size of the problem. As he left the fort he received an absent-minded salute from Decius who was berating a recruit. "Put the sodding stake in spike down, that way it will go in you sad apology for a dog's dick. Morning sir. Soon have this gyrus up. Would be quicker if the tits I have to work with had any common sense at all."

The horses were all corralled away from the river Marcus noticed with quiet satisfaction. Someone had done their job well. As he walked towards them he noticed an older trooper checking the hooves of one of the horses. When Marcus arrived he straightened and saluted. "Carry on. What is your name trooper?"

"Cato sir, Cato Aquilinas eighth turma, chosen man sir."

"The eighth? Ah yes that was Sextus' turma. He was a good man; I had hoped he would recover from his wounds."

"So did we all sir. Me and the lads hope to pay back them bastards someday."

"Don't worry you will." While the man had been talking he had noticed that he continued to work. The horse was obviously in pain but the trooper calmed and soothed the beast with his voice and his manner. The man was a horseman. "Who detailed you here?"

The man looked embarrassed like someone caught peeping. "Er, no one sir. Sorry if I have done something…"

"No, no you misunderstand me. I am pleased. Even more so now that I know you did this yourself without being ordered to do so."

"Horses sir, I love 'em. It's why I joined up. Most of the lads were taken by force. I walked over a range of mountains to join," he added the last part proudly.

Marcus took an instant decision. "Well, Cato. These horses need schooling. I was going to do it myself but I can see that you might do the job. How would you feel about working with me to school these horses?"

Even before he had answered the grin gave Marcus the response he needed. "Yes, sir I would love to."

"Good well start work now. Pick yourself another four or five men who know the nose from the arse and I will join you."

Feeling much happier Marcus headed back to his quarters to change into more appropriate clothes. It was strange but talking to a fellow horseman had put all of his new role into perspective. He just had to do the best he could in each small part of his job and not worry about being perfect. Perhaps that was what had made Ulpius Felix so successful, he had just got on with things. That would be the new credo of Marcus, just get on.

"Macro, stop following me like a puppy dog. When I have a job for you I will tell you. Right at this moment, I am just trying to work out what in Hades name I am supposed to do."

"Right." Macro stood, his apelike arms dangling like useless appendages. Gaius was aware that he was being watched and he hated it. He knew that Marcus had great faith in his ability and saw great things in his future. In reality, Gaius felt he had gone as far as he could. To be spoken of as a leader by Marcus was enough. He was petrified of making a mistake. As he glanced over at Macro he saw himself. This was what Marcus had seen, the raw clay and Macro was the clay. He was taking his frustration out on Macro and it was not the lad's fault. "Macro!" The recruit bolted to attention so sharply that Macro had to check that he had not been cut. "Take the turma down to Decius and tell him that I think they need extra training. When you are done meet me at the quartermaster's."

"Sir! Yes Sir!" Macro raced off as though he had been given a triumph in Rome. Gaius smiled this was how Ulpius and Marcus did it!

Lindum

Cerialis threw down the parchment in disgust. Would nothing go right for him? The prefect of the Pannonian cavalry could no longer command. The best auxiliary unit in Britannia and they had no leader. His legions were well commanded and he knew he could rely on them but it was his auxiliary units, his cavalry, archers and infantry who would hold this precarious toe hold on this last outpost of the Empire. They were the shield that protected his precious legions until they could close with the barbarians. He looked again at the list of available staff officers. He made his decision. "Send for Rufius Demetrius." As much as he disliked this arrogant patrician it would kill two birds with one stone. It would provide him with a proven commander of cavalry and it would ingratiate him into the Demetrius family. His post would be that little bit more secure.

Rufius Demetrius was a career officer; he had served in Spain and in Batavia. He was from a noble family and he needed promotion sooner rather than later. As he strode into the room Cerialis found himself, once again, disliking this noble and it confirmed his view. It would rid him of someone who annoyed him constantly. The man seemed to look down his nose, quite literally, at everyone. Quintus was a career soldier and he fought alongside his men. He got the impression that the patrician would find fighting with mere plebeians beneath him.

He gestured for him to take and seat. "What do you know of the Pannonian cavalry?"

Rufius paused before he spoke. "They are one of the better units in Britannia. They recently lost a large number of men fighting the Brigante. I think their prefect is Flavius Bellatoris."

Cerialis was impressed by the patrician's knowledge. "Excellent intelligence Rufius I am impressed however your intelligence is not up to date. In a skirmish with the," he consulted the tablet," Novantae he was seriously wounded and although he survived he will be unable to continue to command. I am instructing you to take command of the ala."

"Thank you, sir."

"It will take much work to bring the unit up to speed but it is vital that they perform at the same level they did previously. We have few decent auxiliary units and our legions are too thinly spread. You have three months to get them ready for I intend to subjugate the Brigante once and for all. The

Emperor is not happy that a few tribesmen are preventing us from pacifying this rich province."

"Have we enough men to fill the vacant posts?"

"We have sent all the men we had available but they are still short. My clerk will give you precise numbers. Use your discretion but get as many recruits as you can from those who are loyal to us. I take it you have some officers in mind for the decurion posts?"

It was common practice for noble families to send their young sons off with other, influential nobles, to gain experience in warfare before taking up politics. Cerialis knew that Rufius had some young men with him. "Yes sir, a few. Well if that is all I have much to do."

"My clerk had all the details for you. Three months! Be ready!" He waved his hand dismissively but the new prefect of cavalry did not mind the insulting gesture. He had his ala of cavalry. He would show all of them what cavalry could do with a commander who knew how to handle them.

Marcus went to Flavius' quarters. As soon as he entered he noticed that the prefect looked much older and much thinner. In all the years he had known him the decurion had not even thought about his age but now that he was dressed in civilian clothes, without the armour, without the weapons, he seemed smaller. Glancing down at the wound Marcus realised that a serious wound could age a man just as much as time itself.

"Sit down Marcus. How goes the training?"

Marcus face lit up with a smile. "Decius Flavius has everyone hopping around as though their lives depended on it. He is relishing the role. I do believe he was born for the role?"

Flavius nodded. "And the schooling?"

"I have another good man, Cato. He seems to be able to talk to the horses. He has more than half of them ready for riders already. I think he will do well. "

"And the new decurions?"

"Time will tell. You know how it is. New men to the unit are looked on with suspicion until the men get to know them. They seem to know what they are about. I'll know more when I take them out on patrol. I don't like sitting behind walls. You need to ride amongst the tribes to get a feel of them and their mood."

The prefect nodded. "It seems our Governor has acted swiftly, certainly swifter than Bolanus did. I still think we could have avoided the loss of all those men if he had not been so lazy."

"Aye. Ulpius and the others might still be alive."

"There is no point dwelling on what might have been. Ulpius had the warrior's death he wanted and you and I both know," his voice dropped conspiratorially, "that when the queen died the hope went from his heart."

"And one day when I find Gaius Cresens Ulpius and his lady will be avenged."

"May the Allfather grant it. Well, the Governor has appointed my replacement. You are to be commanded by a real Roman. A patrician no less. Rufius Demetrius."

"Do you know of him?"

He nodded. "A good man; he commanded some smaller units of cavalry in Batavia." What was unspoken was the fact that it was unusual for roman officers to be skilled in cavalry. They made good officers for the legions but usually, they raced their cavalry off when they were needed on the battlefield.

"Good. I would hate to see all the good work of Ulpius and you wasted."

"Don't worry. I will recommend you for Decurion Princeps."

"No sir. I didn't mean that. I meant building up such a good ala of cavalry."

"I know you didn't but don't be so modest. Ulpius felt as I did that you are the heart of the ala and you are just as responsible for the reputation we have created. Anyway, I will still recommend you. When do you leave on the patrol?"

I will take the new decurions out tomorrow. We will head east. It has been neglected of late and if we do run into trouble they are less belligerent than their brothers in the west."

"Some of them are almost Roman, aren't they?"

Marcus laughed. "I wouldn't go as far as that." He became more serious. I think we will base a couple of turma at Derventio. It was always a good site for a fort. I hated having to abandon it. This place will be bursting at the seams soon; especially if the new prefect brings us up to full muster."

"I think he will do that." He held out his arm. "I may be gone by the time you return. I will say goodbye now. If you visit me in my villa you will not see the soldier I was but a crippled old farmer."

"To me sir you will always be a soldier." Clasping arms, they said goodbye the soldier's way.

Streonshal

Cresens looked out from his dwelling. It was not a hut. He made sure that it was built in the Roman style and it was the sturdiest house in the village. He watched Atticus as he led the boys back from the shore. He had taken to the role of foster father with relish and the boys adored him. He had helped to build the boats in such a short time that even Gaius Cresens was impressed. They caught so many fish that they had already been able to sell them to

28

inland villages and Cresens had already turned a profit. He shook his head in amazement for no one had worked out that he was talking all the money. They were so grateful to be fed that they appeared to have overlooked it. Even more gratifying was that a few other people came to join their community. Some had fled the killers of Stagh-herts whilst others had heard that it was thriving.

Atticus strode up to the man he still called master. "We have had a good day see the catch." It was an impressive catch.

"Remember to send one of the women to Derventio with the surplus and then come into my house I have another task for you." A few moments later Atticus entered, remembering to take off his sandals. "I need you to go to Stanwyck." Atticus looked up in surprise. "Yes I know it is a longer journey than you are used to but we need some items that we cannot get here." He paused and dropped his voice. "I do worry you know that those men who killed our shipmates will hear of the good fortune of this village and decide to take it. You know that they could." Atticus nodded. He had come to see these people as his family and this as his home. "We need weapons. The Brigante at Stanwyck make fine weapons and we now have a little money to buy weapons."

Atticus could see the wisdom in his words and it made him want to serve the master even better than hitherto. "I shall go in the morning."

Take a boy with you. You will also need to buy a horse and a wagon. You may be able to get those on the way from Derventio but Atticus please be careful. We can trust no one outside of this village." He took Atticus by the arm. "And that includes Romans. I worked for them long enough to realise that there are just as many cut-throats amongst them. Do you understand?"

"Yes, Master. I just hope that some of your wisdom will rub off on me."

Cresens smiled the smile of a crocodile inviting a victim in and said, "Be off with you, I am no wiser than you."

South of Dunum Fluvius

Marcus looked across the mouth of the Dunum. It was indeed a mighty river. One day there might be many bridges across this river but here, at its mouth, it was far too wide. Behind him, he saw the hills rise to a mighty plateau. He had intended to take them south to Derventio but he could see from their faces that the recruits he had brought would not be able to stomach that long ride. He looked again at the escarpment. They would have to camp up on the escarpment. He turned to the trooper next to him. "South."

The one hundred and forty-four men all turned their mounts and the column of twos followed him. The four decurions were wary of him. Marcus understood their reluctance to be open with him. They were new and they had heard of the exploits of the ala. The whole of the province spoke of the ride of Ulpius Felix and his timely intervention. The decurions had been in

Britannia and knew of the significance of the battle. The province had been on a knife-edge. Marcus, Decius and the others appeared as heroes such as Horatio. Added to the lustre of glory was the almost magical sword which the Decurion Princeps carried. As warriors, they envied him the blade but they were all aware of its history. Marcus knew all of this but he needed their trust for, in the heat of battle, the leader at the front had to trust completely in the men at his back; with Gaius, Decius, Lentius and Drusus, Marcus had that trust. He had hoped that this patrol would have begun to build that bond.

Halfway up the escarpment he halted but waved the column past him; he wanted to look at the men's faces as they turned to him. Decius had done a good job in training them to be riders but a good soldier was more than a rider. They needed a level of fitness that did not come overnight. He could see the exhaustion in their faces. "Trooper, keep distance between your mount and the man in front, some of these horses bite."

"Sir!"

As soon as he had uttered the suggestion he regretted the words for he knew Septimus Supero, the decurion of turma six would punish the trooper later. He would have to have a word with all of the decurions. They were all newly promoted and he remembered when he had been in their position; you assumed everyone was a critic and all your mistakes were discussed. He would be glad when the prefect returned and many of his duties would be taken from him.

When the camp had been built and the men were preparing food Marcus called his decurions over. "How do you think they coped today?"

"Some of them will never make horsemen. Should have joined the infantry!"

"True Vettius Martinus, true but we have not got the luxury of trained horsemen. We have to make horsemen of them. Infantrymen are easy to train but horsemen." He paused. "That is why we are paid more than our infantry brothers." The look on the man's face told him that he had not thought of that.

"I don't know how they will hold up in a fight."

Marcus looked at the oldest of the four decurions, Quintus Saenius. "None of us know that until our first action. Do you remember yours?"

Quintus suddenly reddened and looked embarrassed. Marcus Saurius the fourth decurion suddenly laughed. "Well, sir that could be because our friend Quintus hasn't actually been in action, have you?"

He stood up angrily. "We did have action."

Marcus stood between the two men. "Sit down and keep your voices down or you will both be back in the ranks." He turned to Quintus. "What action have you seen then?"

"We chased down some Trinovantes horse thieves and…"

"No battles then?" Quintus shook his head. "The rest of you? Any battles?" He looked at each of them in turn as they shook their heads ending with Marcus Saenius. "It is no shame not to have been in a battle. These men have not only not seen a battle they haven't chased down cattle thieves or hunted slave hunters. We will all have to fight battles believe me. The tribes up here are not pacified and they are tough warriors. Don't believe because this ala beat them that it was easy. We brought back more empty saddles than full ones. I want us to bring back more full saddles than empty ones so be patient with these men. They look to you for your experience and I look to you for your experience. And remember you will not be in trouble for asking for information but if something goes wrong because you didn't ask then you will know what it is like to be in action. Clear?"

Four voices shouted in unison, "Clear!" Marcus was pleased to see that his tirade had resulted in faces that looked happier than when he had started. He would have to ensure that Quintus and Marcus were kept apart and the bad blood would not worsen.

The next day was cold and clear which helped Marcus to sharpen his mind. He would leave two turmae at Derventio under Vettius and Quintus. The experience of controlling such a large area would do their confidence no harm and it would keep apart the two decurions. Should he need the two turmae, they were but half a day away. As he rode through this wild country he realised that there was not as much Roman control as there might be.

Derventio had been an early fort and as such only, the outline of the fort remained. The town had grown quite well and Marcus saw the potential for horse breeding country. He said as much to Quintus and Vettius as he briefed them. "I want you to rebuild the fort. Make it large enough for four turmae. I will send some men to help establish a stud. This would be a perfect place to breed horses. Your task is to ensure that the populace is safe. We have not shown our presence enough and there are bandits and pirates hereabouts. Make it safe."

The two decurions nodded. They saw that the acting Decurion Princeps had the bigger picture. Already in awe of the hero they now realised that he was a thinker; for decurions like Vettius and Quintus, this was like being a leader under the great Julius. When they asserted their agreement, it was heartfelt. Marcus looked at the two men and nodded. He had made the correct decision. He turned to the other two decurion. "We ride. We are going home."

By the time they arrived back at the fort, the prefect had left for the new colony being established at Isurium Brigantium close to Stanwyck. Marcus approved wholeheartedly with the police for it meant that veterans such as Flavius would provide Roman stability in a changing barbarian world. He was also pleased for it gave more protection to his wife and child. He yearned to see them but now that he was the senior officer he could not desert his post.

As he rode past the gyrus he could see a difference in the recruits. Decius had them sparring with the heavy wooden swords and shield. When they first arrived they could barely lift them but as he watched he saw them using them almost as well as men who had served for years. Decius had done his work well. Leaving the two decurions to return to their barracks he headed over to Cato. The sergeant came to attention when he saw Marcus but he could not keep the smile from his face.

"From the expression on your face, I assume you have finished the schooling?"

"Yes sir. Just waiting for some new mounts to start the process again."

"While you are waiting I have another task for you. We always have to wait for wild horses and then train them it seems to me that we could breed them ourselves." Cato's face showed the thought process racing through his head. Marcus was pleased Cato was more than a horseman he was an intelligent horseman. "Select a good stallion and some breeding mares then take them to Derventio. I think we can begin our own stud. We will need to find some civilians to man it but there must be some locals who know horses."

"There are, sir. There are a couple of lads been helping out. I'll have a chat with them."

"Good. I'll leave that with you then eh?"

"Yes sir."

As Marcus led his horse back towards the gyrus he felt more than a little pleased with what he had achieved. He eagerly anticipated the arrival of the new prefect. He felt sure he would approve.

Decius saw him coming and handed over the training to one of his assistants. "I see you managed to lose two turma, sir."

Marcus smiled at the banter. "I traded them for a new fort." Decius looked puzzled. "I left them rebuilding the old fort at Derventio. We are getting a little crowded here. Any sign of the new prefect?"

"Not yet but we haven't had our weekly supplies yet so it may be he's travelling with them. I don't mind. It gives me more time to knock these dog's dinners into shape."

"How are they coming along?"

"Most are coming along well but there are a couple of them who will never make horsemen no matter how much we try. I'd like to ship them out to an infantry unit. They will make good soldiers just not horsemen."

Marcus nodded. He had told his junior decurions they had to make horsemen out of the recruits but he knew that Decius would have tried everything to ensure that they became riders. "I'll see the prefect when he arrives. There's nothing worse than someone who sits on a horse like a sack of grain. Carry on."

Chapter 4

Rufius Demetrius had only stayed long enough in Eboracum to get the latest intelligence from the tribune of the ninth. He looked up at the straight line that was Dere Street. This was always a sight that gave him satisfaction for it meant that Rome had tamed the land and put its indelible mark on the landscape forever. Behind him, the column of wagons and mules moved inexorably northwards. He wished they could get there quicker but he knew that the supplies and men behind him were vital to his plan for the ala. For the first time in his career, he could mould the men to suit him. He would join the great leaders from the past Fabius Africanus, Pompey even Julius Caesar. Soon he would take command of the Pannonian cavalry the Brigante would be swept aside and then the world would know the name of Rufius Demetrius.

Marcus had men posted along Dere Street to warn him of the arrival of the new prefect. He wanted to impress his new leader. The fort was immaculate; it had been cleaned as Decius had remarked, within an uncia of its life. The standards all fluttered in the breeze near the Praetorium and every trooper had gleaming armour. Inevitably it was Macro who galloped in as though the whole Brigante army was chasing him.

"Sir, Sir, the prefect..."

"Take your time Macro. How long before he arrives?"

"Within the hour."

"Good, then you have time to walk the sweat off your horse and clean up both you and him." As Macro slumped dejectedly off Marcus added. "Well done." The spring immediately returned to the keen trooper's step.

So it was that when the new prefect crested the rise above the river crossing he could not help but be impressed. The white stone of the bridge seemed to shine amidst the greenery of the vegetation lining the twisting river. The men of the guard of honour were as rigid as statues on magnificently groomed horses each with the mane and tail braided. As he came level with the guard he halted and without a command, each man saluted in unison. Marcus rode forward, "Marcus Aurelius Maximunius acting Decurion Princeps of the First Sabinian Wing of Pannonians. Welcome, sir."

"An excellent turnout decurion you put us to shame after our dusty ride from Eboracum. After we have washed and bathed we will meet with you and the other officers and I will introduce you to the rest of the new officers."

Marcus watched the patrician ride into the fort. He was the first Roman he had seen who was not in the legion and he felt in awe of the man already. He looked like every statue he had ever seen the sharp nose and chiselled features. Behind him rode more smartly turned out officers and Marcus noticed that some of these had the same look about them as Rufius Demetrius; Decius would have to watch his manners for these were not barbarians, these were noble Romans.

The headquarters office was a little cramped later on as Marcus stood with the other decurions awaiting Rufius and his entourage to return from their bath.

"There looked to be a couple of boys with him. Do you think they are his family?" queried Drusus.

"He looks old enough to be a father."

"Decius…"

"I'm just saying he looks older than the rest of us, maybe not as old as Flavius but older than Ulpius. You know what I am saying and if he has only just got this promotion well…" Decius' further musings were halted by the snap of the sentry's spear and the 'sir' from outside.

As Rufius entered they all stood to attention. "Sit down, sit down." When they were all seated Marcus noticed that two young men, who looked like they could be brothers, flanked Rufius. Marcus looked at Decius who tapped the side of his nose knowingly. "Let us get the formal part out of the way." He grasped the parchment and read from it. "I, Rufius Demetrius am hereby appointed to lead the First Sabinian Wing of Pannonians. I am authorised to make all appointments and to ensure that this ala is ready for battle in two months." A low murmur ran around the seated decurions for many of the recruits would only be half-trained. An impatient stare silenced the mumblings and the prefect rolled up the parchment. "There are one or two other points but the salient point is that we will be ready for action by the end of the month." This time no one dared to speak. "The new Governor, Quintus Petilius Cerialis, is bringing the Ninth Hispana with a number of other auxiliary units to finally suppress the rebellion that is festering here in the north. Julius Agricola will also be bringing the Twentieth Valeria Victrix but they are further away. We gentlemen will be the main cavalry unit. I know that you distinguished yourselves previously and I assure you I expect nothing less from you now." He paused to let his words sink in and then he sat back in his seat. "I will be relying on you experienced decurions to facilitate and smooth the transition. I would like to thank personally Marcus Aurelius Maximunius for taking on the role of acting Decurion Princeps." Marcus looked suitably embarrassed by this praise. "However, for the moment we will not have a post of Decurion Princeps as I want to assess the potential of this ala."

"But sir…" Decius half stood to protest.

"Decurion, perhaps you misheard my orders. I am now running this ala and I will run it my way, the Roman way and I will not tolerate insubordination of any description. Do I make myself clear?" They all responded with a 'yes sir".

"It may well be that when I have seen my new officers in action and seen how they perform their duties I may be able to appoint my own Decurion Princeps. Let me introduce the four decurions who have accompanied me. First my sons Julius Demetrius and Fabius Demetrius." They both nodded in a dismissive fashion as though the rest of the decurions were beneath them. Their reaction was noticed by the rest of the decurions." Over there is Quintus Augustus and Metellus Saenius. I am sure you all have duties to perform and," he smiled wickedly, "things to discuss so until tomorrow morning you are all dismissed. Marcus Aurelius Maximunius if you would stay behind I would like to be briefed on any actions you have taken in your role of acting Decurion Princeps."

As they were all leaving Marcus could feel the resentment from his comrades on his behalf. In his own mind, Marcus knew that the prefect was correct. He could make any decision he wished and, giving it a more positive side, he would have fewer duties to perform and less responsibility.

"First of all, can I say that I meant what I said. I believe you have done a fine job and there is nothing personal in this. The Decurion Princeps is an important role. He is my deputy. As you know there were two Decurion Princeps before this unit suffered such high casualties. When our numbers rise we will need two." He smiled and poured two goblets of wine. "Let us drink to the day when I can appoint you as Decurion Princeps." They touched goblets and drank. Marcus was no wine expert but he recognised that this was un-watered expensive wine. "Now then tell me everything you have done."

Marcus went through all his actions and appointments from the appointment of Decius as training officer through the patrol to Derventio and his plans for a stud. He also mentioned the unsuitable recruits. "Excellent and I think I can go along with most of those actions however the young acting decurion…"

"Gaius sir."

"Yes, quite I think he should return to his turma as we have enough decurions for the twelve turma and as you won't be Decurion Princeps there is no need for an additional decurion. The training officer, I take it he is the one with the mouth?" Marcus nodded. "Yes, well he can use his mouth for training then, for the time being. This sergeant in charge of schooling is a good idea. I will arrange some extra pay for him. Our horses are vital however we haven't got the time to build and maintain a stud to produce our horses and, although I like the idea in principle it will have to wait until after the campaign. By the same token, we do not need to garrison Derventio all of the action will be in the north and west. As for the unsuitable recruits, I am

36

afraid that beggars cannot be choosers. We have ranks to fill and, at the moment even a sack of grain on a horse has value. Thanks again for all your work. I daresay you too have things to do so until the morning."

The four original decurions were waiting for him along with the two newer ones. "Well, I think it is an imperial disgrace!"

Marcus put his arm around Decius' mouth and moved him away from the headquarters building. "Will you keep your voice down? You heard what he said about insubordination." He hurried them out of the fort and towards the bridge. When they were at the bridge he turned to them. "What is a disgrace?"

It was Gaius who spoke up. "Well, sir the fact that you won't be Decurion Princeps."

"And appointing two bloody babies as decurion. I waited ten bleeding years to get it and they haven't even started shaving."

"As he said it is his right to do what he wants." Marcus turned to Gaius, "and one of the things he wants is to have just twelve decurions. I am afraid you are back to being my chosen man Gaius."

Rather than being disappointed Gaius actually beamed a smile. "Suits me. I told you I needed more time." He grinned wickedly at Decius. "Now you only have two babies to watch out for."

"I never meant you, you know that."

"I know. Well, it looks to be an interesting time ahead. I'll go and move my gear back into the barracks."

Marcus turned to the rest of them as Gaius whistled his way back into the fort. "The rest of you be careful what you say. This man looks to be a stickler for convention and wants things done the legionary way. Just do your job and then he can't find fault."

"Whatever you say, Marcus," Drusus put his arm around his friend, "all I can say is that it is a shame. Ulpius and Flavius both wanted you to run this ala and what do we end up with? A 'by the book' man and two whelps for us to wet nurse! Well, I for one am going to get drunk. Anyone join me?"

"That's the best idea you have had in a long time. Come on then old son. I'll join you."

Marcus followed them into the fort reflecting on the fact that he was glad to be back amongst friends. The isolation of a leader was gone.

Fainch

As soon as the priestess reached the uplands of the land of the lakes she began to feel danger. Although she had been close to the Romans on her journey from Mona she had not felt threatened for she felt the holy island of Mona protected her; here in the North, it was a different story for the people were a divided people with some loyal to the Romans and some to King Maeve. Which one could she trust? She had already decided that as Maeve was the successor to Venutius he would be the best choice to manipulate the Brigante and Carvetii to her will. She knew that he was massing an army but she needed that army to be ready at her command. She smiled inwardly to herself; she had always been able to make men do as she wished. Venutius had been the last in a long line of men who had succumbed to her power. The mistake she had made with Venutius was allowing him to make so many decisions. Like all men he made decisions based on heroic deeds; as a woman, she had learned that sometimes the straight line was not the quickest journey.

She had avoided those parts of the North frequented by Romans for she wanted anonymity and so the journey to the lonely lake that was Maeve's home took her longer than she wished but when she arrived on the side of the fell which overlooked the stockaded settlement she felt relief for her journey was over. This time she would not hide as a spy in a hut she would be as a spider in the centre of the web. No more moving at the behest of others here she would mould Maeve and make people come to her. This time she wanted more control over the men who carried out her wishes; that had been her mistake in the first war against the Romans she had not been close enough to Venutius, Maeve would be a different matter.

The guards at the gates gripped their holy amulets as she approached for they knew of her and recognised her for what she was, a witch and a priestess. Had she been a warrior she would not have made it through the gates, as it was the guards parted as grass before the wind when she approached. Others ran before her to warn King Maeve, as he now styled himself. By the time she approached his round house, he was waiting for her. Although he did not know her name he had known of her. The witch who had worked her magic for Venutius was a legend still spoken of in hushed whispers when the warriors were in their cups. The witch who had made the poison that killed a Queen was a woman to be feared and respected.

"Welcome we are honoured by your presence."

"It is my honour to serve a mighty king and enemy to Rome." She glanced around her at the crowd and dropped her voice. "Perhaps if we could sit and talk quietly for I am weary and my words are only for the ears of the king." Maeve nodded. He could feel himself drawn towards this priestess. Her voice seemed to him to be enchanted and musical. To talk quietly and alone would be fitting.

When they entered the darkened roundhouse, lit only by the fire in the centre Maeve spoke to his bodyguards. "We are not to be disturbed. Please sit priestess."

Taking off her hooded cloak her hair cascaded down her back. Maeve suddenly realised that she was still a young woman. He had believed her to be older for she seemed to have been around forever. Her violet eyes were piercing and seemed to search into his head, insinuating their way into his thoughts. "My name is Fainch and I served Venutius. I am a priestess of Mona and I am here, oh mighty king, to help you to defeat the Romans and rid the land of their pestilence."

Her voice continued to enchant and mesmerize him but he remembered the last war and the slaughter of so many of his warriors. "But they are too organised, too well armed; my men are brave but courage is not enough the last time we fought my warriors and those of King Venutius were slaughtered."

"I know wise king that all you say seems true but Caractacus, the king betrayed by Cartimandua, had the right idea. We need all of the peoples of this land to fight, all of them to attack at the same time and then we can defeat the Romans. We will not attack yet we will wait until next year. My sisters are even now spreading the word amongst other kings so that at the feast of Eostre we will all attack. The Romans only have four legions in this land." Maeve looked in disbelief at this woman who appeared wise and knowledgeable beyond her years. "They cannot be everywhere at once and once they are eradicated from one part of the land there will be more warriors to join and fight the ones who remain. We destroy them by all fighting at the same time. We may not be on the same battlefield but we will have the same fight."

"But it is not just the legions. They have the horsemen; the ones who killed King Venutius. They too are mighty warriors."

"I will deal with those men myself." The venom in her voice made the king reel back as she spat the words out. He feared that those cavalrymen would suffer greatly. Her voice resumed its melodic cadence. "You have a spy in Stanwyck."

Once again he marvelled at her intelligence. "Yes but…"

"All you need to know king is that I have power and knowledge and I will use it for you, for us and for the people of this land. This spy has power I believe?"

"Yes, he controls a large number of the warriors in Stanwyck. "

"That will be where we will make our first assault. We will begin a revolt which will draw the legions north so that the peoples of the south and west can have fewer enemies to fight."

"But that means they will be massed against me. I thought we were waiting for Eostre?"

"We are and we will not be fighting the Romans. We will be killing those traitors who have joined with the Romans. Once we have rid our lands of those Roman lovers the Romans will begin to repress the people even more and that oh king will give us even more men. We will wait until next year for once we have the metals and arms from Stanwyck our army will be stronger.

39

The Brigante have to decide whose side they are on; if they are loyal to us they will live, if not they will die."

Her words of steel and hate had convinced him. "We will do it. What is our first action?"

"You need to send more men to join the Brigante in Stanwyck and when we have sufficient numbers we will strike. I will travel to the other tribes, the Novantae, Selgovae, Pictii and they will join our cause." She brushed her hand against the king's cheek and whispered. "Together we will defeat them this time."

This last act was the final enchantment she placed upon him and King Maeve would have sacrificed anything for this mighty witch.

For Marcus, any thought that he would have an easier time without the role of Decurion Princeps were quickly dismissed for the new prefect still expected that Marcus would continue to function in that role. Decius and Gaius were increasingly annoyed at the way that the two sons of the prefect would avoid any of the mundane day to day tasks whilst they were worked twice as hard. Decius took all his aggression out on the recruits with the result that they worked even harder to satisfy the monster that he had become. Marcus took pride in the fact that the ala became even more efficient. To be fair to the prefect he did let Marcus know how well he was performing but it did not help that he had even less time to get to Stanwyck to see his wife and son. He suddenly realised that he would barely recognise his son who, by now, must be walking. He withdrew even more into himself.

His comrades noticed this as they drank in their off-duty times. "He's not the same you know."

"Of course he's not the bleeding same. How could he be? He's worked twice as hard and those two lazy bastards do absolutely nothing. He's doing their work as well. Someone should do something about it."

Gaius suddenly spoke up. "Will you keep your voice down? What you are suggesting is mutiny. That means crucifixion."

There was a short silence as they all drank their wines and reflected on Gaius' statement. "Most of the lads would be with us."

"Will you keep a lid on it? Do you think that Marcus would go along with mutiny?" The lack of comment showed that the other decurions agreed with Gaius. "No, we just try to take his mind off it. Get him talking about Macha and his son."

"That's half the problem," pointed out Drusus. "He hasn't seen them for such a long time."

"Well, there's damn all we can do about that is there? Desertion is the same as mutiny."

The normally harmonious drinking session became bad-tempered. They were not angry with each other, although some eavesdropping would have thought so, they were angry with the prefect and his interference in the normally happy ala. The result of their debate was that they all went to bed extremely drunk and the recruits had a slightly quieter training session the following day although they worked even harder than usual.

Chapter 5

Stanwyck

Lenta lay in her lover's arms. Aed was the first man she had bedded since her husband and she had loved every single moment of the experience. The young man was a powerful lover and they both satisfied each other. Lenta reflected that her life was now complete. The void left by her dead family had been filled with her lover and the vibrant settlement that was Stanwyck. Despite the attempt by the Romans to make Isurium Brigantium the new Brigante capital the influx of warriors and metal workers had meant that the new capital was just a colony of retired Romans and their slaves. Lenta had garnered all the power that she had ever wanted. She was Queen in all but name. True, King Maeve had more subjects but they cowered in the west well away from the Romans. For all that she resented the Romans, she was pleased that their military presence protected her and her people.

She gently kissed the sleeping Aed and went to the door of the house. As she gazed out she could see the bustle and purpose as the newly arrived mingled with those who had always lived here. In the last fourteen days over two hundred loyal Brigante warriors had arrived and it had taken all the industry of her metal workers to arm them but they now had a force that could easily defend Stanwyck from any assault launched by Maeve. Perhaps they could build more stone buildings as they were at Isurium Brigantium; the permanence of such buildings was one of the ways that Roman civilisation was measured. Perhaps one day people would measure her success by such buildings. She suddenly felt the touch of Aed's hand on her back and it sent a shiver of pleasure coursing through her body. "I thought you had left me."

She turned and kissed him hard upon the lips. "I will never leave you my love; I just didn't want to disturb you."

He laughed. "You disturbed me many times during the night."

She laughed with him. "I could see, my love, that you were disturbed already."

"Now that I am awake I will take some of the men on a patrol to the west. I will leave the newer men to guard the fort. It will do them good to have that responsibility"

"Be careful. Maeve has many warriors I don't want to lose you so soon after finding you."

"I am not afraid of Maeve. Besides with our new armour my men are all worth five of his. Remember I am of the Brigante royal family as you are and we do not run away from our responsibilities. I know what I need to do for this land of ours and I will do it." He kissed her so hard upon the lips that it took her breath away and left her wide-eyed with wonder. ". I will be careful for your sake. But we may return after dark; I will warn the sentries, I wouldn't want them to shoot me as a Brigante raider."

Later that day she watched with pride as the column of two hundred mailed warriors left the fort. She could see that there was a mixture of new warriors and the faithful ones who had fought alongside the Romans at Brocavum. She had made the right decision when she had appointed the young Aed to be their commander. He had an old head on a young body. The thought of his young body made her blush like a girl and she found a playful smile playing around her lips. When he returned she would pleasure that young body as it had never been pleasured before.

Aed halted the column close to the steep cliffs above a raging torrent of a river. He turned to Grachus, the oldest of the Brigante warriors and the one who had led them before Aed's arrival. "You keep the more experienced men here. I will take these new men for some archery practice. I think this would make a good site for a fort so cut down some of those trees and we will help to build it when we return."

Grachus looked around. As much as he resented the young pup he recognised Aed's prowess and acumen as a leader. "If we place them by the cliff edge we can lay out the walls easier."

"Good idea, I knew you were the right man for the job. I think the exercise will build their muscles up even more."

"Get those mail shirts off and get your axes. You lazy bastards are going to work today and we are going to build a fort."

As they stripped one of the older men said, "Why here Grachus?"

"He's got a good military eye I will say that. If you look you can see that on this side, where we are going to lay the felled trees there is a cliff which makes it impossible to assault. It is then steep all the way around to that narrow neck. Put a gate there and any enemy would have to assault that one spot. I am just surprised King Venutius didn't put one here."

"He never liked walls he liked to fight in the open."

"Aye and look where it got him? Dead in a battlefield with all his oathsworn. Come on lads let's get those trees down."

Aed led the rest of the men a short way to the west. When they were out of earshot of the builders he halted them. "Today we begin our real work. You have all done well pretending to be Roman lovers but today that pretence goes. We will ride back and kill these Brigante traitors and then return to Stanwyck and join our brothers. We will give them a choice join us or die. Are you ready?" As they all cheered his name he strung his bow. "I want them to die not us. Use your arrows and give them no quarter. Remember we fight as Brigante not copies of the Romans."

Grachus and his men had made excellent progress and many trees had been felled. He heard the thunder of hooves and wondered what it was.

43

Initially alarmed by the noise he relaxed when he saw that it was Aed and his recruits. He wondered why they were galloping in a line towards them. He suddenly realised that they all had bows in the hands. The line suddenly halted and, before any of them could get arms, armour or shields a black storm of arrows rained down upon them. Most were impaled by a number of arrows and died instantly. Those further away tried to run but Aed's plan had been thorough. There was nowhere for them to run for they were on a cliff edge above a river. Within a few heartbeats, they were all dead.

"Strip their bodies and then throw them over the cliffs into the river. Then we ride. Today we begin to make Brigantia ours again." He turned to the young man next to him, "Draghuar ride to King Maeve tell them we have taken Stanwyck."

Macha lay in her bed with Ulpius. He had a slight fever and she fretted. She smiled to herself; she was less likely to run crying to one of the village women. She looked at him nestling in her arms his face puffed up and red. If only Marcus were with her she could share her worries. She had no one; she was as lonely as could be. Lenta seemed far more distant since the birth of her son and since she had taken up with the young warrior, Aed she had virtually ignored her sister. Macha wondered if it was a family trait for her half-sister, Cartimandua, who had left her husband for a young shield-bearer. Would she do the same when she became older? She shook her head as though answering herself, no she loved Marcus and Ulpius too much she would be faithful unto death.

It was indeed nightfall as the column made its way back through the gates of the stronghold. The guards had been chosen by Aed and were oathsworn. Once the gates were closed behind them Aed and his men dismounted and made their way to the hut containing the rest of the traitors. "We want no one to leave. Give them all the same question do they join us. If they say yes then they live. All others must die. The longer we can deceive the Romans the better. Then we will slaughter the Romans in their new settlement." Without the need for further words the two hundred or so men quickly surrounded each of the dwellings. All of the people were inside either sleeping or preparing food; they felt safe and secure inside the newly renovated and repaired walls. There were two exceptions, Nuada, a young metal worker and Bethan, the daughter of his master. They had sneaked out of their huts and were exploring each other's body in the cattle byre. At first, they were so engrossed in the primitive and youthful fumbling that they failed to hear anything outside until suddenly a piercing scream grabbed their attention. Quickly throwing on their clothes they crept to the doorway. What they saw shocked them to their core for Aed and his men were gathering the inhabitants shouting at them and when they received the wrong response they were butchered where they stood. Bethan saw her father stand in front of Aed

44

and spit at him when asked the question, "Who do you support King Maeve or the Brigante bitches?" The sword from behind ended not only his life but that of his wife. Before Bethan could cry out Nuada put his hand over her mouth and whispered. "Quiet. Any noise and we will die. Let us leave while we can." Nuada had seen enough to know that if they stayed they would join his dead master and wife.

They made their way swiftly and quietly around the back of the byre; they were aided in this by the noise of the dead and dying and the crash of doors being forced open. They found themselves close to the main building, the one in which Lenta and Macha lived. If there was one hope that there might be a sanctuary then it might be here where, surely, there would be loyal bodyguards. Any hope that the boy had was dashed when he peered over and saw Princess Macha being dragged out by her hair. A second guard carried a screaming Ulpius under his arm. The two were thrown onto the ground before Aed who had arrived with his handpicked guards.

"How dare you touch us, we are the royal princesses!" Even faced with such terror Macha fought back. She had not survived the attempts by Venutius to kill her to let this young man terrorise her. "If you harm us the Romans will hunt you down."

Aed pulled back the defiant young woman's hair, exposing her neck. He drew his sax and said clearly for all to hear, "Bitch! You and all the other whores who have taken Roman lovers will die. Every bastard child of the Romans will die and then, when we are ready every Roman will either die or be driven from our land," he looked up and nodded. The guard holding Ulpius sliced through the infant's neck so savagely that the head dropped to the floor in front of his mother. Macha's eyes widened in horror and a scream started to erupt from her throat. "I hope the Romans do come for we will be ready for them this time and your man will be the first to die and I will claim the sword of the Brigante for me!"

Even in her terrified state after the shock of seeing her son killed, even the fear for her husband and knowledge that she would die, Macha was still a royal princess and she defied Aed to the end, "The Sword of Cartimandua and you are not man enough to touch it let alone wield it!"

Aed's sax slid across and her jugular was sliced through, her lifeblood seeping into the ground as the life left her eyes.

As they quickly headed towards the ramparts Nuada and Bethan could hear a wail slowly rise from the throat of Lenta as she saw the corpses of her sister and nephew." But Aed, how could you do this? She was my sister." Mesmerized the two young lovers looked back watching the tableaux below them. In widening pools of blood lay the princess and her son. On her knees before them squatted Lenta pleading with her lover and around them like voracious wolves stood the twenty bodyguards of the new lord of Stanwyck.

45

"She was a Roman whore and a traitor and you too are a whore. An old whore at that, just like your dead sister. Tonight, the old Brigante die and the new ones take over but first, my love, as you enjoy lovemaking so much we will see how you enjoy pleasuring my men, all of them!" The last thing they saw before they fled was the sight of Lenta being held down by four warriors. As they slipped over the wall into the ditch they could hear the screams of Lenta echoing into the night as she was raped by each of the men who had accompanied Aed. Nuada held the sobbing Bethan in his arm and he desperately hoped that the Brigante princess died quickly for that was a death no one should endure. "Come Bethan we must find the Romans before they realise that there are survivors. Isurium Brigantium is not far away and there are Romans there. Be strong. Your father was strong and he will be avenged." The young man became a man as he escaped. When he was old enough he would join the Romans and avenge the folk of Stanwyck.

It was barely two miles to the settlement of Isurium Brigantium and Bethan was exhausted both mentally and physically when they reached the outskirts, the barking dogs awoke the farmer as Nuada and Bethan scrambled over the stone wall. Flavius Bellatoris was armed with a spear as he challenged the intruders.

"Please help us. We are from Stanwyck it has been taken." As Nuada blurted out the words Bethan collapsed into Nuada's arms sobbing uncontrollably. Nuada looked at the grizzled Roman veteran. "They killed her mother and father."

"Woman!" Flavius shouted for his housekeeper to help the distressed girl. "Who killed them?"

"It was the leader of the garrison Aed. They slaughtered any who opposed them." He paused. "They killed the princesses."

"Lenta and Macha?"

"Aye and the child."

"Are you sure?" The boy nodded. Flavius sat down. He had lived too long. How could he tell Marcus that his whole world was ended? Suddenly a thought came to him; if they had killed the Brigante princesses then Isurium Brigantium with its veteran soldiers would be the next target. "Boy, get the horses from the stable. Woman, get your things we are leaving." Hobbling with his stick the ex-prefect mounted the first horse which Nuada had brought. "When the woman comes, mount the horses and await me." As the horse raced across the track Flavius hoped that he would be able to gather the people in time.

Mercifully Marcus was not at the fort. The new prefect had deemed it necessary that he return with the two turmae from Derventio himself. Although Decius and the others had been angered at this further insult Marcus was quite pleased for it enabled him to gather his thoughts and to reflect on his position. He had served eighteen years in the cavalry, he only had another seven and, like Flavius Bellatoris he could claim his piece of land. Looking at the land around him as he travelled south-east he could see that it was a good land. Perhaps he could become a horse breeder. He thought back to his childhood in Cantabria and the horses he had raised with his family. It was a long time ago but it was a happy time. Yes, he would wait out his seven years, spend more time with this family and then begin a horse farm. He would have his contacts with the auxiliary and would make a good living. The more he thought about it the happier he became. He let Argentium open his legs as the land became flatter and the horse relished the freedom to gallop. The high fells rolled behind him and soon he could see, in the darkening late afternoon gloom, the towers that identified the fortlet at Derventio.

He slowed his mount down to a walk. Quintus and Vettius had done a good job. The fortlet looked robust and he noticed a great air of urgency and purpose amongst the locals in the hamlet of Derventio. The two guards saluted smartly as Marcus dismounted. "Where are the decurions?"

"In the Praetorium sir!"

"Good. "Leading his horse he walked up past the barracks and could not help but see that all the men, troopers who had been recruits not that long ago now looked like soldiers. All the salutes he received were smartly given. His regret was that he was going to have to tell the men that their work had been in vain. As he saw the effort they had put into it he decided that now was the time for a lie. He would make up a reason for them to return with him.

Someone must have alerted the two decurions for they stood in full uniform outside the headquarters building. "Sir!" From their smiles, they were both glad to see him.

"Good to see you, gentlemen." He waved his arm expansively around. "You have done well. This is better than I would have hoped in the time I have given you." A trooper appeared from nowhere and led off Argentium the decurions were definitely trying to impress Marcus, and it was working.

Their smiles told him that the praise had been justified. "If you would like some refreshment sir?"

"That is the best invitation I have had all day. I would love to and while I eat you can give me your reports."

Marcus didn't know how hungry he was until he started to eat. He listened as Quintus gave the main report with occasional interjections from Vettius. "We found the locals pleased to see us and they provided many of the materials we needed."

"At cost sir."

"Quite. At a cost." Marcus could not help smiling as he munched on his bread and cheese. The clerks back at the fort would demand that every denari be accounted for. He waved his arm and Quintus continued. "We found that the original defences had not been totally eradicated and we made good progress. We also found out why the locals were pleased to see us." Marcus paused in his eating and swallowed a mouthful of watered wine.

"And why were they glad to see you? The money you spent?"

"Oh they were pleased enough about that but it seems there are local bandits who prey on travellers and especially seafarers. Just up the coast in a small inlet just south of the Dunum Fluvius. The people hereabouts said that for a while they could not get fish at all but just lately supplies have started to come in." Marcus nodded fish was always a welcome addition as it could provide food even in winter. This was just the reason he had wanted the fort rebuilding to provide stability.

"Have you had a chance to investigate yet?" He could see from their crestfallen faces that they had not. "No silly of me. You had the fort to build and you have done a good job." He reluctantly put down the goblet. "Now I suppose I had better give you the bad news. The new prefect Rufius Demetrius has arrived and has informed us that the new Governor intend the ala to take to the field in the next month. We need every trooper and you will have to return there with me."

"You don't want us to dismantle the fort do you sir?" Quintus' voice told him that it would destroy the hearts of the men to undo the work. Normally when a fort was abandoned it was made indefensible by the departing soldiers to prevent it from being used against them.

"What do you think of the locals?"

"Nice people sir. Hard-working but a bit worried about attacks from bandits."

"Right. It is not normally done but I will take responsibility. Before we leave tomorrow we will see the village elders and ask them if they would take over its defence. They might not be able to stop an army but I think it would deter these bandits." He could see the relief on their faces. "When we leave tomorrow we will go north first and then follow the river. That way we can poke our noses into this bay and we may gain insight into the size of the problem. And now gentlemen I believe that I will retire and leave you two decurions to enjoy your last night of detached duty." Marcus was diplomatic enough to realise that the two young men would want to spend their last night of command without worrying about a senior officer.

Streonshal

Atticus led the line of horses down the twisting cliff path to the huts at the foot of the cliff. Gaius Cresens had felt slightly uneasy without the powerful helmsman to protect him. Now that he had returned he felt more secure. The villagers were also glad to see the very popular young man. As the villagers unpacked the horses Cresens took him to one side. "Any trouble?"

"Not really but Stanwyck has some very unsavoury characters. The metalworkers were friendly enough but the warriors were not."

Cresens shrugged; he cared only for money and profit. "Did we make a healthy profit?"

Atticus smiled," We made a very healthy profit. It seems they have been making armour and weapons for their own warriors for nothing and they were grateful to get their hands on silver for a change. I made some good contacts. If I return next year I know who to speak to."

"Good. As you can see our numbers have grown and we will have a need for the armour and weapons."

Atticus looked with some misgivings at the dregs who had gravitated to their now successful settlement. They were not the hardworking type; they were chancers and opportunists. From the looks he had seen the villagers give to them they shared his sentiments but they all owed the master so much that none felt they could voice their disapproval. "Perhaps not Master. I came through Derventio and the auxiliaries are rebuilding the fort there. We may soon have peace and stability with the order that Rome brings."

A shiver coursed through the quartermaster's body. He did not need Romans this close and he especially did not need the auxiliary cavalry for they would recognise him. He was not to know they were new to the province. "Good. Perhaps then, if they are making the area secure we might visit our piratical friends up the coast." Cresens was being neither brave nor thoughtful. If the Romans were returning then he needed to maximise his profits and get out of the area. He had made a little money but he knew that the pirates would have hoarded gold and silver and he wanted it. It looked like he would have to pull his disappearing act again except this time he would have an armed bodyguard of powerful warriors.

Atticus nodded his features hardening. Although a kind man Atticus wanted to deal a blow to these murderers and he knew the boys of the village would also want revenge. He had been waiting for the day when they could scour out that pestilential hole. "I will arm the men and prepare them."

"Good. We will leave tomorrow."

The following day Atticus and Cresens mounted their horses and looked at the ragtag bunch of erstwhile warriors. There were ten men and a few of the village boys behind them and they were all armed with a variety of weapons. Atticus had bought what he could and some had bows while others had spears or axes. Some sported the new weapons recently purchased at Stanwyck. Cresens hoped that they would frighten the pirates away but he was not confident. As they made their way along the undulating cliff path the quartermaster became increasingly uneasy. It had seemed such a good idea back in the security of his villa, surrounded by his guards. Out here he would have to test not only their mettle but also their loyalty. Suppose the pirates were better armed? What if the Romans saw them? The panic began to rise inside of him and he began to plot his way out of the dilemma. Fortunately, Atticus gave him the solution. "Are you sure we should be leaving the settlement with so few warriors? The pirates have boats they could attack while we are heading north."

Cresens appeared to think on this. "You are wise beyond your years Atticus. I will return and guard the village. You can carry on and mete out punishment on those barbarians. I would probably slow you up for I am an old man. Remember to bring back their plunder for we need it for the villagers; we can redistribute their wealth amongst those who had everything taken."

"You truly are a hero master." Atticus could not believe how kind and benevolent the Master was, always thinking of others.

"Be away with you. I am just looking after our people." Waving he turned his horse and headed back to Streonshal. Thank the gods that they had given such a keen mind and great sense of self-preservation.

Without the portly Cresens, the column made good time. Atticus knew the route for they had come the other way on the night of their escape and the boys knew it well. The bought guards hung back behind both Atticus and the boys but if they were worried about that they did not show it. Some of the boys had been to the settlement and they warned Atticus when they were close. He tethered his horse to a lone tree in a dell hidden from sight and they set off for the hidden lair. They could see smoke rising from huts and knew that they were almost within touching distance. He signalled for them to spread out and they slowly bellied up the ridge which overlooked the huts again the Master's men showed a reluctance to put themselves in the fore. Atticus glanced around; they would run at the first sign of trouble leaving just him and the few boys. If that happened he would call off the attack. He would not risk those boys for they were the future of Streonshal.

Below them, they could see a handful of huts around the beach and, dragged up on the beach were their boats. From the number of boats, Atticus guessed that there must be twenty or so men in the village and that was too many for the eleven men he had with him. He signalled them to retreat, "There are too many let us withdraw," and they returned to the horse hidden in the dell. It took them some time to negotiate the path unseen.

One of the bigger thugs took him to task as he retreated. "Why did we not attack?"

"There were too many men there. We would have been slaughtered. The Master would not want you to sacrifice your lives. We will return to Streonshal." He could see from their faces that they were disappointed but he did not want the deaths of the boys on his hands. "Had it just been us men I might have considered it but we are too few." He had just mounted his horse when he heard the unmistakable sound of a buccina and the clash of arms. Romans!

Marcus and the two turma had been riding northwards with scouts out. The country was largely deserted and the only tracks they could see were the cattle tracks which meandered up and down the moors. The scouts came racing back, lashing their mounts. "Sir Bandits! They are attacking some traders." The second scout pointed behind them and Marcus could see that the track dipped and twisted away to the sea. It was in the area identified by the headman at Derventio as the base of the bandit bands.

"Draw weapons!" he gestured to the scouts. "Lead the way." Marcus was impressed by the military manner of these young recruits. They might not have seen action but you would not know it from the way they carried themselves.

As they came over the rise they saw the scene clearly. The traders had cloth and pottery on their horses. The twenty or so bandits who had ambushed them were busy killing in the calm, calculating way of men who have done this before and enjoy it when they heard the thunder of the turmae hooves. Panic set in instantly and they ran down the valley sides to the sea. The cavalrymen sliced through them, the bare backs very tempting and unprotected targets. As Marcus sliced through the back of one unfortunate he turned and shouted, "Vettius secure the area. Quintus, sound the charge we'll rid the area of these vipers."

Charging down the track they soon caught up with the fleeing felons who were trying to get to the boats beached by the huts. None of them made it. As the turma halted the huts erupted in a screaming maul of women who came at the troopers with any weapon to hand. Marcus was pleased to hear Quintus take charge. "Disarm these bitches or kill them." His young troopers might have baulked at such an order a month ago but now they obeyed the decurion instantly. Within moments it was over and the women were tied to each other by ropes partly to prevent them escaping and partly to stop them trying to emasculate the troopers with their ragged nails.

"Good work Quintus. Search the huts and make sure no one is still alive then burn the bodies. I'll be with Vettius. When all is secure join us. Good work, men. Good work!"

Vettius was busy seeing to the wounded traders. Two had been killed and the other four were wounded but they would survive. They were incredulous about their escape and all had expected to die. They showed this heartfelt appreciation to Marcus. "Thank you, sir. Thank you. If you had not chanced along we would have been done for. These bandits are a scourge we tried to avoid them but they have grown very bold since the troops pulled out of the fort." The man shivered. "You would not believe what they do with their prisoners and their women sir, why they are worse. We have a saying about them. The men are men and so are the women."

"Where were you headed?"

"Eboracum by way of Derventio."

"Vettius when Quintus comes take six men and escort these traders to Derventio then catch up with us." Vettius almost asked a question and then thought better of it. Smiling Marcus said, "You will catch up with us for we have some slaves and they will slow us down. Any casualties amongst your men?"

"No sir," he grinned and spoke in a quieter voice. "Couldn't have gone better for a first action. They will all think they are bleeding Julius Caesar's now!"

Quintus' arrival was heralded by the wailing of the women who were lashed together. Marcus looked at them properly as they trudged up the hill. They hurled insults and threats at the men but Vettius took his vine staff to them and they returned to giving him the sullen stare and the evil eye. They were a pitiful lot but he could see from their cruel looks and demeanour that they would stand some watching. As the headman at Derventio had told them this village had inflicted as much cruelty and pain as an invading army. Marcus nodded to Vettius as he led his men off. It had been a good day.

"A nice bit of profit here sir."

"It certainly is. The slave traders are always looking out for new merchandise and these," he looked back and quickly counted," fifteen women and children will do nicely. Lead off decurion."

Atticus and the boys climbed slowly and warily over the ridge. They had seen the efficiency of the cavalry and Atticus had prevented the boys from joining in the killing. From his experience of Roman auxiliaries, they would have killed first and apologised later. They spread out and search the huts. One of the boys suddenly shouted and they all converged on one hut. They had found the hoard hidden beneath the floor.

"Right lads, Hael, you ride my horse back and tell the master what we have found. The rest of you load the boats and we'll travel back in comfort."

Chapter 6

When the column of refugees reached Morbium it was late into the night. The sentries sent for the duty decurion. It was Fabius Demetrius. He peered over and saw a motley bunch of Brigante. He already had a low view of the inhabitants, the barbarians and they looked to him as though they were bent on destruction.

"Go away! If you do not disperse I will order my men to fire."

"I am Flavius Bellatoris, formerly prefect of this ala please let us in for we bring urgent news."

"Standing orders state that the gate is not to be opened during the hours of darkness without the permission of the prefect. Go away until morning."

One of the sentries coughed, "It is the old prefect sir. I served with him."

"I do not care who he is standing orders state that..."

"Well go and get the prefect then," bellowed an increasingly impatient Flavius whose knee was now throbbing with the pain of the wild ride.

"I do not take orders from the likes of you. Now clear the bridge or you will be shot."

Flavius suddenly heard a voice he recognised. "Open that bleeding gate!" Even as he recognised the voice of the blunt decurion, Decius, he heard the gate begin to open.

"How dare you disobey my orders! I will have you whipped!" The high-pitched voice made some of the sentries actually smile whilst Decius burst out laughing.

He looked up at the young face of the decurion on the ramparts. "You might not have recognised the prefect but we did and he still carries rank. You might think of that young Demetrius before you order whippings. Now get these people inside and the gate shut."

By the time the gates were slammed shut the whole of the fort had been awakened and a red-faced Rufius was storming towards the headquarters building. "Who has allowed this rabble in here?"

Fabius piped up, "It was Decurion Decius I told him not to. He disobeyed orders." The look on his face suggested that he felt he had scored a point over Decius.

Decius shook his head and said in a voice that was laden with undertones and emphasis. "Sir might I introduce Prefect of Auxiliaries Flavius Bellatoris, the former commander of this unit." Rufius was at a loss for words. "You trooper get a chair can't you see he's in pain." He looked at the new prefect. "Copped a nasty knee wound fighting the Novontae. Sir."

As Flavius sat down with a nodded thank you to Decius, Rufius finally found his voice flashing an irritated look at Decius he said, "Well, er prefect but why have you brought all these people into the fort in the middle of the night and left the security of their homes?"

Flavius beckoned Decius and Rufius forward and lowered his voice. "Stanwyck has fallen to rebel Brigante." He paused and looked significantly at Decius, "and the Princesses Lenta and Macha murdered along with Decurion Princeps Marcus' son."

"The bastards!" He took Flavius hand, "Marcus isn't here at the moment he's out with the men."

"Good I did not relish giving him the news;" he shook his head sadly; "however this just delays the inevitable. For I will have to tell him."

Rufius stroked his chin thoughtfully. "Thank you, prefect. This puts a different slant on things." He turned to Decius. "Have the men stand to and prepare turmae one and two for a scouting patrol. Er, decurion," he said to his son, Fabius, "put these people somewhere out of the way and get them some food and drink. Officers call in an hour."

Decius found Gaius, Drusus and Lentius in their quarters donning armour. "You heard?"

Gaius nodded dumbly. "I can't believe it. Who would kill… and his child."

"He will need our help my friends if he is to survive this."

"Aye especially on top of losing the Decurion Princeps promotion. Talk about kicking a man when he is down." Just then Fabius Demetrius walked into the room. "And you!" He jabbed a finger in the youth's direction. "Your dad might be the prefect but don't you ever question me again or threaten me. Is that clear?" The young decurion paled and nodded. Decius waved his arm around the room. "These men are the experienced backbone of this ala when the shit starts to fall, and I think it has started, you watch us or some Brigante will be wearing what passes for your bollocks as a love token."

As the sun came up the officers all met. Flavius was sat next to the prefect and Drusus was pleased to see that the sons of the prefect were sat with their fellow decurions.

"Good, now that we are all here I can apprise you of the situation. Flavius Bellatoris has told us of the report from the refugees of slaughter at Stanwyck. This however is unproven." The old prefect started to rise in his seat. "However, this can be easily proven. I will send two turmae to the fort and if the massacre is true then I will send a report to the Governor." The senior decurions all looked aghast at each other. If the Brigante had revolted then they needed the legion for they were the only auxiliary unit north of Eboracum. "Decius Flavius and Julius Demetrius take your turmae to Stanwyck. You, I believe, know the princesses?"

"Yes sir!" barked Decius.

"This is why I am sending you. Ask to see them. As we are already two turmae down we cannot afford to lose a single man so be careful." He turned to the other decurions. "We cannot be tripping over these barbarians all the time; build them a stockade over there while we await the report." There was silence. "Now!" The decurions sped into action. When they had left the prefect turned to Flavius. "I did not mean to doubt your word but we only have the word of two frightened children; for all we know they may have fled an irate father."

"In your position, I would have done the same however prefect I would be careful about using the term barbarian in front of the auxiliaries. Many of us were born outside of Rome. These men are all that stands between the Brigante and disaster."

Rufius looked coldly at the crippled veteran. "I thank you for your advice and as with all advice it can be taken or," he emphasised the word," it can be ignored. Now if you will excuse me I have much to do."

Decius rode at the head of the eighty-two men as they left Morbium. He signalled to Gaelwyn and the wiry warrior took off on his pony. The journey was a short one and Decius knew every uncia of the way. They were travelling light for, if the fortress was taken, they would need to return with all haste to the isolated fort on the north side of the river. When they were out of sight of the fort Decius halted the men. He turned in and shouted, "Decurion! To the front." The older men of the turma grinned. They knew how blunt Decius Flavius could be.

Julius Demetrius had the same sulky look as his brother and he joined Decius reluctantly. "I should be with my men."

Decius flashed him a hard stare but ignored the comment. "How long have you served in the auxiliary?" He raised his arm and the column moved off. All the time they rode he scanned both sides of the undulating landscape.

This question non-plussed the young patrician. "Since I arrived with my f… with the prefect."

Decius snorted in derision. "As I thought, you haven't served in the auxiliary and the er, prefect has appointed you as decurion. Look back at those men decurion." Julius turned to view the faces of stone. "Some of those men have served in this unit for ten years. Many of them have fought in more battles than years in your young life. Even the recruits have had more training than you. Can you use a sword?"

The young man smiled a superior smile. "Yes my father hired a famous gladiator to train my brother and me; we are good swordsmen."

"Good eh? How many times have you used your sword while on a horse?"

"On a horse?"

"Yes, we are the cavalry we do use actual horses." There was a sudden eruption of laughter from behind and Demetrius coloured. "I will personally castrate the next man who laughs." He lowered his voice. "Without being too disrespectful decurion at the moment you are a liability and the men know it. You might turn out to be a good officer. For their sakes," he gestured back with his thumb, "I hope so but until we have seen a bit of action I want you to do everything I say and then all of us will live. Is that clear?"

The look on the decurion's face suggested that he might be going to argue but one look at the older man's face dissuaded him. He nodded. "Good now rejoin your men and listen carefully for my orders. I don't give them twice."

As they approached Isurium Brigantium they noticed the burning buildings. They looked as though someone had charged through and fired them; expecting resistance for the damage was not as bad as it might have been. Speaking to no one in particular Decius said, "Well it looks like they were right."

Gaelwyn appeared at his side from a stand of alder trees. "It is a good job that I am not a Brigante rebel or you would be dead."

"Which is why we have you out to make sure they don't surprise us, you cocky little bastard. Well?"

"There are no men between here and the fortress but the walls are all manned."

"What do you think? Has it been taken?"

Gaelwyn shrugged. "It is hard to tell. There are more men than there were but other than that… We will have to get a little closer." There was a wicked glint in the scout's eye.

"You love this, don't you? But you are right." He turned to his men. "Column of fours. We are going nice and steady. Keep your eyes open for the enemy and your ears open for my commands you four get your bows ready. The rest of you have a javelin ready and stow your cloaks." He looked pointedly at Julius who had not moved. "All of you."

The recruit behind Julius Demetrius asked the older man next to him, "Why stow the cloaks?"

"Simple son you need your arms free, you won't be cold if we start fighting and you also stick the cloak in front of you." They looked non-plussed. "Gives a little more protection to your wedding tackle." He grinned at the young man, "Although in your case you'd only need a neckcloth."

Julius followed suit and then loosened his sword in his scabbard. The decurion's words about his lack of experience had hit home. He could fight against a man on foot but for how long? He had seen the recruits training and they spent far longer than he and his brother had. He also realised that he had never fought on a horse either.

The older soldier behind him almost read his thoughts for he said to the recruit next to him. "When we have loosed the javelins be careful with that

56

spatha it's long, the last thing you want is to slice half your horse's head off. Remember what the training decurion drilled into you."

"Thanks."

Julius murmured a whispered, "Thanks", under his breath. If he survived the day he would have to learn how to be a real cavalryman.

The stronghold rose above them in layers of ramparts and ditches. Decius could see the armed men on the top. The old soldier felt uneasy. Something was not right. He had his orders however and he had to find out if the fort had fallen. He turned to the four men with the bows behind him." You four come with me. Decurion!" Julius rode forward. "I am taking these four and this waste of skin," he gestured at the grinning Gaelwyn who took the banter in good part, "a little closer. I am going to try to speak to them. If the fort has been taken I will find out. Should anything happen to me you are in command. Your orders will be quite simple. Get back to Morbium and tell the prefect."

"Should we not come for you?"

"If we can get out we will but you do not do anything other than tell the prefect. Got it?"

"Got it decurion."

"Good lad we might make a cavalryman out of you yet. Right, let's go." The six of them rode in an oblique line towards the gate. Decius wanted to get the best picture he could. "Notch your arrows." He turned to Gaelwyn, "Are you getting the same feeling as me?"

"Yes decurion, the men still don't look right; there are a lot of them and they are not smiling. They should be relaxed and they are not opening the gate."

"I had noticed that." He halted about sixty paces from the gate. Just about in bow range although those inside the fort would have more range. "Ho! Open the gates." The gates slowly started to open and Decius wondered if he had been wrong. Suddenly a phalanx of mailed horsemen raced towards them. "Loose! Treacherous bastards." The four troopers let fly with their arrows and as Gaelwyn and Decius turned to flee he was gratified to see an empty saddle and a fallen horse. He looked up to see that the decurion had brought twenty men forward in a line and they were preparing to shoot their arrows. "Dozy bastard! I told him what to do!"

The pursuing horsemen were still fifty paces behind but the Romans were now pulling away on their superior mounts. He watched with relief as the arrows flew over their head and he took the opportunity to shout, "Retreat! Now!"

Fortunately, the pursuers were no archers and relied on spear and sword. The Romans found themselves out of sight by the time they reached Isurium.

Decius halted the column and rode next to an elated Julius. "Thanks for the help decurion but next time just obey your bloody orders!"

The young man grinned, "Yes sir. I will do."

Shaking his head Decius turned to make sure that they had not lost a man. The stark thought suddenly sank in if Stanwyck had fallen then perhaps the young couple had been right and the princesses were dead. He had tried to hope for the best and even now he perversely hoped that they were part of this rebellion for if they were dead then someone would have to tell Marcus and while Decius would face a thousand enemies he could not be the one to bring that news to his friend.

When they reached Morbium, they saw the progress made on the refugee camp. By the same token, their rapid return showed all in the fort that the news was indeed true. The prefect summoned the two decurions into his office. "Well?"

"Looks like the news was true. We found Isurium burning and they attacked us when we asked them to open the gates."

"Casualties?"

"None sir. Decurion Demetrius discouraged them with a volley of arrows." He paused, "The lad did well on his first patrol."

The patrician was clearly pleased. "Well done. You have both done well. Perhaps I was wrong about you Decius Flavius perhaps you are not as insubordinate as I thought you were."

"Oh no sir you are quite right I am an insubordinate cuss. But I do know how to kill my enemies."

Julius grinned and then quickly covered his smile as he saw the flash of anger on his father's face. "Right. Officer's call now."

Once again Flavius Bellatoris sat in on the meeting although the expression on the face of the Roman patrician showed the distaste he felt for the former barbarian. "My initial thought was to take the ala, retake the fortress and crucify the insurgents," he saw the looks exchanged, "however I am, as you know new to the area and I have not been to this old fort."

They looked to Decius to speak but he looked at Drusus. "I was there with Decurion Marcus and Decurion Princeps Ulpius Felix when we rescued the Queen and I was there again when we rescued the treasure." The new decurions, including Rufius' sons, began murmuring at this but he rapped his hand against the table and they stopped. "If there are few defenders and if they have not improved the defences then I believe that it could be taken but at some cost."

Before the prefect could speak Flavius spoke. "However, they have improved the defences." They looked at him questioningly. "I had to buy some leather and some tools and I took the opportunity to visit with Princess

Macha and Lenta. They have deepened the ditches, raised the ramparts and cleared the woods back."

"Yes sir "interjected Decius, "I reckon that it is about two hundred paces further back. Makes you wonder if they have had this planned for some time eh?"

"We have no time for speculation. Only facts. The decurion mentioned the defences but what do we know of the defenders?"

"The walls seemed to be well manned to me."

"Yes, but did you see the other walls, not just the side from which you approached?"

"No sir but Gaelwyn, the scout, said that the walls were all manned and they didn't see him."

"How many then?" They all looked at each other reluctant to be the one to make a statement that could not be proved. "Come on someone take a guess."

Before Decius could speak a shrill voice piped up. "From the numbers facing us, I would say there had to be four hundred men on the wall." Julius looked to Decius who nodded approvingly. "That would give a total on the walls of about sixteen hundred and then," he went on, "there were more than a hundred who chased after us. If we assume some other reserves then that would make almost two thousand."

"You would be outnumbered by three to one," Flavius stated the obvious for had a decurion said so it would have sounded like cowardice.

"An assault by cavalry appears out of the question."

"The other thing sir is that we don't know how many others are close to hand. I remember when we fought Venutius; these buggers love the ambush. It's how they nearly caught the Queen the first time."

"And how he nearly beat the legions at Brocavum," added Flavius.

"A good point. Well, much as I hate to send bad news to the Governor I will have to." He turned to Drusus. "Detail four men to ride to Eboracum and then Lindum. I will write a report for the Governor. The rest of you had better get the refugee camp built." He looked at the decurions, "Thank you for your honesty."

Stanwyck

Aed was really angry with the commander of his bodyguard. "I wanted the Romans inside the walls where we could have slaughtered them not running back to their fort with news of our rebellion."

"They were too wary. We would have caught them but for those archers."

"You would have caught them had you ridden without mail! How did they become wary and who warned the Romans at Isurium?"

"Someone must have escaped."

"Obviously, the question is did they see the princesses being killed?"

"Does it make a difference?"

"Of course it does. If they think Lenta and Macha are involved in this then that will determine their response." He shrugged his shoulders. "But there is nought we can do about that now. King Maeve will have to make a judgement when he arrives. How far away is he?"

"A day's march."

"And the Novantae are a day further behind. With the troops we have here and those arriving we will have thirty thousand men; more than enough to take on a legion and one cavalry unit."

"Let us rid ourselves of the cavalry now. We outnumber them."

"Yes, fool and they are behind their walls and the river. How do you think we will manage that? You are a better warrior than thinker Ragnar, stick to fighting and the king and I will plan the strategy."

Morbium

Two days later the refugee camp had been finished and they now awaited the return of Marcus and the two turmae. It was even more imperative that they augment the meagre defenders but even Decius was worried that the decurion was well overdue. The messengers would have reached Eboracum the previous day and now would be almost at Lindum. Quintus Cerialis would then take at least a week to get to Eboracum and a further two days to arrive at Morbium. They all knew that it would be ten days before they would have relief, at the earliest.

Julius had changed since the patrol with Decius unlike his elder brother Fabius who still strode around the fort as though the other decurions were animal droppings fouling his world. He was assisting Decius to clear back some of the undergrowth near to the bridge and he asked the question which had been on his mind for some time. "Decurion when you and the other decurions talk about Marcus I get the impression that you are worried about his reaction to the killings at Stanwyck."

"That's right. You don't know, do you? Marcus and Princess Macha they were, well they were together."

"Married?"

"Not formerly. The high ups frown on decurions getting married but yeah I suppose they were what you might call man and wife and they had a son, little Ulpius."

"I can see why he would be upset. Thank you for telling me."

"No, you were right to ask. The rest of us all know and we assume everyone does. I guess I will have to tell the prefect."

"Tell the prefect?"

"This will really upset some people, you know?"

"Yes, I know. If you don't mind could I tell my, tell the prefect?"

Decius looked at the young man with new respect in his eyes. "You are alright, you are. Thanks, son, I would appreciate that."

Rufius had sent patrols out each day and they had reported large warbands gathering food and animals. They had always outnumbered the cavalry and it had galled them to run from their insults.

Decius and Gaius were exercising their mounts when they heard a shout from the sentry in the tower. "Cavalry approaching." There was a pause. "It is Decurion Marcus and he has prisoners."

Decius and Gaius looked at each other. This was the day they had been dreading. How to tell Marcus the bad news? They had had days to get used to it and they no longer thought of the princesses as living but to Marcus, they were still alive, right until someone told him that they were dead and his future ripped to tatters.

Quintus and Vettius beamed with pleasure as they each led in their turma. Marcus allowed them to precede him across the bridge and into the fort. He followed the captives who had lost some of their bluster in the long march from the sea. The prefect emerged from headquarters and the three decurions saluted. "I can see that you have had an eventful patrol decurion."

Marcus looked across at the refugee camp, "And I can see, sir, that we have arrived back just in time."

"You have indeed. The three of you come into the headquarters building and let your men see to the horses. Decurion!" Decius came ambling over. "See to those prisoners. And ask Flavius Bellatoris to join us."

Marcus' head was full of questions as he stood in the headquarters' office. He had missed much since he had left and he could not work it out. He glanced at the other two decurions who looked both pleased and bemused at the same time. They had expected a torrent of questions having brought in prisoners but no one seemed to have noticed them.

They all stood to attention as the prefect and Bellatoris came in. Marcus looked at the prefect and noticed something different. For the first time since he had known him, he seemed to be almost human his face looked sympathetic and caring. Marcus could not work out what the difference was. His speculation was ended when Flavius took him by the arm and said, "Marcus come with me."

The decurion looked up at the prefect unsure of what to do and the prefect nodded. As the door closed he heard the prefect say, "Now gentlemen if you would give me your report and begin with those prisoners…"

Marcus was totally confused. "Flavius what is it? Am I in trouble? Have I done something wrong?"

"Sit down son." The door opened and Decius and Drusus entered. "It's the princess and your son." Terror filled his face along with guilt. He had not thought of them first he had thought of his career. He was a poor father and a bad husband.

"Are they…?"

"There is no easy way to tell you so I will give it to you straight. The garrison at Stanwyck rose and killed Macha, her sister and your son Ulpius."

There was a silence that seemed to fill the room. The three bluff soldiers who gathered there to provide support did not know how to give it. When a friend died you drank to their memory and remembered them that way. Your friends were soldiers and most soldiers expected to die in battle. How did you comfort someone whose family has been murdered? How do you comfort someone who cannot even bury the bodies of their family?

Marcus stood up and grasped each of their arms in turn. "Thank you, my friends. It must have been hard for you to tell me this news and I thank you for your kindness. I now know why there was an atmosphere."

The three of them looked in amazement at the calm figure before them, he suddenly looked a little older than when he had left but he stood before them reacting as though they had told him he had to have a worse room for the night or could not have his favourite food for a while. They could see the pain in his eyes but his voice sounded controlled. They could not know that his mind was raging with anger and hate. "I know you expect tears and there will be tears. But those tears will come when I am revenged on the murderers of my family and when I have laid their bodies to rest." Even Decius was taken aback by the cold anger of the voice which had just been so calm and controlled. "And now I expect the prefect will need my report."

As he closed the door the three of them looked at each other. "Well, I didn't expect that."

Flavius shook his head. "None of us has taken a wife nor fathered a child until we have we cannot judge this man. I will return to my farm but you, his friends must be there for him. I believe he has built a dam in his heart and one day that dam will burst. You will have to repair it."

When Marcus re-entered the office, there was an embarrassed silence. He could see the sympathy from Quintus and Vettius who had obviously been told the news. He became angry inside. He did not need sympathy. He needed revenge. "Have we heard from the Governor yet sir?"

The prefect nodded. He had hoped that Marcus would have a professional manner and was pleased that he was displaying such a professional attitude. "Not yet. The slaves will be useful in rebuilding Isurium Brigantium. Well done decurion. I can see why Flavius Bellatoris holds you in such high esteem. As for the other problem, the unrest in the east, well that will have to wait. Decurion Drusus said that you know the fortress well?"

"Yes, sir I have visited there many times. I have seen the improvements they have made. I assume they said that it would take infantry to assault?"

"Yes they did but it galls me to allow those barbarians to hold us to ransom. And where did those men come from, if there are nearly two thousand inside where did they come from?" There was a silence. "Come on man don't be modest if you have an idea tell me. I am new to the province. Tell me."

"Probably the same place they did the last time from the north, could be Carvetii, Novontae or even Votadini. And then there are the Caledonii and Pictii who have yet to meet us in battle; they are numerous. Normally they fight amongst themselves but if I were a gambling man I would say that the Brigante have some powerful allies."

"So Decurion this could be the start of something far bigger than a warband sacking a Roman town. This could be the war Governor Cerialis predicted."

Fainch

Even as they spoke those powerful allies were gathering in the heartland of the Pictii. The chiefs had come from all over, the Selgovae and Votadini from the northeast, the Dumnoni and Novatonae from the west. There were even chiefs from the north the Caledonii and Venicones. The diminutive figure of Fainch sat amidst them with King Maeve on her right. If any of these warriors felt that the woman's presence was an insult they did not mention it. All of them were in awe of the priestess. They could see her power. For Maeve, it had gone beyond just power and the two of them were now lovers. He was entrapped by his heart as well as his crown.

The war chief of the Novantae was speaking. "It is true that the Romans are gradually moving on my lands. It was not long ago that they destroyed two of my warbands. If we do not stop them soon then they will take all of our lands."

"We of the Caledonii do not fear the Romans. Our lands are far to the north and they will not get there. If they do attempt to conquer us they will find that our land and our warriors will defeat them. No one has ever invaded us. But my warriors are keen to test themselves against these foreign warriors who seem to make others fear them."

"Do not be so certain oh mighty king. In my father's lifetime there were no Romans in the whole of this island and look how much they have conquered. There are parts of the Canti land where there are no local tribes only Romanized tribesmen. They are coming, they are coming."

Fainch spoke and there was silence. "The Romans defeated the tribes in the south because they attacked separately and the Romans could defeat them little by little. We are not asking for an attack now but next year at Eostre."

The king of the Votadini spoke for the first time. "Then why did you take Stanwyck? Surely the Romans will come north to punish those rebels who killed the royal princesses?"

Maeve thumped the table with his huge hand; he could not contain his excitement. "That is the brilliance of Fainch's scheme for they will send their legions north to do as you say but we will fall before them and draw them into the land of the Carvetii, north of the land of the lakes. We have a battlefield chosen between two mighty rivers there the legions will not have the advantage and we can destroy them or we can slip south and ambush them in the land of the lakes and they will be destroyed in the cold winters there."

"Over the winter! Who fights over the winter?"

Once again Fainch's small voice silenced the booming warriors. "The Romans do and once we defeat one legion they will have to send for the others. When Eostre comes the kings in the south will rise and there will be no legions to control them. That is when we will use all your warbands to crush the Romans and it will be on the ground of our choosing." She put her hand on King Maeve's. "The King is excited, as I am for we will defeat them but what is important is that we draw the legions up here, far from their bases so that our brother kings can destroy the legions that will be thinly spread out. We do not need to defeat them in one battle we need to bleed them."

There was much nodding and agreement until Niall the King of the Dumnoni spoke. He had a scarred face and had fought at Brocavum. "That was the plan of Venutius was it not? Did not the Romans defeat Lord Woolgar in the land of the lakes and did not Venutius choose his battlefield which became his deathbed?"

"True King Niall and you fought well on that day but Venutius was a fool, a brave fool but a fool. We will make sure that when we fight the Romans they are surrounded. We will make sure that they cannot use their mighty war engines and we will make sure that they get no supplies. An army without weapons is no army at all." There was much nodding. Most importantly we will make sure we have powerful allies." She swept her arm around the hut." Powerful allies who can help us to bleed and then disembowel this Roman beast and finally when it is lying helpless we will take off its head and Britannia will be ours again."

From the nods and smiles, Maeve could sense that they had agreed but he needed to put it to the test. "Do we fight?"

"We fight!" They chorused back.

Fainch took over. "Prepare you soldiers remember the Romans are well armed and armoured make sure your warriors are. The Romans use all weapons, swords, arrows, horses and javelins; we must do so and the Romans are well fed. If we are to win then we must be well supplied."

King Niall spoke again. "We are all agreed we will fight but I am still concerned about Stanwyck. How will you draw the Romans on and have you men willing to die for such a victory?"

"You are wise King Niall. We have two and a half thousand warriors inside Stanwyck. They all have horses. When the legion arrives it will surround the fortress and build siege engines and assault the walls."

"And the walls will fall."

"And the walls will fall."

There was a gasp. "Then what is the point of such a sacrifice?"

"The walls will fall but not before the defenders have left. King Maeve has another twenty thousand warriors, some Brigante, Carvetii, Novantae and even Votadini. They will attack the soldiers attacking from the west, slaughter them and destroy their engines. The warriors inside will then escape. They can have the fortress but they will not have the warriors. The Romans do not have as many men as we do. They have to send to other lands for their troops. As long as we kill more of them and especially more of their legions then we will win. It is the legionaries who will man the engines and assault the walls and they will not be protected by shields and large numbers as they man their machines. It will be like hunting a wild boar; we do not need to make the killing blow at the start of the hunt we can hurt it and when it chases us hurt it again and again until it bleeds to death. We will bleed the Romans in the lands of the west like the wounded boar it will follow us, follow to its doom."

The kings and chiefs began to bang their table to show their approval. Her hunting image had shown them quite clearly the brilliance of the strategy. Maeve looked adoringly at the witch for she had won over the men of the north with her words and her wisdom. If her sisters were as effective as she was then Rome would lose not only its legions but its province.

Lindum

Quintus Cerialis read again the report from the prefect. He was not angry for he had expected such an act. In fact, the act itself helped Rome for in murdering the last vestiges of the Brigante royal family any action taken by the legions would now be justified as retribution for the murder of a client king. At last, the Brigante could be subdued. They would no longer be a client kingdom but a vassal, a part of the Roman Empire. The tax collectors and officials would move in and the province milked of her riches. He looked again at the maps and writings of the divine Claudius. He had recognised that the Brigante were the largest tribe on this island with the largest power base. When he crushed them, and crush them he would then he would turn his attention to the Pictii and tribes to the north. The prefect had been quite correct the auxiliary unit could never assault the fortress for that he would need legionaries. The Second Adiutrix was untried but they were handily placed in the middle of the province. He would leave them as a mobile reserve in Lindum and then, with the Ninth he would march to defeat the Brigante. Julius Agricola would bring the Twentieth Valeria Victrix up the west coast and between them they would crush the Brigante. Two legions would be more than enough. The reserve at Lindum could march north to support them or west to support Frontinus. The aggressive general was retaining a little caution so far from home.

He shouted for his clerk. "Bring me the rosters of the available auxiliary units." As he waited he tapped the map before him. It was detailed in the east but not so in the west. When the clerk returned the Governor ordered him. "Write an order for the Tribune responsible for the Classis Britannica. I want him to sail around the west coast of this island and meet me at," he looked at the map. "Glanibanta. There is some sort of fort there. He can make his way across the land; the reports say that it is but a day's march from the sea. Make sure he has copies of these charts if he knows his business he should already have them." As the clerk scurried away Cerialis felt his heart sink as he looked at the meagre forces at his disposal. There were but four auxiliary units in reserve, all Batavian: one cavalry and three of foot. If he took them all he would leave the two legions controlling the rest of the province without that useful support. He decided to take just two infantry units. He would have to rely on the Pannonians.

When the clerk came back with the order for him to read he gave him more instructions. "I want a request sent to imperial Headquarters for four more auxiliary units. I do not have enough. Send for the tribune of the Second Adiutrix; he has begged for something to do well now he will have his hands full."

Morbium

That night Gaius sat with Marcus, Drusus and Decius. Lentius would have been with them but his task had been to escort the refugees back to Isurium Brigantium as the prefect deemed they were not in danger as long as there was a patrol between Stanwyck and Dere Street. Lentius had been unlucky enough to have the first duty. The other three had decided that Marcus should not be alone. Marcus, for his part, did not mind their company but he did not need it. He had his thoughts and his memories.

"You've got to let it out, sir."

"Let it out, Gaius? Let what out?"

"Well you must be upset, anyone in your position would be. I mean if that happened to me I wouldn't be able to think straight. I would find it hard to get up in the morning."

Marcus took a long pull on the wineskin and wiped his mouth with the back of his hand. "Do you remember when the Queen was murdered?" They nodded. "I asked the same thing of Ulpius. He said to me, 'Marcus we cannot change the past. Would that the Allfather allowed us to but the past is gone. It is the far shore of youth which is green and growing now we are on the rocks of age and they are grey and they are tired. As much as we want to go back to the green times of youth we cannot.' And that has helped me," he smiled fondly. "The old tyrant is still helping me. "Do you see what he meant

I can't go back and change what happened? Perhaps if I had left the army and been there…well that would have just meant that I was dead as well and besides that couldn't happen. I couldn't leave the army. I wouldn't be allowed to. No, I'll do what Ulpius did. I'll focus on all of you and make you the best ala in the army for by doing that then my family will have a better chance of being avenged. The difference between Ulpius and me, apart from the fact that he was a better soldier," the others shook their heads in disbelief but he waved his hand to silence their protests. "The difference is he knew who to look for, Gaius Cresens."

"Aye, I wish I knew where that fat bastard was. I bet he's long gone to Gaul or Rome or somewhere."

"I wouldn't be too sure but at least he had a goal. And then at the end, he found out about that witch, whatever her name was and wherever she is and I think that made him hurt even more at the end for they had both got away with the murder. He had killed the man who ordered it but not the murderers. I don't even know that. I don't know who killed them. That gives me something to do. Find out their names." They all took another swallow from their beakers and stared, reflectively into the glowing brazier.

Decius belched loudly and then took another drink. "I was talking to the prefect, no not the arrogant bastard, the proper one Flavius. He reckoned he had been in the fortress lately and the man running it was someone called Aed," he leaned in conspiratorially, "apparently shagging the Princess Lenta and that young lad Nuada told me that he was the one who ordered Lenta raped. He said he thinks it was him."

"There you are then sir. You have a name."

"Yes, Gaius I do. Aed and King Maeve. My list is growing. I cannot die until four animals are dead."

"Well, young Gaius you better get off to bed. You are on patrol tomorrow with your turma and our friend the little rodent."

"Rodent Decius?"

"Yes sir I have been improving my vocabulary it just means rat but it sounds better. That young rodent Fabius will chase you all ways to Hades and there is no other Decurion to rein him in so you watch out. At least you have Macro with you."

"Oh, that's some help. The Volunteer."

Marcus looked serious for a moment. "He might be a volunteer and he might be keen but so were you and, more importantly, you can trust him."

"Marcus is right. He will back you."

"It sounds like a lovely patrol ordered around by a pimply face schoolboy and being looked after by Macro."

Laughing they all left the empty wine-skins littering the floor. The slaves would wonder what had gone on when they tidied the next day.

It was getting on towards the shorter days and longer nights and Rufius Demetrius was regretting not lobbying for a better posting in a warmer clime. The alternative had been in the East with Vespasian. He would have been in a better position to impress the Emperor but he also knew that the Emperor did not like him. He suspected it was because he had never served with the legions or perhaps the fact that when they had both served together Rufius had made an unfortunate remark about his family. He had made his bed and although it was a cold one he would have to lie in it. The other reason he was shivering was that he was worried. Today his eldest son, Fabius, would take out his first patrol. He knew that leadership ran in his blood as his brother had shown in his first action. He was now regretting, a little, not sending out two turmae but had he done so his troopers might have felt that he was protecting his son for the other patrols had been a single turma; he believed he did not need to.

He felt a lump of pride as the turma halted in front of the Praetorium. His son reminded him of himself at that age. The troopers were immaculately turned out as he would have expected; everything was polished and gleaming, the sheepskin bleached white against the red saddlecloth, he was his father's son.

"Decurion Demetrius, you have your orders. Carry them out." As he watched them leave he was pleased that the tenth turma had more than half of its ranks filled with experienced men including the man who had been acting Decurion. His son would fulfil his destiny. He turned back into the office. He expected the Governor to arrive soon and he wanted to make sure that all was ready; he still worried about censure over the deaths of the princesses. Even though it was not his fault he had known of officers being punished by death for such acts. He would do all he could to avoid any blame and he already had a report which implicated the former prefect should it be needed. He would have used it already were it not for the fact that the officers and men seemed to revere him and he could not risk losing their loyalty so early in his career.

Chapter 7

Gaius, as the most experienced trooper, rode at the rear of the column. Even though he was very familiar with the country he still kept his wits about him. The Brigante were the past masters of ambush and the country between Morbium and Stanwyck was both undulating and wooded perfect to entrap auxiliaries. He noticed, with dismay that the decurion had deemed it unnecessary to use a native scout. Gaelwyn was still at Morbium. When he had brought it up, as they prepared for the patrol, he had been dismissed out of hand. "Why? We are only going a short distance from the fort and besides, I do not trust these native scouts."

The rest of the turmae, even Macro the keen volunteer, agreed with Gaius but the Decurion was master; the Roman army was not a democracy and the commander's decision was final. Gaius just hoped that it would not come back to haunt them.

At the front of the column, Fabius rode looking neither to the right nor left whereas every other man was on edge anticipating the attack. It seemed as though the decurion felt there was no danger and the Brigantes would stay in their fortress. Gaius knew better for the attack and capture of the stronghold had shown both intelligence and planning; anyone capable of that could easily plan to take out one in twelve of the only Roman force north of Eboracum. Cavalrymen were like gold when fighting the tribes and Gaius knew that the Brigante had the power and the wit to destroy one turma. When they arrived at Isurium Brigantium Flavius came out to greet them.

"Welcome. Would you care for refreshments?"

The crippled prefect was answered with scorn and derision. "Refreshments? We have come barely ten miles." He started to pull his horse away down the track.

Bellatoris ignored the insult and placed his hand on the bridle of the decurion's horse. "Thank the prefect for the use of the slaves. The work is moving much faster now, the walls are repaired and we are grateful."

Ignoring the old soldier Fabius kicked his heels into the flank of his mount and the column moved off. As Gaius passed Flavius he reined in his horse. "I will pass your message on to the prefect."

"Be careful young Gaius for that one is dangerous he has arrogance and believes himself to be invincible. I have seen it before. Be careful. There is something in the air this morning; my knee is playing up that normally means rain or trouble."

He laughed, "In this climate, it normally rains anyway but I will be careful."

"Silence in the ranks or I will have you flogged."

Exchanging looks of sympathy the two comrades nodded to each other and Gaius rejoined the column.

Aed saw the patrol emerge from the woods. Since the Romans had reinvested Isurium Brigantium they had seen the patrol ride out of the woods and then, keeping the same distance from the perimeter, circumnavigate the fortress. The only variation was whether they went east or west first. As soon as the patrol was spotted Aed mounted up two hundred of his warriors and placed one hundred at the south gate and one hundred at the north gate. So far the patrols had kept their distance which meant there was no chance for an ambush. Aed had not launched an attack as he did not want to warn the Romans of his intention. They would need to be patient. Time was on their side for it would take some time for the cumbersome legion to move north. His elite unit was wheeled out every time patrols arrived and then stood down when they followed their normal pattern. If his warriors were becoming bored they did not show it. Most of them were surprised that the Romans had not tried an attack. Aed knew the reason, the legions were too far away but he allowed his warriors to believe that he had frightened the Romans away. They also believed strongly in the power of witchcraft and Fainch's brief appearance at the fortress had given them added confidence. Perhaps with the powers of Mother Earth to aid them, they would finally drive the Romans away. Aed strapped his sword on, perhaps today would be the day when he would get to try his new warriors against the fabled Roman cavalry.

When Fabius emerged from the woods he did not follow the standing orders and ride either east or west instead he kept on going towards the gate. As soon as Gaius realised this he galloped to the front of the column. "Trooper Gaius, get back in line!"

"But sir, the orders are to ride along the tree line."

"Are you afraid? Would you like me to let you stay in the woods where it is safe? Now I can see why you are no longer a decurion for you are a coward. I am not afraid. We are Romans and these barbarians will stay behind their walls."

"Sir I cannot allow you to…"

Fabius's face became red with rage. Were it not such a serious situation the turma would have burst out laughing at his complexion. "You will not allow! You will not allow" When we return to the fort you will receive the appropriate punishment."

By now they were less than one hundred paces from the walls and all of the turma looked up nervously for they expected a shower of arrows at any moment. They could see the armed sentries patrolling the ramparts but they appeared to be making no aggressive moves although they could hear muffled calls and some movements.

"Look you coward! Nothing. Column west!"

Relieved that they were going no closer the men trotted in column behind their leader. At the rear, Gaius was fuming. He could not understand why the Brigante had not attacked but they were surely courting unnecessary danger. The Brigante were a cunning tribe as he had experienced many times in the past. The way they had captured the stronghold showed that. They were unfettered by strict rules and manoeuvres; they could strike in an instant.

Macro was at the front of the column riding just behind the decurion and he was enjoying the danger. He could see the curve of the ramparts as they swept north-west and he eagerly leaned forward to try to see around the corner. In his excitement he allowed his mount to move too close to the decurion's and his newly trained horse bit the rump of the decurion's horse. Although Fabius Demetrius was a highly unpleasant and questionable officer he was a superb horseman and his mount was soon under control, unlike his temper which erupted swiftly.

"Trooper, if you cannot control your horse ride twenty paces in front of me."

"Sir! Yes sir!" If Fabius thought that he was punishing the boy he was wrong. Grinning from ear to ear he rode not only the twenty paces but thirty. Later on, the decurion said that he always intended to do that but it was a happy accident. As Macro turned the corner of the stronghold he noticed a movement from the dip close to the northern wood. In the blink of an eye, he saw a hundred horsemen galloping towards him. He had the quickness of mind and control of his horse to halt and yell, "Brigante!" The whole column halted and Fabius froze. At the rear, Gaius sensed rather than heard the gates open and another hundred men charge their rear. He did hear the thunder of hooves on packed soil. Fabius was still frozen. Gaius willed him to give the order. The recruits with them were as petrified as their decurion.

"Ambush! Retreat!" The trooper cared not that the order had not come from their officer, they had an order and it made sense. Gaius' command had the desired effect and they all obeyed. Wheeling as one they turned and headed straight for the woods; the more experienced troopers slid their shield to cover their back and some of the recruits saw this and emulated their comrades; experience could not be bought but it could be gained. Fabius sat on his mount uncertain what to do when he did decide to retreat he failed to notice Macro riding across his front. The weight of the decurion and his horse crashing into Macro tumbled him to the ground and it would have taken a rider from the Circus Maximus to stay on. He was a big man and the crash took the wind from him. He lay on the ground and his horse rose and followed the rest.

Decurion Fabius looked down at Macro, shouted, "Back to the trees!" and then fled, following the horse of the unhorsed soldier.

71

Gaius could not believe what he was seeing. Macro would be spitted on the spears of the Brigante. He did not hesitate but raced his horse flat out yelling, "Macro!"

Macro realised his dilemma and, rising swiftly for such a big man he discarded his shield and raced after his horse which, fearful of the noise and clamour of battle headed towards the safety of the wood and the company of the other mounts. Many of the turma had reached the woods and were notching arrows. Gaius turned his horse and thundered towards Macro. Leaning forward he yelled, "Take my arm!" Arrows from the Brigante were flying through the air but they were not the best-mounted cavalry and certainly, they were unaccustomed to firing arrows from the back of a horse racing over rough ground. Macro glanced over his shoulder and stopped to face Gaius. Gaius wondered what he was doing as the young soldier hurled the javelin, seemingly at him and then held his arm out. Gaius did not have time to turn around as the javelin flew over his head but he put his right arm out and slowed up his crazed, frightened horse. Fortunately for Gaius, Macro was not only strong he was also tall and he virtually pulled himself behind Gaius. Gaius kicked hard; he could see the trees barely fifty paces away and he risked a look behind him. The Brigante were less than fifty paces behind but he could see a horse wandering around with a javelin in its shoulder and its rider picking himself up. He murmured to Macro, "I thought you were trying to kill me, you mad bugger!"

"No sir, the warrior's horse I hit was getting a bit close and I didn't fancy being knocked off another horse."

Gaius glanced over his shoulder and saw the dying horse and recumbent warrior lying on the ground. They were slowing up now as Gaius' horse struggled to carry the two heavy soldiers. Suddenly the air in front of them darkened as arrows and javelins were hurled at the enemy.

Macro looked over his shoulder, "That took out quite a few. I'll get off as soon as we hit the woods, Metellus has my horse and yours will die with the two of us." The superb athlete vaulted off Gaius horse in two actions and quickly remounted his own horse still wide-eyed and frothing but stationary at least.

Fabius glared at Gaius but he had gathered enough wits to shout," Retreat but in an orderly fashion. Alternate troopers."

The order meant that in each column pair one would retreat and prepare their missile while the other fired and then they would ride behind that trooper. It meant that the enemy always had to face twenty arrows or javelins and soon became discouraged. The two hundred Brigante had neither order nor cohesion. Each of them was trying to get to the Romans; they crashed into each other, trees, roots and the recumbent bodies of horses and men slain and wounded by missiles. By the time the troopers had reached Isurium's walls the pursuit had petered out. The Brigante knew that the troopers could easily hold them off from behind the safety of the colonia's walls. The decurion realised that the horses were winded and ordered a halt. Flavius came out of his villa. "What happened?"

Before Gaius or Macro could answer the decurion said, "This trooper disobeyed my orders and this other one tried to mutiny." He pointed at Macro and Gaius. "They will be flogged when we return to the fort." The troopers and Flavius stood in shocked silence for mutiny carried the death penalty. "We will wait here for a while in case the Brigante decide to attack but I think they have had enough now."

Flavius glared at the decurion and then said pointedly to Gaius and Macro, "Refreshments lads?"

They both turned to look at the red-faced decurion and then said, as one, "Love to...sir!"

Aed was disappointed that they had not ensnared the patrol but pleased with their discipline. He knew that his war chiefs would need to work on their cohesion and their reaction to orders but they had, for the first time, driven the Romans from the field. It was a start; it was a difficult time; they were changing from a rampaging barbarian army to an army that fought more like the Romans but with heart. He turned to Scanlan, one of his young war chiefs, "Tomorrow send out a warband to harass the next Roman patrol as they leave; they will be wary and will not make the same mistake again so we will try something different. Put men in the woods. We know how they like order. They will not make the same mistake they made today but they may become careless. The more we undermine their confidence the better."

He wondered how long it would be before the legions arrived. He was in a precarious position and he knew it. He was the bait in the trap. His scouts were, even now, hiding outside Eboracum. He would know when the legions arrived before the Romans and when he knew then he could tell King Maeve and the trap would be sprung.

Macro looked about ready to burst into tears although Gaius had a stoic blank expression on his face as they stood in the Praetorium listening to the ranting of their officer. "This trooper disobeyed an order and stayed thirty paces in front instead of twenty. I want him flogged."

Even Rufius looked up at that statement. He would have already dismissed it were it anyone but his son. He had to be seen to back him.

"And this other man, Trooper Gaius?"

"He disobeyed my orders after he had tried to countermand my order."

Rufius felt more secure, he could legitimately back up his son for disobeying orders was a major offence. Marcus and Decius exchanged looks

73

for they had an idea already what had happened. Macro was looking terrified, almost quaking. He had just escaped death and now he was to be punished. Gaius, on the other hand, had a face of stone. He believed in the inherent justice of the Roman army and felt certain that when the facts became known he would not be punished.

"Have you anything to say for yourself, Trooper Gaius?"

"Sir I did not disobey any orders."

"You did, you did, when I said back to the woods you went and rescued this trooper."

All of them looked at Fabius for this was flimsy evidence at best. "With respect sir, I ordered the men to retreat before Trooper Macro was unhorsed."

"See! Do you see what I mean? He is always trying to give orders and I am the decurion." He sounded to the whole room like a petulant child who could not get his own way.

"Let us go back to this more serious offence of countermanding orders. What exactly did trooper Gaius do?"

"I ordered the men forward from the woods and he told them not to."

"Is this true?"

"Yes sir."

"You realised that you are condemning yourself?"

"Yes, sir however your standing orders were that we should patrol next to the tree line. The decurion was taking us towards the walls."

Rufius looked at his son almost willing him to change his story slightly and say he meant to be further away from the danger. "Towards the walls?"

"I felt there was no danger…"

Marcus intervened for the first time. He was quietly angry and this had been growing for some time. He had worked out most of the events but even he was surprised at how little Gaius and Macro had done. "No danger? Despite the fact that in a few heartbeats you were nearly ambushed and but for Trooper Macro's position and Trooper Gaius' quick thinking you might all be dead."

"Yes," sneered the arrogant young man, "and who placed this man ahead of the column so that we could be forewarned of any attack!"

"Yet you said he disobeyed orders."

"He did! I said twenty paces."

"Had he been at twenty paces you might have all been killed so which is it did Macro's presence save the turma or jeopardise it?"

The silence was so heavy the Decius wondered if he could cut it with his sword. Marcus looked at the prefect. "I think, with respect, that Trooper Macro be dismissed I cannot see how we can punish the man who was responsible one way or another for saving the patrol from disaster."

After glaring at his son for a moment the prefect murmured, "Dismissed Trooper Macro."

"But sir…"

As a relieved Macro left the room the prefect said loudly. "However, Trooper Gaius did not obey his officer's orders."

For the first time, Gaius' face showed concern. "But sir he was taking us away from the tree line and disobeying standing orders."

"He did give an order trooper and you do not know what other orders were given to him as your officer. You do not know, for example, if the prefect of cavalry had asked him to ride closer to the walls to inspect them. "Decius and Marcus both looked at Rufius, he was going to save his son by lying. "If Roman soldiers question their officer's orders then we will have anarchy and the barbarians will win. Fifty lashes."

"Lashes is that all!"

"Decurion Demetrius you are dismissed. Now leave us and see to your troopers." The voice of the prefect was that of a scolding father. "Trooper Gaius you are dismissed. Punishment will be at first light."

When they had both left Marcus stood to leave. "Sir I think that was unfair. Trooper Gaius is a good soldier and he should not have the punishment on his record."

"He should not have questioned his orders."

"But your standing orders were disobeyed."

"How do you know I didn't give him other orders?"

"Did you?"

The prefect stood up, his patrician face angry. "Be very careful Decurion Marcus. If you even imply that I have lied I will have you crucified. Do I make myself clear? Now go, both of you!"

Chapter 8

At Streonshal Gaius Cresens was enjoying life. There was a certain irony in the fact the very Romans who were hunting him had killed his fiercest rivals. He now had two settlements under his control; both of them paid him his taxes and called him master. He had even developed the pirates plunder into a profitable and legitimate business. It had become obvious to him that ships would still be wrecked; now, instead of killing the victims his people rescued them and their belongings but made a charge for their service. The survivors were so grateful that they all paid without question. Things were going so well that he had had a stone-built villa erected at the top of the cliffs. He had insisted on walls and towers so that it could be defended. Now that he was master to nearly four hundred people he had his own bodyguard of ten hardened warriors who were without leaders and looked to Cresens for financial support. They had gravitated to Streonshal after hearing of the money the master paid. Atticus did not approve of them believing them to be little more than bandits but the master thought it prudent and in his eyes, all of his decisions were good ones. Cresens had to pay them a little from his increasing horde of money but it was worth it for they gave him absolute loyalty and made him less dependent on the noble Atticus. Life was good.

On the morning of the punishment, Decius came into Gaius' barracks. As soon as he entered he could feel the resentment the men of the turma felt about authority. He gave them a hardened stare which quickly made them disperse. Gaius just looked up his eyes wide with terror; there were few floggings in the ala but they had a reputation of being so painful that men cried and Gaius did not want to do that. "It's not fair Decius and you know it."

"I know son but life isn't fair is it? Look I have had floggings; most of us have. Just take your medicine. Marcus has wangled it so that you are to be moved into his turma and I have Macro. You won't have to serve under him again. Now," he looked furtively over his shoulder and then produced an amphora from under his cloak. "Get your shirt off and I will rub this on your back."

What is it?" he asked suspiciously.

"Just oil and a few herbs and stuff. It will make your back a little numb but it will stop any infection, Trust me it will make life easier."

"Thanks, Decius. Who is going to do the flogging?" Decius paused for a second and then continued to rub in the slightly herby smelling mixture. "Who?"

In the quietest voice, Gaius had ever heard he mumbled, "Me."

"You but…"

"I was ordered and before you say anything if I go easy on you they will have someone else give them to you, the whole fifty and then give some to me. This will help and, "he looked directly at the young man, "for the pain I will be giving you, I am sorry."

This was the first flogging the ala had seen for Ulpius and Flavius had not needed to use such harsh and severe punishment. The troopers looked neither at the figure of Gaius, stripped to the waist and tied to a training stake nor even at the man who had ordered it, the prefect. Instead, the combined hatred of over seven hundred troopers was directed at the young decurion Fabius. His younger brother Julius had managed to stand some way away from him as though he was trying to distance himself from the crime. Fabius appeared oblivious to the whole thing, almost bored as he stood at attention with an evil smirk upon his face.

It was an ashen-faced Decius who flexed himself to lay on the first stroke. He looked over to the prefect, part of him hoped that he would rescind his order but in any case, he had to have the command to punish. "Carry on with the punishment Decurion."

Gaius had a stick in his mouth, mainly to stop him from biting his tongue off but also to make his screams less loud. In addition, Marcus had made sure it was laced with a strong spirit which, allied to the salve on his back might diminish some of the underserved pain. The sound of the flail cracked sharply across the silent parade ground, making a noise like lightning as it snapped across his white, unmarked back. The first stroke sliced a thin red line across his back and Gaius stiffened as the tendrils of blood oozed down his back. The shock of the pain was so excruciating that the prisoner almost stopped breathing. Decius took his time with his second stroke and placed it well above the first one. Marcus and Decius had discussed how to administer the punishment with the least damage and they had both agreed that Decius should try to avoid the previous whip mark. Although apparently cruel they had both seen enough floggings to realise that the deeper the wound the longer it took to heal. The concentration on the placement of each blow made it easier for Decius to forget that this was a friend, a friend whose life he had saved. By the tenth stroke, the whole of Gaius' back was traced with dripping, bloody wheals. Julius was looking decidedly green but Fabius still had the smug smirk on his face which fuelled the anger of the troopers. Marcus looked at the young man with sadness. As Decius had shown with his brother given the right support any man could become a better officer but that would never be the case with Fabius for these men might follow him to battle but he could never trust them; a blade in the back, a tripped horse, tardy support any of these could result in his death. As Marcus knew, men had to trust their officers and the officers had to trust that when they went into action their men would be right behind them. He glanced at Julius. He hoped that the young man would not faint or vomit for although the men would understand it would diminish him in the eyes of his patrician father.

Mercifully Gaius passed out at the thirtieth stroke and the ala breathed a collective sigh of relief. His bloody back looked as though his skin had been sliced off in chunks; the parade ground was covered in gobbets of blood and skin. As soon as the punishment was completed Marcus roared, "Parade dismissed!" Drusus, Marcus and Decius ran up to cut down the unconscious trooper. Macro brought along the bucket of salt and water. All of the troopers had given some of their own valuable supplies to put on his back. If he had been awake the pain was unbearable but his present state meant that they could apply it liberally. The antiseptic qualities meant that the wounds would not become infected. Marcus wrapped the bandages tightly around his upper body and they carried him back to his barracks.

Marcus turned to Decius, "I am going to see the prefect."

"Don't do anything stupid. Gaius took his medicine, that little bastard can't hurt him again. The last thing we need is to have you punished as well."

"Don't worry I am not going to give either of them that pleasure." He strode over to the headquarters building. He was about to talk when he heard the thundering of hooves as a messenger halted his sweating horse just behind him.

"Orders for the prefect, from the Governor."

Perhaps Rufius had been waiting behind the door or perhaps he had anticipated the arrival for he was out of the door before the sentence was ended. He imperiously snatched them from the rider without a word. Marcus looked up at him and shouted over a trooper, "Take this man's horse and rub him down then take him for something to eat and drink. He looks like he needs it."

Gratefully the man said, "Thank you" and went with the trooper.

"It seems the Governor wants a conference with his senior officers." He scanned the officers gathered around him. "In light of the unrest, I will take a turma with me as an escort. Fabius Demetrius, I will take your turma." He paused, "You can accompany me. It will be a good experience for you to see how the staff works."

Smirking his pleasure Fabius snapped off a, "Yes sir!"

As they left to gather their belongings Decius said to Drusus, "Thank Mithras for that. If he had left that little bastard we would have had to explain how come he had his throat cut and bollocks sliced off, accidentally."

Eboracum

The Governor looked around the temporary fortress that was Eboracum. The Ninth had done a good job but with the extra mules and staff officers, it was a little crowded. The auxiliary units were camped out on the other side of the river and had built their own marching camp. In the slog up the east

78

coast, Quintus had been pleasantly surprised by the landscape which was not the harsh, wild one he had expected. The rolling hills and rich lush valleys showed him the potential of this part of the province. Once he had wrested control back from the natives it would make Rome and himself very rich. It gave added impetus to his mission. As soon as the prefect of the only cavalry unit available in the northern part of the province arrived he could begin to make his plans. Indeed he could do nothing until Rufius Demetrius arrived for no one on his staff had any idea what they were facing. The intelligence they had assumed that the Brigantes were allies and, as events had shown, this was not the case. While he waited he considered his limited though professional forces. He would need to take a sizeable number of legions with him. He would leave a couple of centuries to garrison the fort along with a couple of auxiliary centuries. He had decided not to wait for new auxiliary units from Gaul and Rome but instead, he had one of his tribunes, Antoninus Saenius, raising one from around Lindum. It wouldn't do to raise one in Brigante country as he would never be able to trust them but he needed more troops.

The tribune of the Twentieth, Agricola, remembered the Brigante well from his previous visits. He now wished that he had spent more time around Stanwyck rather than just building the bridge and fort at Morbium. The Governor called him over. "You have made good time Julius."

"I travelled light." He gestured at the hills in the distance. "It is more pleasant here than the wild and rugged place which is the spine of this land. It is almost peaceful here."

"It is. This is a rich country and we will harvest it. I only await Rufius Demetrius. Do you know him?"

"I know of him rather than the man himself. He seems to be a competent officer," he said guardedly.

"You mean his mistakes are well covered? No do not answer I know what you mean. You know the ala though?"

"They are a formidable force. I have fought with them. At the battle of Brocavum, they were the difference between defeat and victory."

"Good then if he is competent he should not be too much of a liability and the ala should carry on performing well," he shook his head, "I remember when I commanded the Ninth at Londinium when the bitch Boudicca rebelled. They were not the legion they are now and they nearly caused us to be defeated fortunately I managed to rally then and I am a half-decent commander."

Julius grinned at the man's candour. He had brought up the one disaster in his life making it clear he wanted honesty. "Rather like me at Brocavum. Were it not for the Pannonians my head might well have been decorating a Brigante trophy spear."

"So Julius what is the best way to crack this persistently irritating nut?"

Morbium

The prefect had been gone for barely half a day when Marcus ordered all the troopers to the parade ground. The previous day, as the prefect was preparing to depart, the senior decurions noticed sullenness about the men and, whilst they did not disobey any orders, they did not obey them with any degree of cooperation. As they sat in their barracks quaffing their watered-down wine Drusus summed it up. "The prefect was wrong, he backed up his son and he shouldn't have. That is not so bad but he then had one of the most popular men in the ala flogged. There's neither sense nor reason in it."

"No, "agreed Marcus," but then think of the battlefield. Does that always make sense?"

"But morally the prefect was wrong. He has put all of us in jeopardy. The older men know the difference between that little shit and the rest of us but the recruits, and we have a lot of them, think we are all the same. We will have an officer no one can trust and us."

"Lentius is right Marcus. We need to do something about this."

After Decius spoke they all looked deeply at the ground as though trying to divine some inspiration. Marcus almost welcomed the mental challenge as it drove into the dark recesses of his mind, the recent losses he had suffered. He felt strongly about Gaius for he and Ulpius had nurtured the young man and, while Marcus could do nothing about his dead family, he could do something to help Gaius. "I'll just call in on Gaius."

"You have a plan then?"

Marcus looked at Decius, "I'll call in and see Gaius; he paused," and yes I do have a plan."

After he had gone Lentius said, "I don't know how he is coping. If my wife and son had been butchered… well I don't know what I'd do."

"I suppose that is what makes him Marcus. He was always a deep one. When we were both troopers he always thought more than the rest of us. I guess that is why Ulpius marked him down for promotion."

"Well he will need all of his strength now," grumbled Decius, "we are going to war again soon and I for one want the men behind me to follow me without question not wondering if I am going to make a stupid decision and then hesitating."

The men stood at attention in their turma the decurions in front. They were in a hollow square with the same sullen expressions they had worn since the flogging. Marcus did not say a word; he just walked along each line looking into the face of each man as he passed. When he arrived at his own turma he halted and cracked his vine staff sharply on his greaves. In the still silence of the parade, it sounded like the sound of the flail on Gaius' back and some of the men started in alarm. From the sickbay, Gaius emerged in full armour. He

80

marched up to Marcus, saluted and then stood in front of the men. Decius looked over to Drusus and winked.

Returning to the centre of the parade ground Marcus began to speak. His voice was neither angry nor censorious, it was calm and measured. "Troopers, when the prefect returns we will be going to war. We will be fighting for our lives against the Brigante. Those more experienced amongst you will remember how fiercely they fought last time and how many comrades went to the Allfather." Even though they were on parade and at attention, some of the men nodded. Marcus deliberately ignored the minor misdemeanour. He walked around and as he spoke he gestured towards the decurions. "These men are your leaders. These men are your officers. These men will make the difference between life and death. These men are your decurions and you must obey them without question." He stopped next to Gaius. "Without question!" He shouted so loudly that some of the turma swayed backwards as though struck. "This trooper is a fine soldier. He is my chosen man and that means he is, in my opinion, a leader and the best man in my turma. That doesn't mean he is perfect and he can and has made mistakes. He made a mistake the other day didn't you trooper?"

The whole parade held its breath; the decurions wondered where Marcus was going because he was in danger of making the situation worse rather than better.

"Yes sir."

"What was your mistake trooper?"

"I questioned my officer in front of the turma sir."

"And what should you have done? No, I will rephrase that trooper. If you felt I had made the wrong decision or interpreted an order wrongly what would you do?"

"I would approach you sir and quietly explain what I thought." He smiled, "Respectfully."

"Good and I, "he paused in front of Julius, "as a good officer would listen to your ideas and act on them. That is what a good officer does. I might not agree with you trooper for I might know just a little more than you but I would listen and I might ignore that advice. Then what would you do trooper."

"Realise that you might know a little more than me sir and obey the orders."

"Thank you, trooper. And it is likely that had I received your advice I might have acted on it." He turned to face the parade which looked less sullen and more focussed on the words of Marcus. "Before we leave Morbium I want all of you to realise that we are not only the finest cavalry in the northern part of the province, we are the only cavalry. That means that we will have to do the work of three or four alae. It is highly likely that we will be operating in small units. Your decurions will have to make decisions without senior officers to advise us. That is where the teamwork will come in for your decurions will need to know that you will support and back all of their actions. Looking around me now at the decurions and troopers I am proud for I know that all of you will not let me down. The memory of Ulpius Felix and Flavius Bellatoris will be in all of you. I have total faith in each and every one of the decurions before me." Marcus had paused before Julius Demetrius to let him know he was included." So let us stop walking around with long faces. Let us remember who we are. We are the Pannonian cavalry and there is nothing the Brigante can throw at us that we cannot handle. They have never beaten this ala and they never will. Are you with me?"

The cheer was so loud that a frightened flock of crows rose from the nearby woods terrified by the noise.

"Parade dismiss." Marcus walked over to Gaius and said quietly, "Thank you."

"No sir, thank you. What you said was right. I think I let him get to me, sir. And thank you for having me back. I won't let you down."

Marcus gripped the young man's forearm. "You never have and you never will."

"Remind me never to gamble with you, sir," snorted Decius. "I was almost getting ready to defend you in case they attacked you. You are a crafty bastard. Is that why you went last night to see Gaius, to set this up?"

"It wouldn't have worked if the ala hadn't seen that we are one unit and that Gaius didn't resent authority." He lowered his voice. "Of course it could all be back in the melting pot when the prefect and his son return."

"Yes, I noticed that you only spoke about the men before you." He became serious. "You had better watch your back some prefects might see that you were trying to undermine his authority."

Marcus shrugged. "When we are in the field fighting the barbarians what the prefect thinks will not matter. The sooner we go to war the better."

Later that day Septimus returned from patrol, the first patrol since the near disaster. Decius noticed that some of his men had bandaged wounds. "What happened?"

"We were ambushed in the woods. Luckily for us, we had Gaelwyn with us and the old fox seemed to smell them out. They shot their arrows from too great a distance. We didn't lose any men but a couple of the lads took hits."

Marcus had arrived during the report. "Looks like they are getting to know our routine. I think we should vary it from now on. Well done Septimus. You better see the surgeon about your men."

Eboracum

"Now that all the commanders have finally arrived, "there was a note of censure in Quintus Cerialis' voice. He had let Rufius know that he should

82

have left sooner, "we can begin to plan this campaign. Julius Agricola will move up the west coast with the twentieth. I will bring the ninth and the two Batavian units up the east coast and we will meet at Stanwyck. The cavalry under Rufius Demetrius will act as a screen for the advance of the ninth and they will also patrol north of Dunum Fluvius." He looked around at the men he would need to rely on in this coming campaign. They were all unknown to each other but he would have to meld them into a fighting team who could trust each other. "Until we defeat this rabble at Stanwyck we are blind. I do not want to fall into the same trap as my predecessor. I have been told by the prefect of cavalry that the fortress can be taken by siege weapons which means that once we have defeated the rebels we can carry on the invasion north. Prefect, I will need one turma detaching to act as liaison and scouts for Julius Agricola. As you have thoughtfully brought one with you they can leave this afternoon with the general. Do they need a decurion?"

Rufius coloured for Fabius was on his right. "No sir. This is their decurion, Fabius Demetrius."

"Your son?"

"Yes sir."

"Is he not a little young?"

"He is more than able sir as the general will discover."

"Yes well, that remains to be seen."

"What about Morbium sir, it guards a valuable river crossing."

He turned to Cominius Sura, the prefect of one of the Batavian infantry units. "Detach one century to guard Morbium until the return of the ala. Any further questions?"

"How will we coordinate our attack?"

"I thought I had explained that Prefect Demetrius. Your cavalry will be the liaison between the two columns. You will ensure that messages are successfully passed from one unit to another."

It was a red-faced and angry prefect who spoke with his son just before the cavalry left for the west. "When I get to Rome I will see to it that that man never commands again. How dare he question my decisions?"

"I didn't like the look General Agricola gave me."

"He is a good general and, he has the ear of the Emperor so be careful my son. Curb your tongue and think before you try to gain some glory. There will be many opportunities for brave deeds but they will be in battle not while scouting and acting as a messenger. When we are together again with all of our cavalry there will be an opportunity for a glorious charge to win the day. Keep that in mind."

"Yes fat… sir!"

Morbium

"Prefect approaching," there was a pause and then the sentry added, "alone."

"If he didn't have some good trooper with him I could almost hope that the little bastard of a son of his was dead."

Marcus looked at Decius coldly. "I'll have no more of that talk. We support the prefect and all the officers. Even those we don't like."

"You are right but I don't need to like it."

As the prefect entered the gates Marcus could see him glancing around assessing the fort. 'Judging me eh?" thought Marcus, 'Well you won't find anything amiss here."

"Officer's call now."

The buccina sounded and within moments they were all stood in the headquarters' office at attention. The prefect did not bother to change, wash or even drink. "Right gentlemen our war has begun. As you can see Fabius Demetrius is already in action with the twentieth and Julius Agricola. Tomorrow the fort will be taken over by Batavian infantry. We have three tasks; firstly, we will have to keep the Ninth and Governor informed, that will be turma twelve Metellus Saenius." The decurion saluted. "Secondly we will need to screen the Ninth. I will take charge of that with turmae six, seven, eight, nine and ten. Decurion Marcus Aurelius Maximunius will take the remaining four turma and patrol north of Dunum Fluvius as far as Brocavum. Any questions? No? Then I suggest you make your preparations. We will be away from the fort and what passes for civilisation in this barbaric part of the world so we must make sure we have everything that we need. That means spare tents, weapons, uniforms, everything. See to it."

As the decurions moved away Decius grabbed the arm of Julius. "What the? Oh, it's you, sir."

"Listen, son, you are going to be on your own sometimes with forty men hanging on your every word. Now I don't think for one minute you are like your brother." Julius looked at him. "You know what I mean?" Julius nodded. "You will be a good officer but you need to lead these men not just shout at them and think they are less than nothing. What Marcus said was true we are a team, we work together. You probably know more about battles in the past and Hannibal and Caesar and all of them but some of these lads have fought the Brigante and the Carvetii they know what war is between you can become something more. They won't take advantage of you, trust me and you trust them. Right?"

Julius clasped Decius' forearm as he had seen Marcus and Gaius do, "Right... decurion."

"Go on, you'll be alright."

The next day the prefect left with his vexillation, before he did so he called Marcus over. "You will have to wait here until the Batavians arrive, whenever that is. You must keep me informed. I need intelligence. My turmae will be spread out in a line between the ninth and Stanwyck. We will be easy to find. Do not waste any men on glory charges or suicidal attacks just make sure the Brigante don't try to get around our flanks. I want the ala ready and in one piece once we have taken Stanwyck. We will gain our glory on the battlefield not being glorified bodyguards to the infantry. Although so far I have seen little evidence of strategy from these tribes. Good hunting."

"He is still a bastard you know? He has stitched you up. North of Dunum Fluvius!" Decius snorted as he watched the prefect ride out at the head of his men. "Every bugger up there is an enemy. He knows where his enemy is, tied up in a fortress. We have three hundred men and we will be facing thousands."

"Excellent Decius I thought for a while there you were becoming an optimist. We have done this before. We know the land. Remember Ulpius and I scouted all the way to Brocavum with one turma and we came to no harm."

"With respect sir, the whole of the north was not up in arms and ready to slit Roman throats. This isn't just the Brigante remember the Novantae and the Votadini? They have had a couple of years to re-arm and retrain. This is going to be harder."

"Yes, Decius but look on the positive side. We have the best decurions with us. The old guards are back together."

Grinning Decius clapped Marcus on the back. "That's why I like you; you clever than the rest of us put together and, what is more, you are the optimist who sees the cup as half full. You are right. Well, the sooner these Batavians get here the better. I'll go and make sure we have left bugger all for them to drink. I know these Batavians they like their ale more than I do."

Chapter 9

North of Dunum Fluvius

Drusus had taken his turma close to the river. It was not easy for here the river was wild and fierce with waterfalls and savage rocks but it meant his southern flank was secure. He had four men to the north to warn of an ambush. In the three days they had been on patrol they had not seen any sign of the enemy but he knew they were there. His new recruits had begun to make comments about his caution until the older troopers told the tales of what the Brigante did with their captives and they began to look on their decurion with more respect.

It was one of the older troopers who found the evidence of warriors, it was a dead fire but it was only hours old; around the fire were the signs that a warband had been here. There were also droppings from horses and ponies. Somewhere ahead of them were Brigante. He called over Agrippa, one of his more experienced troopers he was a reliable and cautious man. "Find the Decurion Princeps and tell him we have found Brigante sign. Despite the prefect's orders the troopers still referred to Marcus as Decurion Princeps. In their eyes, a new prefect would not eradicate a man's reputation. "And Agrippa, be careful. I don't want to see your head adorning some Brigante spear." Drusus spread his men out looking for signs of the direction the warband had taken.

The land here was bare and rocky without much vegetation. The Romans felt slightly more secure for it meant there were no woods from which the Brigante could launch attacks. The Brigante however were more cunning and the ambush ahead was cleverly laid out. A hundred warriors lay in the stream which fed the mighty river, forty more were hidden beneath mats of grass and finally, a hundred mounted warriors lay in wait to the north of the river hiding in a low swale which kept them hidden a short sprint to where they would attack the Roman flank driving them towards the river, their comrades and certain death.

Riding at the head of the column but moving very slowly Drusus wondered if he should have waited at the dead fire for something that didn't seem right. There was no birdsong, only the rush of the fast-flowing water over the rocks. Recent rains had raised the level and it was quite noisy. It masked other sounds from their left. "Keep your eyes open men!"

The first that Drusus knew of an ambush was when a line of men to their left rose, seemingly from the river and hurled a variety of missile weapons at them, slings, arrows and javelins were all used. Even as the Romans protected themselves with their shields from the warriors to their side, from their front the hidden men rose from their mats and with axes and swords hewed at the legs of the cavalry mounts. Quickly realising it was a trap

Drusus ordered a retreat. Even as he did so he saw a number of his men dead or dying with others unhorsed and at the mercy of the barbarians who swarmed over them. His instinct was to rescue them but his head looked at the overwhelming numbers and decided to save those that remained if he could. The remaining twenty or so troopers turned their mounts and headed east towards safety. The mounted Brigante appeared to their left before they had managed to get to the trot. It was a massacre. Even the well-armed and well-armoured Romans could not cope with odds of five to one with no avenue of escape. One or two tried to ford the river but were dashed to their deaths on the deadly rocks.

Realising he was doomed Drusus and his chosen man turned to face the horseman. He did the only thing left to him, he charged. His actions took the Brigante by surprise. The two trooper's javelins took out two men and then their spathas began to cleave an avenue of death through the Brigante. Their initial success was short-lived for the Brigante closed around them. Drusus' chosen man was the first to die with a spear thrust under his arm and into his neck. He fell lifeless from the saddle. Drusus was either more skilled or had more luck for the warrior who tried to spear him had the misfortune to find a hare hole and broke his neck as he fell from his horse. He was beginning to think he might outrun them as clear sky appeared before him when a warrior behind him slashed at Drusus with his sword and caught the flank of his horse; it reared to the side and crashed into another warrior. Two horses and two warriors crashed in a heap. Drusus was the first on his feet and he turned to face the enemy who were just behind him. The axe took his head off even as he turned and the decurion died, almost the last man of turma two only Agrippa, racing to find Marcus survived the massacre at the falls.

Agrippa knew nothing of the slaughter behind him. A steady trooper, he had been in the province for four years and felt he knew it well. He did not ride on the skyline instead he darted from cover to cover and gully to gully. He headed northeast for he knew that the other turmae were riding at an oblique angle to them and he had more chance of meeting them. Within an hour he had found the turma of Lentius who listened to Agrippa's report. "We have seen nothing yet not a single sign of anyone friend or foe. "He pondered for a moment then made his decision. "Aelius, ride first to Decurion Decius and then to Decurion Princeps Marcus and tell them that Decurion Drusus has found evidence which may be of a warband. Tell them I will wait here for orders." Aelius galloped off north-eastwards and Lentius took the opportunity to rest men and horses.

He turned to Agrippa who he knew from their time under Ulpius. "Did Drusus say anything to you about numbers?"

As he chewed on the dried horsemeat Agrippa shook his head. "No, but I got to look at the ground. There were signs of horses and that normally means warriors."

"Right. And how long ago did you leave him?"

"Must be a couple of hours; I took it slowly as I didn't want to miss you."

"Not far away then?"

"No."

He turned to his men. "Alternate troopers mount up. I want a picket line a hundred paces all around. Keep your eyes open, there is a warband out there."

Agrippa looked searchingly at Lentius. "You think they are nearby?"

"If they are mounted they could be anywhere. We weren't a tight line and they could be laying an ambush for us. Did you see the direction they left?"

"It was quite rocky. It may be that the decurion discovered that after I left. I have no way of knowing. I saw no sign on the way here which means that the warband might have headed north or south rather than east."

"You may be right. That could be bad news, especially if they have gone south. That is why Decurion Maximunius gets paid a little more, he has to make those decisions."

They had exchanged sentries twice when they heard the drumming of hooves and the other two turmae arrived. Lentius reported to Marcus and the three decurions discussed their options. "I saw nothing at all neither sight nor sound. Not so much as a misplaced blade of grass. How about you sir?"

"Nothing at all. The land seems empty. There were no fires and no travellers. It is strange."

"Strange sir?"

"Yes it is past high summer and there should be people out gathering for the winter. You know how quickly it comes up here in the northlands."

"I know it gets bloody cold."

"I think the three of us should converge on Drusus. By now he should have worked out their direction of travel. As he hasn't sent any more messengers I can only assume he hasn't caught up with them."

"I hope not."

"Don't worry Decius, Drusus is too cautious to follow them into a trap and the good news about the land here is that there are few places for an ambush."

Lentius looked over at Marcus. "Do you think that is why we have seen no locals; they spotted us on the skyline and hid?"

"Could be. Mount up. Where is Drusus' man?"

Agrippa had been waiting close by knowing that Marcus would need his knowledge. "Here sir."

"Right lead us to your decurion and the rest of the turma. Let us hope we find him before dark."

The evening was beginning to fall when Agrippa's hand came up to halt them. Marcus rode up beside him. "What can you see?" he peered into the darkening gloom to make out what Agrippa could see.

"It was near here but I thought I saw someone standing there. A guard."

"Could be a sentry," he looked at Agrippa, "or it could be the warband." He signalled twice with his arm and the first turma came up behind him in a line.

Decius rode forward. "A problem?"

"Don't know. Agrippa thinks he saw someone, from the helmet it looks like a sentry from the turma. I'll take my lads forward in skirmish order. You wait with the rest. Be prepared to cover our retreat."

"Will do." Riding back to the two turmae he ordered bows to be strung.

Marcus turned to his men and said quietly, "Be on guard we don't know what is up there yet. "He signalled them forward and then shouted. "First Pannonians coming into camp!"

The silence was eerie and Marcus could now see the figure which did not move. Agrippa shouted out, "Wake up you dozy bugger it's the Decurion Princeps."

The fact that no one had run and no shower of arrows had fallen on them made them relax a little. If it had been Brigante they would now be in action. Agrippa was the first to realise that the reality was far worse than what they had imagined. He gave a gasp of horror which caused every trooper behind him to draw his weapon. Then Marcus saw what Agrippa had seen. The figure was not a sentry but the head of a Roman trooper sat hideously grinning from the top of a spear. The grin had been inflicted post-death with a slash of a knife across the mouth. As they drew closer they saw all forty of the turma on forty spears. In the centre was Drusus his lifeless eyes staring out at them. Agrippa remembered the last words spoken by his decurion and swore a silent oath that he would have his revenge on the barbarians who slaughtered his friends and comrades.

Marcus turned in his saddle and yelled, "To me! To me!"

Decius, Lentius and the two turmae were there in a heartbeat. There were no words to be spoken but Marcus knew that orders had to be given. "Turma one alternate troopers, half set up a picket line the rest of you search around and see if you can pick up signs." He turned to Lentius and Decius, "Get your men to take these," he paused a catch in his voice, "troopers down and see if you can find their bodies. These warriors will be buried with honour."

It was completely dark by the time the tasks had been completed. Decius brought the worst news. "They have dismembered the bodies you can't tell one man from the next."

Marcus nodded, cold anger coursing through his veins. "Build a pyre. In the morning we will send them to the Allfather."

Later as they sat together they pulled together what had happened. Agrippa sat with them for he knew exactly where they had been prior to the massacre. "So the river was on our left. There was nowhere for anyone to hide except in the rocks near the river."

Marcus looked sadly at the sole remaining trooper from turma two. "It seems likely that is where they hid."

Lentius spoke up, "And we found some pits dug they must have hidden there. Looks like they might have hidden under the turf. No one would have been able to see them."

Marcus nodded, "If only they had had Gaelwyn with them. He would have been able to smell them." He gestured to the north, "The ground to the north looks torn up by horses. It looks as though they waited out of sight and then when our men retreated they would only have one way to go, right into the enemy."

"The lads did well though sir."

Marcus nodded. They had found a nearby grave and over thirty bodies lay there. Drusus may have been ambushed with no hope of survival but he and his men had fought to the last. "He will be remembered and, Lentius, he will now be with Ulpius and they will talk of the times of glory."

Lentius smiled sadly not daring to speak in case he broke down. There were now just three of them left from Ulpius' turma, himself Marcus and Gaius. Thirty of their comrades had died in this desolate outpost of the Empire.

They lit the fire in the early dawn and they stood with heads bowed each with their own thoughts for the friends they had lost. Macro had found the tracks in the last darkening of the previous night and Marcus had sent him off as the rest of the vexillation prepared to leave. As they mounted he saw him to the west signalling. "Right men we ride and before we return home we will avenge our comrades."

It was noon when they crossed the river. It was much narrower and shallower this far from the sea. Marcus began to recognise some of the features from his patrol with Ulpius Felix. He turned to Decius, "We are not far from Brocavum."

"Typical. I bet the bastards are there already. This could be a waste of time."

"I don't think so. They had mounted men but they were mainly on foot. We have been going at a healthy pace. We could be closer than you think. Besides I was going to head down that way soon. I expected a messenger from the prefect before now." He signalled Agrippa. "Agrippa, take Macro and scout ahead of us. I think they are close. When you find them send

Macro back to me." He looked sympathetically at Agrippa. "We will all be revenged on them Agrippa not just you. Use your head." Agrippa nodded and he and Macro raced off.

Decius smiled as Macro passed him. "Look at that mad bugger. He thinks all this is a lark."

"Yes, Decius but he has not lost any comrades yet. It is still a game to him. You can only realise the stakes when you have gambled. Had it been Gaius and Drusus who had perished he would have a different attitude. Let us hope he always thinks of this as a game."

Decius looked at Marcus. They might be of similar ages and experience but there the resemblance ended for Marcus was a far deeper thinker than Decius would ever be and, as he chewed on some salted horsemeat he was glad. Action, not words that was his motto.

It seemed like a few hours before Macro came racing back along with Agrippa but in reality, it had been less than half an hour. "Found them, sir. There is a small lake in a natural bowl with hills around it and they are resting. They are going slowly because they have litters. It seems some of them are wounded."

"And they are not all mounted sir!"

Agrippa glared at Macro but Lentius grinned and said, "You'll get used to him, Agrippa. He tends to open his mouth and then think."

Decius mumbled," I'm not sure he even knows what think is."

"There are about a hundred of them with about twenty wounded."

"What about the approach?"

"There is one hill which overlooks it and they have two men there. I think we could sneak up and kill them. The hill would hide us and we could take them."

"What tribe are they?"

"From their standards, they look to be Carvetii but some of them are mailed with similar shields to our own."

"That bastard Aed! I knew we shouldn't have given them ideas and help to become better warriors. It's a bit thick being hit by the weapons we gave them using the tactics we taught them!"

"We had to Decius; they were our allies remember/"

"Treacherous allies."

Marcus turned to the men. "Leave your supplies here we go in armed and ready to move. I don't want any to escape. "He turned to one of the older troopers. "Metellus you stay here with the mule train and guard them." When the older man looked disappointed Marcus added. "You have had much glory. Let the younger ones find their strength. There will be other battles."

The men began to prepare for battle. They tucked their cloaks into their sheepskins and put their food and waterskins along with their sleeping blankets in neat, ordered piles. Metellus began to strap the tents and other supplies onto the mules. Once that was done he lashed each mule to the one behind. Although he was to remain behind the decurion had not said he could not follow slowly.

"Lentius you take your turma right. Decius left. I will go through the middle. Gaius take Macro and Agrippa, they know where the sentries are. Dispose of them without the Carvetii becoming suspicious. Can you handle that?"

"Not a problem sir. I wondered why you were not using me. My back is fine, "he glanced at Decius, "that salve I was given helped."

"Good lad, now be careful."

The three of them tethered their horses some way from the hill. They left their helmets with their horses. There was gorse and scrubby, stunted trees to disguise their movements. They noticed that the sentries sat talking to each other and would only turn around occasionally. The three of them spread out and went up in short bursts. Whenever one of the sentries started to turn they lay flat and managed to get within thirty paces. Agrippa was the smallest of the three and they had agreed that he would take the sentry on the left; he would crawl up and slit his throat. Macro would throw his javelin at the one on the right while Gaius would have his javelin in reserve in case either man missed.

As soon as Macro's javelin thudded through the sentry's back Agrippa leapt up. His sentry looked at his stricken comrade and he began to shout when Agrippa's hand covered his mouth and his razor-sharp knife sliced through his throat. If those by the lake had noticed anything it would have been a momentary movement for Agrippa and Macro sat in the same places as the dead sentries. Gaius raced down the hill and signalled to Marcus who was just out of sight below the skyline.

The three turmae came in an extended line. The hill masked their movement and they would make an unwelcome appearance on the hilltop. Gaius gathered their horses and took them to just below the top of the hill. Out of sight, he said," Any movement yet?"

"They haven't noticed us but it looks like they are beginning to move. A couple of them are heading towards the hill on the other side."

"Right as soon as we attack our job is to get those men so mark them."

Marcus halted the men in a line and Gaius explained what he intended to do. Marcus nodded his approval. He silently drew his sword. There would be nothing spoken until they were noticed. The closer they came to the enemy the more chance they had of inflicting heavy casualties. The horses walked over the hill and then, on the other side, they began to trot. Their momentum naturally increased their speed and they were halfway down before they were noticed. Gaius and his comrades were already racing around the lake to the other side unnoticed by anyone.

The Carvetii were surprised but they did not panic. Their leader quickly shouted an order and twenty warriors planted their spear hafts into the ground so that their points were a deadly hedgehog. Without breaking stride, Marcus signalled the man next to him to move right while he edged left. He would not risk the blades and there were not enough to deter them. Because the land was steeper on the right Lentius' line hit first and there was a mighty clash of sword on sword. On the left, the wounded were protected by a thin line of warriors and Decius soon found himself through them and at the water's edge with a line of bodies scattered in untidy heaps. Marcus and his turma had been split by the hedgehog and were being forced back. Decius shouted above the din, "Leave the wounded we can finish those bastards off at our leisure. To me! Protect the decurion," His men formed up behind him and the phalanx thrust through the heart of the defenders. It was the final act that turned the tide. Some of the men flung down their weapons and tried to race into the water only to be struck by arrows. Within less than half an hour it was over and the lakeside was red with blood. The auxiliaries were in no mood for prisoners and went around dispatching the wounded, not as an act of kindness but to ensure their demise.

On the far side of the lake the three cavalrymen had spread out and the two men they were pursuing were jinking left and right to avoid capture. Gaius rode his man down and thrust his javelin into his unarmed back. Agrippa and Macro had a slippery opponent who managed to find the places the horses did not like. He suddenly turned and ran towards the skyline. With suddenly dawning horror, the two troopers realised that it was a small cliff. The Carvetii jumped down a short cliff. The fall turned his ankle but he was able to hobble away. Macro and Agrippa knew their horses could not make the leap and Agrippa cursed as he knew that the man was escaping and would raise the alarm. Suddenly Macro produced a sling and took out a lead ball. He spun it quickly around his head and then released it. The Carvetii warrior thought he had escaped and did not turn around. The missile plunged into the back of his skull and he died instantly.

"Nice shot!"

"Used to hunt hares and squirrels when I was little. How do you think I got this big?"

By the time they reached the lakeside Agrippa and Gaius knew the size, number and even sex of every animal Macro had killed. Agrippa looked at Gaius and shook his head. "Just think Agrippa by the time we have finished this campaign young Macro will be able to give details about every one of the three thousand warriors he is going to kill."

"Sorry sir, er Gaius but I was pleased. It was a good shot wasn't it?"

"Yes, son and this is just gentle ribbing. A word of advice; be a little less when you tell Decius or you'll be shovelling horseshit from here to Alexandria."

Marcus had made his troopers strip the bodies of all armour and arms although this was a distasteful and unpleasant task it was vital that it was done. As he explained to Decius, "We don't need these arms and this armour but they do. If we leave the bodies as they are then another hundred warriors will become as well-armed and armoured as these. With the legions hunting them, they will not find the time to make such fine weapons."

"Yes sir but what will we do with them?"

"Pack them on those horses and take them with us. When we have left them at the fort we will have some remounts for Cato Aquilinas to train up."

One of the sentries suddenly shouted and every man became alert, scanning the skyline and gripping his sword. Decius let out a snort of relief, "Thank Allfather it is just Metellus. I will have his guts for breakfast scaring me like that."

"Yes, but it shows that all of the men are keen to get into action and can think for themselves. This is not the sullen rabble we had after Gaius was flogged. They have their spirit back."

With the arrival of the pack mules and once the horses had been loaded with arms and armour, they set off. As they drifted over the skyline they saw the carrion birds swooping overhead. By nightfall, the wolves and foxes would have joined in and soon there would just be bones to show where a warband died and a reminder to the rest of the tribe that the Pannonians took revenge very seriously. "Where to sir?"

"South, it is time that we gave our report to the Governor. I don't think there are more warbands north of the river. This was the only sign. If we head due south we should find ourselves closer to Stanwyck. My decision."

Gaius murmured to Macro and Agrippa, "If he decided to ride to Hades then the men would follow him.

West of Eboracum

Julius Agricola found Fabius Demetrius to be a most disagreeable and opinionated young man. It was obvious he thought himself superior to everyone including the general. Early on in their trek north Agricola had had to censure him for inappropriate remarks to both centurions and his own men. It also galled him that he was a very poor officer; his men obviously hated him and there was no rapport between them. For all of that, however, the general recognised that he was a good cavalryman and he was able to keep an effective screen ahead of the legion to discourage ambushes. His thirty-eight men were also very well drilled and confirmed his opinion of the ala; if the rest were as good but better led, then they had a good chance of defeating their tricky enemies...

For his part, Fabius hated his duties. He hated having to take orders especially from those he felt were inferior to him and that was most of the army. When he became a general he would improve discipline. He had noticed that the general addressed his centurions by their first names and drank with them! They were plebeians and rough plebeians at that. He hated the land. It was treeless, cold, wet and windy! He longed for the lands around Capua where he had grown up, the blue water the beautiful trees, the olive, groves, the vineyards. He hated the food and drink. The wine was just upmarket vinegar and the slop they served was beneath his contempt; he would not serve it to his dog! The only thing which kept him going was that he would soon be rejoining his father and under his command. It kept him keen to move the legion along which, ironically, also pleased Agricola and his men who yearned for the comradeship of the ala and other officers who could be pleasant.

Isurium Brigantium

Quintus Petilius Cerialis sat with the ex-prefect of cavalry discussing how the new settlement might be strengthened when Stanwyck was reduced. Although he had been impressed by the extensive fortifications the Governor knew the fortress could be reduced in days not weeks. He had two legions for the twentieth was but a day away and he had siege engines. He had no doubts that it would fall and this time his men would tear down the towers and the walls. They would demolish the buildings and fill in the ditches. The two soldiers were working out the best way to defend the new administrative capital of the region.

"Eboracum can supply soldiers to put down any rebellion."

"Yes, Governor but it takes time to get to Eboracum doesn't it?"

"You would like regular patrols from Morbium then?"

"It is but hours away," he paused significantly, "they saved us last time."

Quintus drank deeply the wine; it was a good one for he had brought it himself. "I suppose a wall and a gate would make you secure enough from border raiders. Yes, that will be no problem." He relaxed back into his couch. "They are a good unit of cavalry, I am impressed. You have done a good job."

Flavius shook his head, "It was Ulpius who made them what they are. Oh, I allowed him to have a free hand and encouraged him but what you see is the result of that long vexillation during the winter. It made them what they are."

"He was an interesting character I believe."

"He was that."

The Governor gave a half-embarrassed laugh. "I did hear a rumour that he was Queen Cartimandua's lover and they were to have a child?" If silence could echo then this one did. "Oh, so it is true. I would have liked to have met him."

"When you meet his decurions it is like meeting the man for they are all like him."

"Good. Well, I had better turn in we begin the assault tomorrow. "I have sent for Rufius," he looked around him and then lowered his voice, "you know he may be a damn good officer but he is not exactly likeable, is he? No, don't answer. Too much wine. Do finish it off there's a good fellow."

At the officer's briefing the next morning Fabius saw his father but it would have been most inappropriate to speak as technically he was still part of Agricola's staff." Good. We are all here then. Excellent." He took out a detailed map of the area and spread it out in front of the officers, all the tribunes and senior centurions were there and it was a crowded tent. "The ninth will begin the assault today. We already surround the fortress. My engineers assure me," two elderly officers nodded vigorously, "that it will fall within two days. The ninth will assault once the gates are breached. The onagers and ballistae will be brought up today. I want the Batavians to defend the engines," their prefect nodded and spoke to his senior centurion quietly. "The twentieth will be in reserve to the west. They are close enough to close on any advance to relieve the fortress. Demetrius, I want your cavalry to the north and west. Has your vexillation returned?"

I expect them in the next day or so. My scouts have not found them yet."

"I do hope nothing untoward has occurred. It would not be helpful if half our cavalry had been eliminated before the battle. Oh and Julius you had better let the prefect have his turma back. He appears short of men." The officers in the room all laughed gently while Fabius and Rufius reddened angrily. "I want to make short work of this fort and then the ninth will return to Eboracum and the twentieth will go into winter quarters at Cataractonium. Your Batavians can erect a fort here which will help protect Isurium and then in the spring we can advance north and rid this land of the Brigantes once and for all. Questions? None? Good. Get to it, gentlemen."

Fainch

Fainch was having her work cut out to soothe King Maeve. He had begun to worry now that the Romans were outside his fortress. "I think we should move the whole army to the land of the lakes. It will suit us there."

"I have told you before oh mighty king that the Romans could surround that land, supply themselves from the sea and you would have your whole army trapped. The Romans could then conquer all of your lands. Keep to the plan. When Aed is rescued retreat north. The Romans will think they have won. While they rest in the winter we will build up our army and you will send small bands to destroy the isolated settlements. It will drive those who waver to our side when they see they cannot be protected.

Mollified the king lay back in her arms and she continued to run her tapered nails up and down his chest gradually arousing him. "You must learn to relax and be more patient. The war band is in position and will attack the Roman engine the day after tomorrow, be patient for just a little while longer.

Chapter 10

North of Stanwyck

The journey back to the Roman-controlled parts of the province was slower than Marcus wanted. The mules and pack horses did not like the rough terrain over which they travelled. In addition, Marcus had to be certain that the Roman right flank was secure. These were some of the reasons the scout failed to find them. It was Gaelwyn who did so. "News Decurion."

"Good to see you Gaelwyn."

"The prefect has riders looking for you. He needs your turma. The prefect has arrived with the legions."

Marcus nodded. "Do we head for Stanwyck?"

"The orders were for the cavalry to protect the north-west of the fortress."

"How far are we from there?"

The scout looked with distaste at the pack animals. "With those at least a day."

"We are with those so let us be about our business."

Stanwyck

The newly built defences did not last long and Quintus looked with pleasure at the gaping holes. The defenders had kept well hidden, especially when the bolts began to fly. The Governor conferred with the engineers about the time it might take and he was hopeful that it would be soon. Decius Brutus, the Princeps Piles entered the headquarters. "Sir?"

Yes, Decius, things are going well are they not?"

"Yes, sir really well. I think we can take these today. Those gates are almost in. The defenders keep hiding. I think today."

Cerialis pondered Decius' words. He had known him a long time and trusted his judgement implicitly. He had fought at Glanibanta and was the nearest he had to an expert in the Brigante and the way they fought. "What about casualties? We only have three legions in the north."

"They don't have the artillery to cause us problems sir and they are brave but disorganised."

Vespasian would be happier with a speedier return to peace and whilst the action would not end the war it would bring it considerably closer. Ever the decisive general he nodded. "Assault when you are ready." He turned to his aides. Find the prefect and the general let them know we assault now. There may be survivors heading their way."

Aed watched with interest the legionaries beginning their preparations for the assault. His men were becoming increasingly nervous about their predicament and he wanted it ended sooner rather than later. He turned to the man next to him. He had a highly polished shield. "Send the signal now."

On the nearby hills, the one thousand horsemen saw the signal and prepared for their moment of glory. While the onagers and ballistae at the northern section between them and Stanwyck were attacking the walls they would charge them and destroy them. As soon as the weapons were destroyed, along with the auxiliaries who guarded them, Aed would leave the fortress and escape.

Rufius Demetrius had received his orders with disgust. The last thing he wanted was to chase after the few survivors. He addressed his decurions. "We will position ourselves at the eastern end of the fortress just in front of those onagers then when the legionaries go over the wall we can support them."

All the decurions apart from Fabius looked aghast at this. Only Julius had the courage to speak. "But sir, I thought we were to pursue survivors. If we are here we will not be able to get past the machines."

The prefect smiled in a patronising way, "But if we are in the fortress then there will be no survivors, we can move more quickly than the legionaries."

Decius Brutus led his men from the front. They moved in a steady line their javelins ready and their shields held tightly. As he looked down the line he was proud. There was not a foot out of step or a man who was not looking eager. "Be ready for the arrows lads. They should launch them soon." He heard a cheer from behind him as a mighty rock finally knocked down the gates. There was no defence left from the Brigante. Decius smiled grimly; they would all die. A few arrows were fired and he heard the thud of slingshots but only one or two of his men fell and Decius noticed that only one stayed down. He had been right the fruit was ripe for the plucking.

The Batavians were so intent on watching the walls crumble that they failed to hear the thunder of hooves. The first they knew of the attack was when the horses thundered into their unprepared backs. Dozens were killed without seeing the enemy. The centurions quickly shouted their orders, "Form ranks."

They had time because the Brigante warriors were throwing lighted torches onto the onagers and smashing the ballistae with axes, their crews slaughtered beside them.

Fabius shouted, "Sir, look to the north. They are attacking the engines."

"Damn!" The prefect realised he was in the wrong place he would have to ride in front of the ballistae and onagers. He had no choice, "Pannonians follow me." The artillery managed to stop firing when they saw their own cavalry ride in front of them but then looked in amazement as the mighty northern gates opened and the garrison emerged to charge the Batavians and artillery being assaulted from outside.

The Governor could not see what was happening. His only view was of the ninth clambering through the gate and over the ramparts to a seemingly deserted fort. An aide rushed up to him. "Sir the Brigante are attacking the artillery to the north."

"Where are the cavalry?" The aide pointed and Cerialis could see the turmae trying to make up ground and help the beleaguered Batavians for the artillery was now burning mightily. "Damn the man!" This was the unexpected turn in events that Cerialis had not anticipated. If he lost the Batavians and the legionaries who manned the artillery it would diminish his force added to which it looked like his quarry from the fortress would escape relatively unharmed. Had the prefect obeyed orders then some of the enemy warriors might have been captured and some of the Roman losses might not have happened.

Gaelwyn brought the news to Marcus. "The Carvetii are attacking the Romans! The Batavian auxiliaries are being slaughtered! It looks like a large force of cavalry, probably an ala."

Ever decisive Marcus shouted, "Hobble the pack animals. Weapons only. Decurions to me!" When Decius and Lentius arrived he quickly outlined his plan." Looks like we are in the right place at the right time again. The Brigante will have their backs to us but they outnumber us ten to one. The advantage we had is that there is a legion just the other side of them and, I assume, the prefect with the rest of the cavalry. We go in the same way and hit them hard. Don't bother chasing those escaping for our mounts are exhausted just protect the Batavians."

They quickly mounted and formed their line. They could not see the battlefield but they could see the smoke rising from the burning engines. "Ride for the smoke!" They rode in three columns for speed and soon found themselves riding up a low embankment. At the top, they could see the force of cavalry charging from the fortress and the Batavians in hollow squares fighting for their lives. In the distance, Marcus could just make out the rest of the ala trying to cover the ground to their auxiliary comrades. "Form line!" Marcus could see that they could not defeat the enemy but perhaps they could save roman lives. "Charge!"

The Pannonians were on the downhill slope and quickly gained momentum. When they were just a hundred paces they gave an enormous roar which could be heard across the battlefield. The Batavians saw the standards of the Pannonians and took heart. The Carvetii suddenly heard an enemy force to their rear. Aed saw the cavalry and decided that discretion was the better part of valour. He took the Stanwyck defenders through the gap in the western corner of the Roman assault works for there the siege engines had burned away.

Marcus and his line hit the disjointed Brigante in a solid line for they were riding knee to knee. Their javelins were thrust before them like lances and they hit the unprepared Carvetii like a tidal wave. The barbarians were stationary whilst the Pannonians had great speed; those not speared were crushed and trampled to the ground. The three turmae crashed through the whole line in less than a heartbeat. Although the Carvetii outnumbered their attackers they had been split in two and, worst of all the war chief had fallen in this first attack. The two bands of Carvetii milled around uncertain of their course of action.

Marcus reined up next to the Batavians who had lost half their number. A centurion with a split helmet and blood running down his head greeted him. "Good timing!"

Marcus nodded. "We will attack this band." He gestured to the warband to his right. "Just hold the other one. Help is coming from the fortress." They both glanced up to see the larger half of the ala thundering towards the remaining Carvetii. "Pannonians form line." The experience turmae formed a line in quick time." Charge!" The horses were tired now and the charge was delivered at little more than a trot. The Carvetii were more prepared and Marcus found himself facing a mailed war chief with a huge sword. The first blow almost shattered his shield and Marcus knew he would have to end this sooner rather than later. He slashed with his sword not at the man but at his horse. He half severed the head and the horse crashed to the ground taking the warrior with it. As he groggily rose to his feet Marcus stabbed down at the gap between his helmet and mail shirt. The eruption of blood told the decurion that the man was dead. The battle, however, was swinging in the direction of the Carvetii and although the Pannonians had killed many enemies they were still outnumbered and on blown horses. There could be no retreat. As the auxiliary cavalry fought desperately their numbers were being whittled down inexorably.

Gaius watched in wonder as the decurion wielded the sword of Cartimandua calmly and efficiently. Although his shield was shattered his enemies were scattered by the blade which seemed to sing. Gaius edged his mount to the left, more vulnerable side of his mentor as did Macro who was tucked in behind him. The three of them were carving their way through the diminishing ranks of broken barbarians. Macro was thoroughly enjoying himself and his mighty arm hacked and slashed almost without effort. His blade went through shields and mail, bone and bodies.

Suddenly out of the corner of his eye Gaius detected a movement, a Carvetii warrior armed with an axe was charging towards Marcus unprotected right side. Gaius could not manoeuvre his mount to that side and he did the only thing he could he launched himself from his horse with his sword held before him like a spear. His blade went straight through the

101

unprotected neck of the warrior and Gaius crashed to the ground. Macros saw his friend fall and saw the Carvetii racing to finish him off. Screaming in anger Macro wheeled his horse around and rode straight for them. Before any blade or spear could touch the auxiliary, who was dragging himself to his feet Macro had killed two one with a forehand and one with a backhand slash. "Come on you bastards! Who thinks they can take me?"

Even as he was rising to his feet Gaius was amazed to find that Macro knew enough Carvetii to insult them. He quickly thrust his sword into the side of the man who was trying to spear Macro's horse and the two of them made a killing circle as the wary warriors tried to approach the two blades of death. This might have gone on for some time but for the sound of the buccina. Glancing over Macro saw the soldiers moving from the fortress in two columns. "It's the legions!"

The Carvetii had seen them and they began to disengage and follow the fleeing Brigante. "That's right run away. You survive today but I'll have you yet."

Looking up Gaius saw that Macro was grinning with delight as he hurled insults after the routing warriors. He then turned to survey the battlefield. He could see little islands of Pannonians with seas of bodies spread around them. Marcus had survived and as he scanned the field he saw Decius and Lentius waving at him. Once again they had defied the odds and emerged victoriously. He looked up at the exultant Macro, "Thanks Macro I owe you."

"And thank you Gaius once again I am indebted to you. You are making a habit of saving my life."

The front ranks of the legionaries had just arrived and Marcus heard a familiar voice shout out orders. "Open order. Kill any bastard who moves!"

"Decius Brutus! Good to see you." Leaping down from his horse he grasped the First Spear by the shoulders.

"And you too Marcus and Gaius," he looked up at Macro who loomed above him, "and who in Hades name is this giant?"

"This is one of our recruits, Macro."

"Did you see that sir took one out with the forehand and one the backhand?"

Gaius patted Macro on the leg, "You'll have to excuse him Decius he has a tendency to relive every action blow by blow." He lowered his voice, "but he is a good soldier."

"Thank you, sir!"

"Never mind that go and find my horse!"

"Sir, yes sir."

Decius Brutus drew Marcus aside. "Very close call that. I don't think the general would have been pleased if one of his only two auxiliary units had been slaughtered." He gestured over his shoulder to where Rufius and the rest of the ala were chasing down survivors. "He's a funny bugger. I hope he has a good story for the general." Marcus looked at him quizzically. "He was supposed to be behind the Batavians to support them. Looks like he was after glory and was trying to get in the fortress after my lads had cleared the ramparts."

"He does like his glory but he is a good cavalryman. The thing is, Decius, he is no Ulpius."

"Who is? Although from what I have heard you aren't doing a bad job."

"The prefect doesn't think so. I was demoted from Decurion Princeps."

"No? So he has no common sense either?" They both laughed and then Decius became serious. "Sorry to hear about the princess and her sister. I liked them and your son…"

Marcus face hardened as he steeled himself no to show emotion. "I will avenge them Decius I swear by the Allfather. The men who did it are even now fleeing west. It will be a long war but I will avenge them." He looked down at the battle-hardened veteran. "Did you lose many men?"

"A handful wounded and that is all. I don't think they ever planned to hold us for long."

"That's probably our fault." Decius looked up quizzically. "The Brigante we thought were allies; we helped to train them and we told them of the prowess of the legions. Don't you remember the Brigante who fought with us at Glanibanta? They would have remembered how effective artillery can be."

"You are probably right but there has to come a time when we will fight alongside them. That is the way Rome works. The Pannonians fought hard against Rome but now provides warriors. These are but setbacks. And now I must get back to my men."

Aed halted his fleeing warriors just north of the river. He had been right to leave the fortress when he did for the trap had nearly been sprung on them. He rued the fact that the Pannonians had managed to intervene again. It was time they were eliminated. He looked down as the survivors of the Carvetii began to trickle in. There were not many of them. One of them a huge man who was bleeding from a scalp wound spat out blood and teeth and then snarled up at the mounted Aed. "I see you did not lose many men Brigante. Are you Roman now?"

Riding up to the warrior Aed kicked him hard in the face and then shouted to the Carvetii who were arriving. "We obeyed orders; you were the diversion to allow us to escape. You should have been better prepared. My warriors will now protect you on the way back to the west." He turned to one of his trusted warriors. "Ride back and watch the Romans. If they pursue come immediately if not then watch them for a few days and report to me."

Riding away Aed reflected that, while they had not had the success they hoped they had had a success of a kind. The two auxiliary units had been badly mauled and the elite fighters, those of Aed's warband had survived unscathed. It all depended now upon what the Romans did. He found himself eager to hear the words of Fainch for so far, her prophesies, predictions and plans had all borne fruit.

The Governor had made his temporary headquarters in the main hall at Stanwyck. Thanks to the Romanisation of Lenta and Macha it was almost comfortable. As it was such a large space he had all of the officers from the legions and auxiliaries present, the tribunes, prefects, centurions and decurions. The only ones not present were the optios and sergeants who were busy running the camp. "We have done well, he glanced over at the prefect of cavalry although not well enough in some cases. I will see each unit commander after this briefing to give specific orders." Marcus smiled to himself. This new Governor was certainly a man for the detail and Marcus approved of this. It was in complete contrast to his own leader who just expected his subordinates to carry out his wishes; he sometimes expected them to read his mind. "We will go into winter quarters. The Ninth at Eboracum, the twentieth at Cataractonium, the Batavians will build a fort here although the vexillation at Morbium can remain and will share quarters with the Pannonians."

"Sir," blustered a red-faced Rufius.

"When we have our meeting prefect you can raise all the questions and issues you wish but let us get the bigger picture first eh?" The Governor waited for the sniggers and whisperings to cease and then went to the hide map pinned to the long wall in the hall. "We are here and control the land to the south and east. General Agricola assures me that the land to the west is secure right up to the land of the lakes. The Dunum Fluvius will be our northern border and this will be our western border. Winter approaches and those that know the land better than I assure me that nought can live and travel the high lands in winter." He smiled at his officers. "Actually, I am not certain the summer travel is advisable." All present laughed at this attempt at a joke, all that is except for the grim-faced Rufius and his sulking son Fabius. "I want the Pannonians to continue their patrols north of the Dunum Fluvius." He looked pointedly at the prefect, "which is why the century of Batavians will be useful in guarding the fort whilst the cavalry are on patrol. I want the twentieth to re-invest and rebuild Glanibanta. I am not at all sure why it was abandoned in the first place this way we will have a base from which to invade up the west coast should it be needed. I have asked Rome for more legions and auxiliaries but in all honesty, I do not expect any before the spring. The Second Adiutrix at Lindum is busy recruiting suitable replacements for the Pannonians and the Batavians but gentlemen that is all we expect." He put down his vine staff with which he had been pointing and turned to face his officers. "In the spring we will invade the lands of the Carvetii and the Brigante and we will destroy them. Then we will begin to plan how to conquer the rest of this barbaric yet rich province."

One of the centurions from the twentieth put up his hand and the Governor frowned although he allowed him his question.

"Sir some of the men are worried that we are on the edge of the world and are fearful of what we may find in the north and west. What shall we tell them?"

No one laughed at this for some legionaries had refused to fight in Mona and even Caesar had found it difficult to make his soldiers fight with the same zeal at this remote part of the world. "

"A good question, centurion. Tell your men that I have some of the Classis Britannica sailing not only up the west coast but also around this land which I and Julius Agricola believe to be an island. When that ship sails up to the docks in Eboracum I will be there to find the news and you, centurion will be the first to know. Any more questions?" Heads were shaken and Cerialis rose to dismiss them. "As he is so keen with his questions I will see the prefect of the Pannonians first. Dismiss."

Marcus strode away with the rest of the Pannonian officers. The exception was Fabius who hung around outside waiting for his father. Decius turned to Julius and bantered, "Thought you would have wanted to wait with your brother?"

Julius grinned back, "What and miss all the witty remarks and comments from you, sir? I don't think so."

They all laughed as Decius playfully cuffed him about the head. "Cheeky little bugger."

Marcus smiled; his first impressions of the youth had been right he would fit in and make a good officer. In his mind, he was going through the casualties and the effect on the ala. It should have been the worry of the prefect but that sort of logistics seemed beneath him. The banter and chat of the officers who were relieved to be alive still seemed to be going on somewhere else. It was not that they had forgotten Drusus it was just that this was not the time to mourn and each man would remember their friend in their own way. He went back to his ruminations on their strength. They had begun the campaign with twelve turmae. Each had been up to full strength but now, with the casualties they had incurred, they had less than seven turmae anywhere near full strength, three were half strength and one no longer existed. The recruits they had left at the fort to complete their training would make the numbers up in most turmae but that would still only leave them with eleven turmae, about four hundred men. Their full strength was a thousand men but it was some time since they had had the luxury of twenty-four turmae with complete ranks. Even if the prefect could not see it Marcus could. They would be spending most of the winter either patrolling or training raw recruits, and training raw recruits in winter would severely tax Decius' temper and patience. Marcus smiled at the thought.

On their way back to Morbium the prefect gestured for Marcus to join him. He had returned from his meeting with the Governor with a face as black as thunder. He had not spoken other than to tell them to follow. Stanwyck was some way in the distance and the prefect obviously felt he could speak without being overheard. "Damned impertinence! Said I should have obeyed orders! The Batavians might have been saved if I had been there. The man doesn't realise the function of cavalry. We need to be free from the legion's apron strings eh?" Marcus noticed the use of 'we' to include him in this rant against authority. Marcus believed that cavalry could be used closely with the legions; he had seen Ulpius do so at the battle of Glanibanta when Decius Brutus and he had destroyed a much bigger Brigante army.

The prefect looked carefully at Marcus, noting that he had not spoken. "I was going to bring charges against you, you know?"

Marcus looked surprised. "Me sir why?"

"Losing me a turma and not being there when I needed you and your men."

"I couldn't get back any quicker sir and the loss of Drusus; well I would have given anything for that not to have happened. He was my friend." Although he spoke calmly inside he was seething with rage. What did this pompous self-centred snob know of friendship and comradeship? Absolutely nothing.

Mollified the prefect went on, "Quite, quite. Not my orders anyway; the Governor... again! And you did well to attack when you did. The Governor was quite impressed. Seems you have friends in the legion."

"Have I sir?"

"Don't get coy with me Marcus Aurelius Maximunius. Julius Agricola and Decius Brutus both seem to think you are a brilliant soldier. What do you say to that?"

Marcus was taken aback. He had never coped with compliments and he was wary for he thought the prefect had an ulterior motive and would end up punishing him or embarrassing him in front of the men. In the end, he just said, "Not for me to say, sir. I can't control what others think of me."

"Quite right, quite right. The thing is I need you to carry on doing what you do well. Manage the men train the men."

"Yes sir, not a problem."

"But not lead them."

"I beg your pardon?"

"I am the leader and I will lead the men into action. These detached duties where you go off and fight little battles they won't do you know." He leaned into Marcus and spoke quietly, "Confidentially I will only be here a short time. My family has a much better position for me with Emperor Vespasian so you see if you help me out then I will recommend that you become prefect when I leave. With friends like the Governor and Agricola that shouldn't be a problem. So what do you say? Will you manage and train the men and run the ala?"

"Of course, sir, that goes without saying but when you talk about not leading, will I be stuck in the fort?"

Rufius laughed. Marcus had never heard him laugh and it sounded like the cackle of an old crone. "No, no. You will take your turma out on patrol and so on and so forth but when the ala goes into action I will command and I will lead. The glory will be mine. Clear?"

"Clear sir."

"Good."

Marcus now saw how petty the prefect was. He was only interested in glory and honour. Marcus cared for neither. The prefect saw the ala and its men as a vehicle. Marcus saw them as his family. He would go along with the prefect but he would be damned if he would stop leading the men.

"Of course that means that you will be Decurion Princeps. Extra pay and all that."

Murmuring 'thank you sir' Marcus saw just how pathetic the prefect was. The men still regarded him as Decurion Princeps and he had more money than he needed. Once again, he had an insight into the prefect and his petty ways. The prefect spent the next few miles explaining his ideas to Marcus. Surprisingly Marcus found he liked some of them.

Chapter 11

Morbium

They had only been in the fort for hours and the decurions had barely unpacked when Rufius asked for the officers to attend a meeting. He had not yet spoken to his friends about the prefect's plan and he wondered how they would take the announcement. When he entered he was somewhat surprised to see Fabius sat on the prefect's right. He had no chance to think further for the prefect began without preamble.

"The Governor in his wisdom has seen fit to house a century of Batavians in the fort. I made my objections known of course. I have just been informed that we have another one hundred and fifty recruits to add to the one hundred we left here untrained. It should be obvious to even a blind monkey that we cannot be housed here."

Decius interjected, "We have the camp we built for the refugees, sir."

The prefect glared at the decurion. "When I want questions or advice I will ask for it until then kindly remain silent. As I was saying we are too crowded. Decurion Marcus Aurelius Maximunius has had a good idea. Oh before I go on I should add that Marcus Aurelius Maximunius is hereby promoted to Decurion Princeps." The prefect found it hard to continue as the other decurions were congratulating and patting Marcus on the back. "When you have quite finished. He had the idea of re-investing the fort at Derventio. Although this was curtailed because of the rebellion I think it has merit. Decurion Princeps Marcus Aurelius Maximunius will take turmae one three and five along with all the recruits. The fort will be enlarged and the Decurion Princeps will train troopers. I will retain the other turmae, all eight of them and we will patrol. When Decurion Decius Flavius and Decurion Princeps Marcus Aurelius Maximunius have trained the first turma he will appoint a decurion and that will bring the garrison up to four, from then on trained recruits will be sent here to eventually build us up to twenty-four turmae. Any questions?"

Marcus had waited until he was in a big meeting to ask this one question. "Any restriction on who I appoint as decurion sir?"

The prefect beamed a smile and looked at his son. "Of course not you are Decurion Princeps after all."

"In that case, I can appoint him now."

"You have someone in mind already?"

"Yes sir, Gaius Appius Figulus." The prefect coloured and Fabius tried to rise only to be restrained by his father. Decius and the other decurions grinned but kept silent. Even Julius looked pleased.

"Very well. We shall spend the winter building up our stock so Decurion Princeps if you wish you can use your sergeant to start the stud. If the last battle was anything to go by we will need many horses. Any further questions? No then in that case Decurion Princeps you may take your men to Derventio in the morning and one final matter. As you know I shall be very busy visiting the Governor and so forth my deputy and the other Decurion Princeps is Fabius Octavius Demetrius."

Even Julius was shocked but no one could say anything. They all had to suffer the smug expression on the young patrician's face. They left in stunned silence. Marcus turned to Lentius and Decius. "Find Gaius and bring him to my quarters we'll need to plan." He held his hand up to silence Decius and looked at each of the other decurions in turn. "And we need to think before we open our mouths. We can have a farewell drink later when, perhaps, we have reflected on all of this."

Marcus' quarters were quite crowded with the ten other decurions. As soon as they had entered all of them had effusively praised Gaius who was really taken aback by it all. Earlier when Decius and Lentius had brought him along to Marcus he could not hide his disbelief that Marcus had managed to get this promotion for him. "I don't think the prefect was too happy about it."

"Not just the prefect Decius did you see his son? I thought his head was going to erupt with rage," added Lentius.

Even Marcus smiled at this image. "All you need to know Gaius is that you are now a decurion and we will be going to Derventio for a while."

Septimus was the first one to bring up the prefect's decision. "I have been in the auxilia for ten years and I have never heard of such a young man being promoted so highly and so early." He turned to Julius sat next to him. "No offence young Julius."

Julius grinned; he was so unlike his brother that some of the decurions thought he must have a different father. "None taken, Septimus. I too was surprised but my brother is ambitious and he was ever the favourite."

Decius grunted, "Well he's not our favourite," and ruffled the young man's hair.

"It doesn't matter. He is the prefect and he can do as he wishes. "

"Yes, Decurion Princeps," said Lentius, "but if it is any consolation to the rest of you when we field the whole ala Marcus has seniority because of his service."

"Didn't know that," said Vettius a happier look rising on his face like a new moon. "I think I'll drink to that."

"You had better make that your last one, I suspect that the new Decurion Princeps will be exerting his authority tomorrow and you will all need your wits about you."

They took the hint and began to drift off. "Now that they have gone, Marcus, do you think this is going to work? I can't see him changing at all. Someone else will be flogged to cover his mistake. It makes me angry to think that all the good work you did to get the spirit back into the ala will be eradicated by one man, sorry boy!"

"If one man was able to do that Decius then I wouldn't have done such a good job would I? Tonight, you saw all of the decurions. They might argue about little things, they might even not like each other at times and have different ways of doing things but they are united in one thing, their determination to make this ala great again. I don't think they will have too many battles to fight over the winter. Remember when we went on our last little jaunt? We saw neither hide nor hair of the tribes until spring. He might exert harsher discipline than we might but it isn't going to kill them. If we trained the decurions right, and I think we did, then they will survive and, in the spring, we return and when we return we will be stronger because you Decius will have trained the new recruits our way."

Decius swallowed the last of the wine, gave an almighty belch and then asked, "What is this place Derventio like? I have never been there."

"Totally different from here. It is in a vale between two moorlands and is about fifteen miles from the sea. Great country for horses for it is gentle upland, not rocky crags as here. It is a perfect place for training and I think Sergeant Cato will enjoy the places he can train the horses."

"And the people?"

"Good question. Ulpius and I patrolled there a couple of years ago and although they are more Romanized than the rest they don't welcome us there with open arms. I think they put up with us and hope we will be gone sooner rather than later."

"They are in for a shock then. We've never left anywhere we have conquered."

"Once we have built the gyrus…"

"Again?"

"Again. And the stud I will take a patrol out with Lentius to get the lay of the land and let the locals know that the Romans have returned to Derventio."

"While I get to train all the recruits."

"Yes, but you will have Gaius and Macro with you. One other thing about the recruits, they are likely to be from this province we will need to be very careful about their loyalty."

"Especially after Aed."

"Have you any thoughts on a weapons trainer, I know you could do it Decius but you have your hands full getting them to sit on a horse, and we will need a quartermaster."

"I have a couple of lads in mind. How about Agrippa for weapons trainer? He is handy with a sword and a javelin. Perhaps Macro could assist him by all accounts he might be a bit of a big head but he can use every weapon easily."

"Good idea. I will talk to them tomorrow while we ride. And quartermaster?"

"Bit more difficult that. They have to be trustworthy and not afraid of the really boring work. No one springs to mind." He reflected for a moment. "Wonder what happened to that fat bastard Cresens? He was an evil swine. Robbed every trooper blind."

Marcus' face became hard. "He has more to answer for than robbing troopers. He robbed Ulpius of a Queen. I don't know where he is but if he is in this land I will find him and then he will die."

Streonshal

At that very moment, Gaius Cresens was very comfortable. Nor was he as fat. The life he had led had been harsher than hitherto and he was leaner. He was however becoming increasingly rich. His informal taxes, which amounted to protection money, were very lucrative. Because the locals did not live in fear of bandits and pirates they were producing more and did not notice the money that Cresens was accruing. The only dark cloud on the horizon was the Romans. Although their attack on the bandits' lair had been timely and saved them from disaster if they returned in numbers then they would bring with them all the trappings of civilisation, like taxes and the people, would not pay to two tax masters. As they had not been heard of since the summer he hoped that they were off fighting more belligerent locals. Now that autumn was here and there was food aplenty Cresens hoped to make even more money. Jared had also told him of the winter storms which brought a bountiful crop of wrecks and plunder. Life was good.

Atticus entered his villa. It annoyed Gaius that he did not knock but he was still playing the kind master. Atticus was another cloud on his horizon. He was too good and questioned the taxes. He pointed out that they had more than enough so why take so much from the people. Cresens could never have enough. He also wanted to make contact with the Romans. Having served as a freeman on a Roman ship he saw them as a good thing. Cresens had yet to come up with a sound argument against more contact. The young helmsman had filled out and grown up in the time he had been in the settlement. He was seen by all the young men as a hero and leader whilst all the young women ached for his body between their compliant legs. Atticus was a problem that would have to be faced and soon.

Atticus looked at the pile of silver on the table. "That is a mighty pot Master. You have done well." He hesitated. "Perhaps we could allow the villagers to keep more of their goods?"

"Atticus, Atticus, I have told you," he used his silky rather than his hectoring voice, "who pays the guards who protect the goods travelling to Derventio and Eboracum?"

"You do master."

"Yes, and they cost money. This may look like a handy pile right now but what about during the winter when there is little trade and yet I will still have to pay the guards."

"You could let them go. Some of them are little better than bandits themselves. I have had to bang a few heads together before now to stop them from abusing our charges."

Cresens knew that they were thugs and that pleased him but he could not let Atticus know that. "Good. I will have a word with them perhaps I will threaten to withhold some of their salary eh?" He laughed a mirthless laugh which Atticus ignored.

"Now that the Romans are back in Derventio we may not need to protect the merchants on the roads?"

"As you told me last week the Romans haven't been seen for a moon and besides it is not just on the road what about the forests to the south and west? Many bandits still hide there."

"All the more reason to speak to the Romans for they could easily clear the forests."

"You seem to have all the answers Atticus. I will think on it."

Atticus beamed like a child rewarded with a toy. "Thank you, master." He kissed his hand," Thank you."

"Be off with you." As Atticus left watched by the smiling Cresens he did not know he had signed his own death warrant.

Brocavum

Aed felt confused when he arrived at the Carvetii stronghold. Although he had not expected to be welcomed with open arms he had at least expected a welcome instead he was greeted with sullen stares, mumbled curses and open hostility. King Maeve barely acknowledged him and seemed besotted with the young witch Fainch. He had followed his orders completely. He had built up the guards, disposed of the loyal ones, killed the royal family and successfully extracted his force without loss in the face of the Roman army. What more could he have done?

Fainch found him alone and brooding at the south tower. He stood up as she ascended to the top of the tower. He was taken away by her beauty; she had always been beautiful but she had hidden her beauty under grime and dirty clothes playing the part of a witch and hiding from stares. It no longer suited her to be invisible. She was the thread that held this tenuous coalition together and she needed Aed as much as King Maeve. Aed was true Brigante and had many followers he was the future and had more claim to the throne than Maeve. She could not allow dissension. In truth, he was also a good-looking youth. She had deliberately dressed to attract him; the blue woad was not applied as a sign of war but used over her eyes to deepen them and highlight the colour, her lips were red with the body of a crushed beetle and her cheeks blushing with diluted beetroots. Her hair was no longer wild and striking but sleek washed and oiled to sheen and shimmer in the light of the setting sun. She had bathed in a hot bath filled with fragrant roses, jasmine and honeysuckle. Her shift although simple was cut low to give him a glimpse of her ample and full breasts and was drawn in at the waist to reveal her curvaceous hips. Fainch was not at all unsettled by her own actions. She served Mother Earth and as such, she was as Mother Earth fertile and fecund. She was not ashamed of her body, indeed she would have walked around naked were she not aware that this would have created problems for those around her.

"Aed why do you keep alone?" He did not answer, in fact, he was finding it hard to speak let alone think. He just shook his head. She walked behind him and put her hands around the sides of his head. "I have powers, some you have seen, some yet to see. I will look into your mind and then your heart." Aed found his heart pounding harder. It also seemed to be throbbing in his chest more than during the fiercest battle he had ever fought. "You wonder why the Carvetii treat you as they do when all you did was what you were ordered." Aed started and tried to turn around. She was reading his mind! "Be still my warrior. You will not be harmed. You also want to be at the head of the army when it attacks and defeats the Romans for you feel you are a better and braver warrior than King Maeve." His eyes darted from side to side, afraid that someone would overhear for those were his very thoughts and she was speaking them. "There is no one to hear my words and only I can read your thoughts." At least there was nothing more she could discover. "And there is more." His heart began racing. "You desire me. You wish to hold me in your arms you wish to enter the sacred world of my fertile places. You wish to have me."

He broke away and fell on his knees before her. "Please I beg of you. I cannot control my thoughts, do not kill me for desiring you."

She walked up to him and, putting her hands behind his head drew his face into her breasts which had suddenly, and he knew not how, appeared from inside her shift. "Your thoughts are natural, oh warrior, as are mine." He found his mouth around one of her breasts and even though he fought the urge he found himself kissing the pale breast and then found his tongue touching the erect nipple. He felt her tense and put her head back then she pulled his head away, bent down kissed him full on the lips her mouth opened and her tongue darted into his. Before he could respond she pulled away. "Not now but I will come to you. Do not be afraid." She raised him up and as she did so he noticed that her breasts were back inside her shift. She put her arm through his. "As for the Carvetii they believe, wrongly, that you should have attacked the Romans and aided them when they were attacked."

"But then my men would be dead!"

"Exactly! You did what was right for the war. They wanted you to do what was right for the battle and in that they were wrong. Your warband is the finest in the army." He started to say no but she stopped walking and stared at him her voice suddenly harsh and commanding. "No false modesty and no lies. I can read your mind but I would prefer the truth. Always the truth. Understand me?" He nodded. "Good. You have the elite warband. The others can be thrown away needlessly but you are the cutting edge. You are the only force that can defeat their auxiliary cavalry. Without that cavalry, our army can move around the slow cumbersome legions and destroy them. That is why I was happy, no delighted," her voice now purred and soothed, "when you returned complete and I want you to stay that way," she lowered her eyes and then looked straight into his eyes, "for me and one day you will be the most powerful man in this land and I will be by your side." Suddenly she was gone and Aed found himself wondering if this had all been a dream. She had read his mind, she had offered herself to him and she hinted that there was more to come. Striding from the tower he suddenly felt empowered. Let the Carvetii treat him insolently he cared not; he had had a glimpse of the future and he wanted everything in it.

Derventio

"Well I am glad the lads did a bit of work on it but there's a lot for us to do."

"Never mind Decius it will get rid of some of that flab and give you a chance to see what these recruits are like." The recruits Marcus had spoken of were a mixture of tribes from the province, Regni, Atrebates and Canti and more traditional recruits from Cantabria, Pannonia and Batavia. Marcus noted that the provincial recruits were all from the far south and had neither allegiance nor knowledge of this land which was a good thing.

"The first thing I'd like is if they knew their own name."

"Don't you remember what it was like when you joined? I can still remember wondering who this Marcus was when inside I was Himli." When recruits joined they were given Roman names so the first few months were a difficult time. Marcus realised now that it helped you to join in to become more Roman. It stopped you from being a barbarian. He smiled as he realised he was a barbarian born but he regarded the peoples of this land as true barbarians.

"At least they can speak Latin."

"That's the advantage of being the first to be conquered, you learn it from birth. Right, I'll get Lentius' turma and mine to finish off the fort. You get Gaius' turma and the recruits to build the gyrus and let Cato have six or seven men to build a holding pen for the horses. He can build something sturdier later on. You get on with that and I will go and have a word with Agrippa and Macro. I didn't get the chance on the way over"

"Right boss."

He strode over to where his turma was busy unpacking. He shouted over, "Lentius, Gaius, Agrippa and Macro." Lentius and Gaius strolled over to him, Agrippa wondering why he was in the company of decurions came at a fast walk, Macro who was convinced he had done something wrong ran over so hard he barely stopped in time to avoid the Decurion Princeps. "Steady on Macro I am going nowhere. Gaius, get your turma to give Decius and the recruits a hand to build the gyrus."

"And stop him killing them as well?"

"That would be a good idea. Lentius take your turma and mine and finish off the fort. The lads did a good job but it isn't quite ready."

"We'll have it looking like the Imperial Palace!"

"Now then I suppose you are wondering why you two are here?"

"A secret mission sir? Capture the Brigante king eh sir?"

Marcus and Agrippa exchanged looks. "Not this week. Macro first we build a fort. No, I have an offer to make to both of you and I want you both to hear the other's offer." Macro looked confused.

"The Decurion Princeps is going to offer both of us something and the roles are linked, right sir?"

"Right, Agrippa. I would like you to be the sergeant in charge of weapons training. You up for that?"

"Yes sir. That would really suit me. Thank you."

"I know that Drusus would have offered you something had he survived. There will be a pay rise."

"Always welcome."

"Now the thing is we are training another twelve turmae and I am certain that we will need more decurions and also that you will become a decurion sooner rather than later."

"Thank you again, sir."

"So, I would like you to consider taking on Macro as your assistant and training him, at the same time to become a weapons training officer at some time in the future."

"Thank you, sir."

"Thank me for what I haven't offered you anything yet."

"But sir you said…"

"You weren't listening son if I want you as my assistant you will be offered the job."

"But you do want me, don't you?" pleaded Macro.

Agrippa looked at Marcus, "Well I don't fancy him bursting into tears so I will say yes but Macro."

"Yes, sergeant?"

"You need to become a man quite quickly for you will be giving other men orders. Do you understand?"

To Marcus, it looked as though he grew a whole head taller. "Yes, sergeant."

Grinning Marcus said to Agrippa, "Work out a schedule with Decius. Take the ones who become riders first."

The two men snapped a, "Yes sir "and strode off.

Decius had been right he thought they were a perfect match. The older sober Agrippa and the keen as mustard Macro. It would be building for the future. The weapons training had always been handled by Ulpius and, after his death by Drusus. Marcus had felt that the role needed someone who was not a decurion for they had to deal with every man in the ala.

Chapter 12

The nights were drawing in and the first frosts of the year had made the men build their fires a little higher by the time the fort was finished and the gyrus up and running. Marcus felt he could take the opportunity to go with Cato and select some horses for their stud. Decius was more than happy to take charge of the fort. As they rode south to the farms that dotted the rich soil of the east of the land Marcus noticed the change in Cato. Not only was he happier he looked younger, but he was also more inclined to smile and he seemed less nervous around Marcus. The change was due entirely to Marcus and the gentle way he had had with men. Ulpius had been a barker and a shouter. Marcus preferred persuasion.

"So, sergeant, what do you think we should look for today?"

"I'll be happy with one stallion and four or five broodmares. It doesn't do to start these things too fast."

"Explain your thinking, sergeant."

"If we have two or three stallions we increase the friction between horses, fights and so on. More than one stallion means that you can't be certain who sired which foal and if you are trying to breed certain characteristics."

"I can see the logic in that and the four or five mares?"

"The same really sir. We will make mistakes at first. Too many mares mean too many mistakes. I need to train my men up as well."

"Good I like your thinking let's get some horseflesh."

The land they were travelling through was the land of the Parisi. There were many farms and most had numbers of horses that were well suited to the land. It was coming to the time of year when fodder was becoming scarce and the two auxiliaries were hoping to pick up bargains. They were lucky at the first farm for the farmer there had a large number of horses and he happily sold them three mares. They asked about other horse farms and he directed them north of Derventio.

"It means a ride of about twenty miles sir."

"I don't think decurion Decius will mind being in charge a little longer eh sergeant?"

"No sir."

"What about the actual stud? Any thoughts on where that should be?"

"Away from the fort sir. You don't want the other horses being spooked by the mating. It is also better for the foals sometimes they can be hurt if there are a lot of horses nearby."

"When we get back you had better find somewhere suitable."

They crossed the small river which ran through Derventio about ten miles downstream. The autumn rains had not swollen it yet and the water only came up to the horses' withers. They made such good time that they reached the first farm just before sunset. There was a rudimentary palisade around it but the farmer happily let them in when he saw their uniform.

"Would you care to spend the night here? The wife has cooked a nice game stew and we have space in the hut."

"We will share your food but we don't want to put anyone out."

The farmer, a man as round as he was tall laughed. "You'll be putting no one out. The roundhouse is big enough."

The farmer's wife was as skinny as the farmer was fat but once he tasted the food he realised why. She was a wonderful cook. Army food was plentiful but dull. This stew had hare and squirrel and was flavoured with elderberries and brambles. After the meal, they comfortably sat and talked horses.

"Excuse me sir but are you from the fort?"

"Yes, I am the commander actually."

"So, you are putting men back in there?"

"Why is that a problem?"

"No, we are delighted. It means we can send our produce to Derventio and we'll be safe."

Cato and Marcus exchanged looks. "Why would you not be safe?"

"The bandits."

His wife interjected, "It was a lot worse last year."

The farmer looked crossly at his wife, "Who is telling this tale you or me?" She quailed. "Right. Sorry about that, sir. The wife's right, until last year we couldn't send anything anywhere. Bandits would rob us. Sometimes they would steal slaves. Two years ago, they took Sceolan, he has the next farm up the valley, and they took his two bairns. Two lads."

"Didn't you go to the authorities in Eboracum?"

"The problem is sir if you go off there what happens to your family and your farm when you are away? We all thought that when the Romans came life would be better but once the fort was abandoned then all the worst kind of rogues came out like woodlice from rotten wood."

"You say it is better now?"

"Well a little better. About a year ago some new men came to Streonshal on the coast they started sending their fish here for us to buy and we sold them grain and the like and then seemingly the pirates up the coast were killed."

"That was Romans. Was it a little place almost near Dunum Fluvius?"

"The big river. Yes, that was it. Didn't know it was Romans. The people in Streonshal made out it was them."

"What changed?"

"Well it is safer and we can move our goods but we have to use their guards and they charge us a tenth of the goods to protect it."

"Do all the farmers pay this," he paused to let the word take effect, "tax?"

"If they want their goods to get to market."

"And of course you don't pay Roman taxes?"

"Couldn't afford to," the farmer replied bluntly, "and besides if you Romans could collect taxes it would mean you had tax collectors and soldiers and the bandits wouldn't be able to have such a free hand."

"Well, farmer, I can promise you one thing you won't need to pay for guards. As soon as I have bought a stallion and a couple of broodmares I will get patrols out and the first place I shall visit will be …what was the name of the place?"

"Streonshal."

"Right and what is the name of this man who runs it?"

"Don't know. They call him the Master but I think he is Roman."

"Roman eh? Leave it with me. Thank you for an excellent meal we'll be away in the morning."

"I might be able to save you a journey. I have a couple of stallions. We were going to eat one this winter and I have got more broodmares than I need. If you want to have a look in the morning you can take your pick."

The farmer was as good as his word and Cato picked out two excellent broodmares to go with a magnificent young stallion. The farmer was pleased they took that particular stallion for he had four white socks and they believed it to be unlucky as a result they paid a low price.

As they rode away Cato said to Marcus, "In my tribe, it was one white sock that was unlucky."

Marcus laughed. "Thank the Allfather for their superstitions. What do you make of this Master?"

"Seems to me he has just taken advantage of the folk hereabouts."

"My thoughts exactly. Let's get back to the fort and see what wonders the decurion has performed."

It was almost two days later that Marcus was satisfied enough with the state of the fort to send out a patrol. He decided, in the end, to send out two for he wanted the complete picture for the area. Lentius was to travel northeast with a specific task, to visit, 'the master' at Streonshal. Gaius had the shorter and somewhat easier patrol due east. Marcus was aware that Gaius had little experience of independent command and he would need to get to know his turma. With Agrippa and Macro assigned other duties he would have no one to whom to refer. Lentius was given a thorough briefing by Marcus. "You had better take rations for a two-day patrol. Streonshal is some way up the coast. There is a route over the moors but if you go one way and back the other it will give us a better picture of the area and show more of the locals that we are back. Keep a map of your journey." He looked earnestly at his friend. "I want this informal tax stopped. Sometime in the next year or so a Civitas will be established and I want any taxes to go to us, not to some local bandit. I am also concerned that he is Roman. That suggests a military man and all the Roman military men who are here legitimately are settled on farms or in service. Any problems just bring him back for questioning. Any doubts bring him back for questioning. Clear?"

Lentius grinned, "Yes sir. I'll bring him back."

Marcus shook his head as he smiled wryly. "Sorry, Lentius didn't mean it to come out like that. Use your discretion."

"Yes sir."

"Oh, and take Gaelwyn with you he might be useful."

Lentius groaned, "He'll be moaning all the way there and back and telling me how much better the Brigante are at tracking, fighting, loving, everything."

"No problem Lentius, just ask him who always wins in a battle. That should shut him up."

Lentius and Gaelwyn found themselves in agreement over their route, which surprised both of them. They decided to go east, travelling part of the way with Gaius and then up the coast. Gaius for his part enjoyed the early part of the journey because it delayed the time he would take his first patrol. He was excited about the responsibility but he had over twenty men in the turma he did not know. When they reached the last ford on the river Lentius waved his goodbyes and his men waded across to the northern bank.

They had only travelled a few miles when they reached the sea. They found a huge bay with a small settlement of fishermen. It was a good place to talk. The headman knew no Latin for they were an isolated community but Gaelwyn translated. He too had heard about the master but as they didn't trade with anyone they did not pay the taxes. He agreed that the destruction of the pirates had been a good thing. Having been briefed by Marcus Lentius made sure he let the headman know who was responsible; they did not want this master claiming the credit. As they trekked north Lentius pointed out the high cliff to Gaelwyn. "That would be a perfect place for a tower. You could signal all the way down the coast."

"What is it with you Romans? Why signalling? Why all the roads? You follow the land. You do not control it."

"That's the difference between us old man. We Romans like order and control it makes for peace."

"Yes but living the Brigante way makes for life."

They found that they could follow the cliff tops which rose and fell gently. A few miles further on they found another bay but this time uninhabited. Lentius made a note on the map he was compiling that this would be another good place for a tower. It was soon after leaving this second bay that Gaelwyn returned. "I have found the settlement." While the men fed their horses and took the opportunity to eat themselves, Lentius and the scout went to one side to discuss their options. "They have a palisade around some buildings. One of them is a large building. It looks Roman to me. "

"How many people did you see?"

"There must have been five turmae."

"Warriors?"

"There were some armed men. A handful."

"What do you suggest for an approach?" Lentius did not mind asking the old scout for advice. He knew ambush and assault as well as any of them. It was enough for Lentius that Marcus trusted him with his life.

"It is nestled against the top of the cliff but it is on this side of the river. The gate faces the river so it would seem to be the place which is most heavily guarded."

"Here is what we will do. You lead half the turma to their north wall and hide the men. I will ride to the west and follow the river to the gate. From what you say I have more than enough troopers to defeat their handful of warriors." Gaelwyn nodded. "Your task is to stop and capture anyone who flees. If this master is a Roman he may be known to us. If I need you to attack I will sound the buccina."

Gaelwyn nodded and Lentius smiled as he saw the grudging respect in the Brigante scout's eyes.

Streonshal

Cresens had invited Atticus to his villa to discuss plans for the winter. That was the lure to draw in the now expendable sailor. He carefully mixed the poison he had retained from his murder of the Queen. He only needed enough to kill one man and he could save the powerful killer for another such opportunity. He mixed it in a jug of the beer he knew the young man liked to drink. Outside his thugs had been briefed to stop anyone approaching. After this murder, there would be a new regime in Streonshal.

Atticus walked into the villa as a mouse stumbles into a trap. He believed he had persuaded the master to be less harsh with the villagers. Today could be the start of a better life in this newly prosperous village.

"Ah, Atticus come in. Have a drink. There is cheese and ale on the table."

"I have just eaten master but thank you."

Outwardly smiling but inwardly cursing Cresens continued. "You have some good ideas for the settlement, Atticus. I think we can make this a much better place."

Atticus looked at what he perceived to be a kind man. "Master there is one thing. Those guards. Do we need them? They frighten the villagers and now that the Romans have returned we no longer require their services."

"It is still a rumour about the Romans."

"No master I saw them."

"You saw one small turma. Have you seen any since? No." Atticus shook his head. "I thought not. Do have a drink."

Just then there was an almighty noise outside and Cresens became angry. He was just about to rid himself of a moral encumbrance he did not need this distraction. "What is it?"

One of his thugs entered red-faced and flustered. "Romans. Roman cavalry!"

Cresens had to think quickly. Roman cavalry meant Pannonians. It was likely that, despite their losses, there might be someone who recognised him as a murderer and deserter. He would use Atticus to stall them while he made good his escape. He had had a small door built into the palisade on the north wall for just such an eventuality. "Romans. You were right after all Atticus. Well if you will go and greet them I will make myself and this hovel presentable." As the two men left Cresens grabbed his money bag from its hiding place and his cloak and went out of the rear door.

Lentius rode his men through the gate noting the disparity between the villagers and the armed guards. The guards looked like the bandits they had killed in the past and yet the villagers looked like hard-working fisher folk. The tall well-built man who emerged from the villa was different again. He had a noble look about him. He further surprised Lentius by speaking Latin. "Welcome to Streonshal, decurion. I am really happy that the Romans have returned. My name is Atticus. "

"Roman?"

"I was a Roman sailor and I was wrecked upon this shore."

"Your friends there do not look happy to see us." Lentius pointed to the sullen crowd of guards who had gathered.

Atticus turned to the motley crew of thugs and bandits, "They are not my friends but my master finds them useful. Would you like to see him? He is the headman of this settlement."

"Yes I would," Lentius was perplexed for this young man seemed honest and trustworthy and did not marry with the image of someone who was taxing the people illegally.

"Follow me then for he is preparing his villa for visitors."

When they entered Atticus looked around in surprise. The room was empty and there were items scattered all over the floor as if someone had left in a hurry. "It seems your master has left and somewhat hastily judging by the upturned furniture." Lentius turned to the trooper next to him, "Cassius find the back door and see where he has gone."

"I cannot understand why he has left. He said he was preparing the room for you." Atticus looks more perplexed and confused than Lentius.

"Sit down and explain to me how you came to be here." Atticus sat down and began to tell the story of the storm and the shipwreck culminating with their arrival and the destruction of the pirates by the Romans."

Lentius nodded. It all sounded true and backed up what the other locals had said and what he knew of Marcus' attack. "Now what of this protection tax?"

For the first time, Atticus looked uncomfortable. "I have to say that I did not agree with the protection the Master sold. At first, I could see a reason for it but once your soldiers returned I felt we did not need it."

They were suddenly interrupted by a noise and disturbance outside. Lentius heard the words, "How dare you. Take your hands off me. Do you know with whom you are dealing?"

"That's the master. He has returned."

They both went out into the road. There was the Master with his hands tied and Gaelwyn holding a sword to his back. The prisoner began to threaten and rant. "This is an outrage" and then he looked up. His face went ashen and his hands dropped to the ground.

"Gaius Cresens! This is an unpleasant surprise."

"Do you know him? Asked Atticus surprised on all levels by the turn of events.

"Know him? All the troopers of the first Pannonian cavalry who served with Queen Cartimandua know him."

"You are mistaken I am not the man you think I am. I am…"

Lentius savagely slashed him across the face with his vine staff and said in a voice that was so cold and chilling that the men in his turma looked at him in shock never having seen him so angry. "You are Gaius Cresens once quartermaster of the Pannonian cavalry. You are a deserter, the man who poisoned Queen Cartimandua and tried to murder three other people. You are a base, vile creature who does not deserve to live."

Even the villagers who were somewhat bemused by the events looked shocked for they had all heard of the murder of their Queen. "No that is wrong I…"

"I will tell you what; you bloated excuse for a man. I will take you back to Derventio where others will testify to your identity and where you will be tried and found guilty of your crimes." Lentius noticed the thugs and guards beginning to move away from the scene; they had realised that the man with the money would be no more and they were making good their escape. "Stop those men! Disarm them!"

Some of his troopers immediately tried to grab the man nearest them. Two of Cresens hired men drew swords and tried to hack their way out. They stood no chance against the well-trained troopers. Others tried to fight back with bare hands. When peace was restored there were but six bandits still remaining. "I do not know of your involvement in this but you six will return with me to Derventio and the inquisitors will get the truth." The six survivors began to shake for all had heard of the inquisitors and the torture they employed.

"And me?"

Lentius looked at Atticus. "I do not believe you had any knowledge of wrongdoing and besides the people will need a new leader and I believe if they could choose they would choose you." He noticed some of the villagers nodding. "I will return to my commander and explain what I have done. It may well be that he comes to question you or request your presence at the fort but for the moment I ask if you will stay here and look after these people. Do I have your word?"

Standing just that little bit taller he replied, "I would be proud to and decurion I will gladly come to Derventio at any time to give my testimony."

Realising he had made the right decision Lentius grasped the young helmsman's arm and then shouted, "Put ropes on this scum they have a long walk to Derventio."

From the happy noises emanating from the palisaded settlement, Lentius knew that Atticus was popular and would do a good job. He turned to the figure tied by a rope to Lentius' horse," How on earth did you dupe such a fine young man to do your wishes, you evil spider?"

Cresens response was to spit in the direction of the decurion. Lentius just pulled so hard on the rope that the ex-quartermaster crashed to the ground. "If you want to play then I can accommodate you all the way back to the fort. But remember this you will arrive in one piece; you may be bloodied and you may be in pain but I will return you for justice and then you will be tried and when you are tried you will be found guilty. Guilty Cresens. And you know what that means, the death penalty. The bastinado!"

The troopers of the turma were surprised with the speed with which they travelled for Lentius was normally a considerate commander. They did not understand what had happened in Streonshal but whatever it was it had angered the normally mild-mannered decurion. They had heard his words and seen the look on the prisoner's faces but they were all recruits and knew only part of the story of the murder.

They reached Derventio just before dusk and it was Decius who was on duty. When Lentius identified himself Decius stepped forward to peer into the twilight gloom. "You are back early. Was the ground too hard to sleep on? Fancy a drink?"

Smiling Lentius pulled the rope so that the prisoner was forced to walk forward. "No, I couldn't wait until the morning for I have a prisoner and I am sure the Decurion Princeps will want to see him."

As the light fell on the prisoner's face Decius suddenly exclaimed, "Gaius bleeding Cresens. At last, we have you, you fat evil bastard." Spurning his vine staff Decius hit him so hard with his fist that the deserter was knocked out. Grinning he looked up at Lentius, "I have waited two years for that, drag the scum to the headquarters."

There was a marked difference in the reaction of the recruits and the older troopers; almost to a man, the older troopers had a mixture of hate and delight all over their faces while the recruits looked confused at the violent treatment meted out to this prisoner, this Roman prisoner.

Chapter 13

The Decurion Princeps decided to hold the trial of ex-quartermaster Gaius Cresens in public. The gyrus was used so that all of the troopers could attend. Lots were drawn amongst the recruits to see who would pull guard duty on the empty fort but the trial would be a short affair and they would not be left alone for long. The prisoner was manacled and sat in the middle of a hollow square.

Decius read out the charges, "Gaius Cresens you are charged with desertion. Gaius Cresens you are charged with operating as a spy for King Venutius of the Brigante. Gaius Cresens you are charged with the murder of Queen Cartimandua. Gaius Cresens you are charged with the attempted murder of Ulpius Felix, Princess Macha and Princess Lenta. Gaius Cresens you are charged with fraudulently taking monies from the troopers of this ala. How do you plead?"

He remained stubbornly silent for he could not deny the charge of desertion. "Why doesn't he say anything?" Macro asked Gaius.

"No one can prove he killed the Queen. We could have used inquisitors to find that out but the decurion wanted a quick trial. The most serious offence which can be proved is the desertion which he can't deny and the punishment for that is the fustuarium."

"What is that?"

"The soldiers whose lives he put in danger beat him to death. You might have heard some of them mention it by its other name, the bastinado. For us, that means the troopers who are still alive and were serving when the Queen was killed will be the ones to exact punishment."

"That's why it was the recruits who had to pull the duty."

Marcus had given the prisoner plenty of time to answer. "If you have no answer to these charges then have you anything else to say?"

"I do not recognise this court. I am a civilian and any charges should be brought by a civilian court."

Marcus spoke for the first time. "You are a civilian eh? Where are your discharge papers? Show them and I will personally escort you to a Civitas Capital for trial." The silence echoed around the gyrus. "Quite. If you have nothing further of value to say then I will pass the sentence. The sentence for your crime is the fustuarium."

Cresens fell from his chair to his knees. He began sobbing and pleading. "No, please. It was a mistake. It wasn't me. It was that witch. I know her name. Spare me."

Marcus' voiced seemed quiet and threatening after the screams of the prisoner. "What is her name?"

"If I tell you will you let me go?"

"If you don't tell me you will be tortured by these men," he gestured at the three decurions who sat stone-faced.

"You can't."

"I can and I will and you know it. What is her name?"

"It was Fainch. She is a priestess of the Druids and a witch."

"Carry on decurion."

"Have mercy!" screamed the doomed man.

"Silence!" Decius' voice boomed out. "All troopers who served under Ulpius Felix from a square around the prisoner."

Gaius took his place and was surprised at how few of them remained. There were less than twenty. He noticed that although some of the others had cudgels and stones, having anticipated the punishment some like Decius and Marcus had bare hands.

It was Marcus who gave the command. "Let the punishment begin."

As Macro watched, mesmerized, he was stunned by the cold and efficient manner they went about the task. The men with the cudgels broke every bone in his legs and feet. Others then broke his arms. His screams echoed and thundered up to the hills. The troopers with stones then hurled them at his body and even Macro winced as he heard a rib break. Finally, the four decurions were left and they pummelled his body with their fists. His bloody though still heaving body lay on the ground and the final act took place. The silent soldiers used fists, feet, stones and cudgel to finally eradicate every sign of life from his body. When the panting troopers stood back all that could be seen was a bloody piece of meat.

Decius roared, "Dismiss!"

"Burn that." For Marcus, this would indeed see the end of an evil that had haunted him since the death of the Queen. Unconsciously he fingered the hilt of her sword, the sword he carried in honour of her and her dead lover.

The passing of the evil Cresens seemed to mark a turning point at the fort. The recruits saw how harsh the discipline could be whilst the older troopers finally saw justice. For Marcus and the other decurions, they were halfway to fulfilling their promise to a dying comrade. Now that they knew her name they would seek out Fainch.

"Next time we are in rebel lands we will have to keep a prisoner or two. At least until they tell us where she is."

"You never know Decius she may have left these lands."

"Something tells me she has not. She spent a long time close to Eboracum. I think she may be closer than we think but it doesn't alter what we have to do with her and," Marcus added, waving a hand around the departing recruits, "here, to build a force ready to take on the Brigante."

Morbium

The first frosts of winter had struck the northernmost fort in the Roman Empire. Most of the troopers left at the fort were new to the province and the cold hit them hard; it permeated every part of their bodies and seemed to rip into their skin. It seemed that they were never warm unless they were in their barracks. The winds during the day were harsher and colder and the sudden rainstorms seemed to tear into their flesh like whips. What exacerbated the situation was the Decurion Princeps, Fabius Demetrius. The prefect was frequently absent visiting Eboracum where the Governor was planning the invasion of the north. When he was away the newly promoted decurion took delight in engaging in the most punishing and pointless activities. He held parades where punishments were handed out to any man whose equipment failed to satisfy the incredibly high standards of Fabius Demetrius. Troopers were sent on long training runs and patrols without a horse. They would have to practice charges in straight lines which the more experienced decurions realised was not the way one used auxiliary cavalry. Their best weapon was a looser and more flexible formation. What particularly annoyed and irritated the other decurions and troopers was that his turma never had to engage in any of these activities. All the difficult and arduous patrols north of the river were conducted by either Julius or Vettius both of whom, for some reason, had been selected by Fabius. Both decurions, although angry, knew they could do nothing about it and made it into a sort of ironical honour that their turmae were the only ones who could cope with the duty.

As new recruits arrived from Derventio the ones at Morbium realised what Elysium it must be at Derventio with the healthier regime of Decius and Marcus. Fabius had his own sleeping quarters next to the prefect and at night the decurions not on duty would discuss the two different approaches. "I think there will be a problem in the spring when Marcus returns."

"I don't know about that Septimus. He will be senior Decurion Princeps."

"But my father will still be the prefect and in any conflict who do you think he will back? My brother or Marcus?"

"And what about the men, especially the new recruits for they will back Marcus."

"In that case," put in Quintus, normally the most reflective of the decurions, "it is up to us to exert our own discipline and make sure that we obey the rules. However, much we might dislike them."

"I wish spring were here now."

Julius laughed, "Metellus that is just because you hate the cold. Your homeland in Cantabria is even warmer than mine. Your legs are permanently blue."

The rest all laughed including Metellus who found he liked Julius almost as much as he hated his brother. "There is that but it means that we will be in action again and we will have a leader with us that we can trust."

"Well at least the prefect is back and that means life is just a little bit easier."

At that moment the prefect and his son were sharing a fine amphora of wine which the prefect had brought from Eboracum. "But father did the Governor not give you any clue as to how we might be used in the campaign?"

The prefect scowled. "All he talks about are his legions his precious ninth and his little favourite Agricola's twentieth. He talks of us in the same way as he talks of those damned Batavians. As if we are at all similar."

"Does he still blame us for their losses at Stanwyck?"

"He always manages to make some snide comment in front of the others. I fear we will just be used as a screen for his precious legions and to protect his Batavians."

"While you were away I had the men practising the charge but I get little cooperation from the decurions."

"I think that is because their loyalty is not to you but to Decurion Marcus."

"That is not fair what can we do about it?"

The prefect sipped his wine and stared into the brazier which burned brightly in the well-appointed room. "Your turma, it is loyal to you?"

"To a man."

"Good. We will be creating turmae thirteen and fourteen soon and we will need decurions. I am sure you have two men who could fill those posts and their replacements will then become loyal to you."

Fabius's eyes glinted with excitement. "When we create the other turmae we can promote more men which means that, eventually, more of the decurions will be loyal to me."

"Exactly."

"I'll drink to that."

Brocavum

Aed rolled over onto his side the sweat pouring off him despite the cold outside the hut. Fainch sighed with satisfaction. While she enjoyed going from one lover to the other there was no denying that the more powerful man in her life was the younger, more virile Aed. Although the older Maeve satisfied her she didn't feel the thrill she felt when with Aed and perhaps she thought Aed would be the better leader for he had a power about him which Maeve did not.

"I do not like sharing you with that old man."

"He is not that much older than you and only a little older than me. Are you calling me old?"

"No! I do not mean that. It is just I hate the thought of sharing you with anyone but especially not him."

129

"No man owns me. I choose my men. If you do not like that then that is your problem."

Having backed himself into a corner Aed had nowhere to go. Instead, he began stroking her hair and nuzzling her ear. "Does that mean you will still visit me? Will we continue to have these times?" She remained silent but made no effort to pull away. "I will behave. I promise."

She rolled him over on his back and kissed him full on the lips at the same time gently running the backs of her hands down his chest towards his groin. Soon he felt himself growing again and they once again made love. This time it was more tender with a deeper climax for both of them. They both rolled onto their backs and stared at the tendrils of smoke rising into the thatched roof of Aed's hut.

Fainch raised herself on one elbow and ran one finger down the side of his face. "Be patient my love. One day you will lead the Brigante but first, we have to defeat the Romans and we need a king to be sacrificed to make all the tribes rise against the Romans."

"You have a plan."

"I have a plan which will give you the throne not only of the land of the Brigante but the whole of this province which the Romans call Britannia."

"Tell me!"

"I said that I had a plan not that we had a plan. In my experience, a secret plan shared is not a secret any longer. Do not worry," she put her hand against his lips, "you will know when the plan comes to fruition and your innocence will protect both you and me. Look like the flower but be the serpent beneath. Obey him and follow him faithfully. Make yourself indispensable to him. Take every insult with a smile for in doing this you will make the people love you and men will follow you seeing in you nobility absent in him. Keep your elite riders faithful and loyal to you."

"They are but they are impatient and wish to fight."

"Good that is how we want them keen. You can find an opportunity to fight. For the Romans are ever-present."

"How?"

"There is a Roman fort at Morbium with cavalry. They send patrols out in the winter. Find their pattern and then take out some of your warriors and kill them. When you return with their heads, horses and weapons it will make men love you even more and it will test your men against the Romans. Let your warriors show their bravery. Outnumber the Romans but not by too many for you want your warriors to know that one to one they can defeat the Romans. They must fight with discipline as the Romans do but with the hearts of the Brigante. When the other warriors see your success and when the other kings hear of it you will become the hero of the whole war host."

"You are as wise as you are beautiful. I will need to do this before the snows come otherwise we shall leave a trail for the Romans to follow and we know that the Romans fight in winter."

"Good. Now you are using your head instead of your heart. Be cold and be calculating. Remember I have cast a spell about you and you will not be defeated but you must be more careful and use your head."

Morbium

Once again the prefect was absent. Like a cockerel in the farmyard, Fabius strutted around the fort as though he owned it. He summoned Metellus. "Take a patrol north of the river. You know the routine."

Even as he replied, "Yes decurion", and apparently accepted the injustice with resignation, Decurion Metellus was angry and frustrated. The whole fort knew that it was Fabius's turn for patrol. Every time the prefect was absent he pulled this trick. It meant that his turma stayed in the warmth of the fort and, more importantly, did not risk running into a Brigante warband.

Julius and the others sympathised. "It is not right," objected Quintus Saenius. "He abuses his power."

Julius spoke up, "I will go and speak with him."

"Is that wise? You may be his brother but that does not seem to matter to him."

"Vettius it is my duty."

If he expected anger then Julius was mistaken. When he made his request that Metellus should not go as it was his turn his brother merely nodded. "You are quite right brother." The word brother was emphasised and imbued with as much venom as he could muster. "A Demetrius should go on patrol today. Take your turma south of the river."

Realising that his honour demanded that he take the patrol out he nodded. "I will tell Metellus that he is to stand down."

"You misunderstand me, decurion. Metellus will still patrol but they will be north of the river."

Julius had been outwitted. There was nothing he could do. The others, however, showed what they felt by what they said. "The little bastard!"

"Quintus he will hear you."

"I don't give a damn. He may be your brother but he is a bastard."

"Well, my men may enjoy a trip south of the river. None of us has patrolled there for months. Who knows, we may catch King Maeve."

The other decurions smiled at the young man's attempt at humour. As much as they hated his brother, they loved Julius more for his high spirits, good humour and, above all, his honesty.

As he left Morbium he pointedly avoided looking in the direction of the headquarters for he knew his smirking brother would be there and he did not want to give him the satisfaction of laughing at him. He could sense the resentment of his men, not resentment towards him but towards his brother. "Well lads at least we are south of the river, who knows it might be warmer." The laughs and guffaws told him that he was not the object of their hate. "Let's see if we can make good time. Attius! Out scouting."

"Yes sir."

Once Attius headed off into the distance Julius had time to reflect on his relationships. He found the concept hard to come to terms with but he preferred the decurions in the ala to his family. He respected Marcus more than his father! A year ago that would have been unthinkable but he had seen not only the way that Marcus ran the ala but the way the men responded to him. It was a frightening thought but he wished to be more like Marcus than his own father. He was woken from his reverie by the thunder of hooves. Attius!

"Sir! Found tracks. Must be fifty or sixty horsemen and they are coming from the west."

"Brigante!"

"Yes sir that's what I thought."

"Halt! Right men. We have a force of Brigante horsemen north of the river. We are going after them." He could sense immediately the excitement of the men. They would be going into action for the first time. This was what they wanted; the chance to fight the enemies of the Empire. It was a shame that his brother could not see it.

Metellus hated this patrol; the same sights, the same paths, the same river the same hills. The problem was you did it so often you often saw what you expected to see. He had his scout out; it was Cassius, a recent recruit who was just like Macro but without the bulk. There was something different about this day. The birds seemed quieter although at this time of the year that could be normal as many birds seemed to leave this bleak upland area and travel further south. Perhaps it was a sixth sense but Metellus was wary. "Be on the lookout lads. I smell trouble." The men smiled. Metellus was known for a huge nose but also the ability to smell out trouble.

Suddenly Cassius' empty horse thundered towards them. "Ambush!" His men quickly drew weapons and, without being ordered formed into a single line with Metellus in the front. Before they could move forward ninety mailed warriors wielding long spears hurtled towards them. "Javelins!" Forty javelins flew towards the Brigante warriors. Although ten of them struck home only four warriors were hit although six horses fell to the ground taking their riders with them. The turma drew their swords and moved forwards. It was not a charge it was a walk for they had been caught unawares and the mailed warriors crashed into them with a clash of metal and horses. The Romans were outnumbered almost two to one and the enemy had the advantage of surprise. Metellus found himself facing two warriors who hacked and slashed at his sword and shield. From the noises behind him, he realised his men had the same problem. His young recruits fought as well as they could but this was their first action. Metellus despatched one of his opponents with a slash at his head. The lucky blow caught the man on the unprotected part of his face and his mouth was ripped open. The other warrior managed to smash at Metellus' shield and break not only the shield but also his arm. It was all he could do to slice down at this enemy's horse's head which collapsed, instantly dead, throwing its rider to the ground.

Quickly looking around he saw that more than half his men were dead. He had no option. "Retreat!" Although the order was simple, the implementation was almost impossible. His men had too many opponents. They were all going to die. His young men would be spitted upon Brigante spears in their first action. Steeling himself to die with honour Metellus looked for an opponent. Suddenly he heard a Roman roar as Julius and his turma smashed into the rear of the mailed warriors. The surprise was overwhelming; the raiders had no idea that another turma would arrive and Julius' turma had unprotected backs to attack. They instantly halted the attack. Even so, it was a near run thing. The Brigante still outnumbered them. But the sudden attack had unnerved them for they knew not if this second turma was alone or perhaps part of a Roman ambush. Once again Metellus yelled, "Retreat!" and this time they managed to extricate themselves. There were so many dismounted enemy warriors and so much confusion with Julius' turma attacking their rear that the two turmae managed to escape without further loss. By the time the raiders found out that Julius' turma had been alone the Romans had used their head start to lose them. They only halted two miles from the action and then only because their horses were blown.

Metellus rode next to Julius. "Decurion, I owe you a debt of honour. Had you not arrived my men and I would have been dead." Looking around Julius saw what he meant. There were only nineteen of Metellus' turma left alive and Julius had lost four; a sorry encounter.

"I think Metellus that, in the circumstances, we might return to the Decurion Princeps and report. But first, let me splint that arm." It took some time to bandage those who, like Metellus, were wounded, and to rest the horses. They would not have enough time to build a camp and the Brigante were just too close for comfort.

Back at the battlefield, Aed was raging but as Fainch had advised him, he kept his anger inside. True he had the twenty-five heads of the dead and soon to be dead auxilia but he had not had the victory he wanted. He had wanted to destroy a whole unit and give his men the exultation of a complete victory. However, from the elated behaviour of his men, he realised that Fainch had been right and they had achieved their objective; the men felt like gods. Even though they had lost forty of their number they had chased the Romans from the field and that was a first. His men bickered and fought over the heads they took from the butchered Romans. Weapons were shared, bodies stripped of valuables and the horses roped together as true trophies of war. He realised that Fainch was right. Now that he had thought about it the goblet was half full; they held what they had won.

The prefect had already returned and was briefing his son when the sentry shouted, "Patrols returning! With wounded."

They both looked at each other. Rufius said, "Patrols?"

"Yes, I sent one north and one south of the river but they should not have returned yet. I didn't expect them back until tomorrow."

Both of them were thinking the same thoughts; they both wondered about the wounded for so far they had not received even a scratch on the many patrols. A patrol normally stayed out overnight; if this were an early return then it meant there had been problems. The prefect hoped that it did not presage further problems. Now that it was heading into cold winter they expected the patrols to be less likely to run into the enemy. As the gates opened they saw that there were more than twenty men missing. The two decurions saluted and then dismounted; Metellus with some difficulty. His face was ashen. The prefect took one look at him and said, "Get to the surgeon. Decurion Demetrius can make the report in your stead."

Even though they were family Fabius and Rufius did not make life easy for the young Julius. They sat and he stood whilst he made his report. "I followed the river as ordered until we came across the tracks of a large Brigante force of horse warriors. We followed their tracks as swiftly as possible. We discovered them just as they began to ambush Decurion Metellus. We were able to surprise them and kill many but they still outnumbered us and they had the advantage. We felt it prudent to return to the fort rather than risk annihilation. We both felt it was more important to report the presence of such a large force of raiders north of the river."

Fabius looked scornfully at his brother. "And just how many warriors attacked you then brother? Fifty? Sixty?"

"There were more than one hundred. They were dressed in mail as we are and they had long spears which outreached our javelins. In addition, we did not know if this was an advance force. The purpose of patrols is to gather intelligence. We thought this was sound intelligence." His voice was calm but inside he was seething and his eyes bored into his brother's. His honour was being impugned. He was under no illusions; had they stayed they may have inflicted a few more casualties but the end result would have been the same. They would have been slaughtered.

"Why were you south of the river decurion?" The prefect's voice was both calm and measured.

"The Decurion Princeps ordered me to patrol south of the river."

The prefect looked at his elder son. "Two patrols?"

"I thought it advisable and we may have been able to catch more of the enemy. Perhaps if the decurion had been a little bolder..."

"Did you not hear me," he paused to choose the right words but he put an edge to them, a challenge to his elder brother, "Decurion Princeps Demetrius. They outnumbered us and their arms were superior to ours. Had I been bolder then you might have had to send more patrols out to find our bodies."

"Enough!" the prefect's voice seemed to boom in the confines of the office. "What is done is done. There is no suggestion of cowardice. It is as we feared; the Brigante has begun to copy us and our arms. There were mailed warriors who fled Stanwyck. These must be part of the same force. You did well decurion. Go and see to your men."

Julius saluted and looking scornfully at his brother turned and left. Fabius began to half rise in anger but his father restrained him. When Julius had left the prefect looked long and hard at his son. "Why did you send your brother out on patrol?"

"He implied that I should have taken a patrol out. It was my way of punishing him."

"But it was your turma's patrol was it not?"

Fabius began to redden and blustered, "With you away I felt I needed to stay at the fort for discipline."

"I can see that I will need to visit Eboracum less frequently then in future. Anyway, enough of that. Have we received the trained recruits from Derventio?"

"Yes, they came in yesterday. Eighty men. I was going to form turmae thirteen and fourteen."

"In light of the casualties, you will just have to form one and use the others as replacements. Appoint a decurion. I assume you have one of your men in mind?"

"I had two but I will just have to appoint one, Modius Varro."

"Good see to it."

Modius Varro was a bully. He was almost as big as Macro but he was ugly and this had been made worse by a knife scar that ran all the way down one cheek. He had not received it honourably but in a back street when he and another thug had attacked what they took to be a helpless old man but who turned out to be an ex-legionary. He still died but he took Modius' companion with him and left a reminder to Modius of the dangers of attacking people when you did not have all the advantage you could. Since that time he had made sure that when he bullied anyone, they were weaker than he was and he had back up. In the turma, he was known as the enforcer because he enforced his will on everyone. He had the turma both afraid and in awe of him. The fact that their decurion supported him influenced their view.

His new turma were all recruits and had enjoyed the training they had received. For all his bluster Decius had been a good trainer and Agrippa and Macro had worked the men hard but made them stronger, fitter and adept with a variety of weapons. Within a very short time, they found out that Modius did not use the same methods as Decius and Agrippa and the thirteenth turma soon had the lowest morale in Morbium. The winter was an even harsher time for the new thirteenth turma than the rest of the demoralised ala.

Chapter 14

Derventio

"Sir I have an idea."

Inwardly groaning but keeping an expressionless face Agrippa turned to the incredibly keen and energetic assistant weapons' trainer. "Yes, Macro what is this idea?"

"The practice swords help build up the men's strength but if we introduced strength training for the whole body they would become fitter and be able to fight better."

"That's all we need a regiment built like you!"

The crestfallen young man said, "You mean you don't like the idea?"

"I didn't say that. It was a joke, Macro. Take me through how it would work."

"We get the men for four hours a day for weapon training well if we spent the first hour lifting rocks, squatting with weights you know all the exercises I do every day then spend three hours with weapons. "

"How will that help them?"

"I was talking to Cato and he said that one of the problems the men had is that they don't like to let go of the reins. They are afraid they will lose control of their horses. If they used their legs they would be able to manoeuvre their horses that way," he looked at Agrippa. "It's what you do sir. It's what every good rider does."

He realised that the callow youth was right. If they could control their horses with their legs then they would be free to use their weapons more effectively. "Right we'll try it for the next two weeks with the new batch of recruits then we can have a little tournament between them and the last batch. How's that?"

"Great idea sir. Right, I had better get some weights sorted out. I know where there are some rocks that would be perfect."

Agrippa shook his head as he ran off whistling; would that all young troopers had the same attitude.

Morbium

"Salvius Cilo you are the most pathetic trooper it has been my misfortune to meet." Modius stood towering over the young man who had, once again failed to turn his horse quickly enough for the bullying decurion. His shoulders bore the scars from the repeated beatings he had received. Modius had decided that Salvius would be the object of his fury because he had not done as the others had done and relinquished part of his pay. Cilo was saving to send money back to his family in Durobrivae. The main reason he had joined the auxilia was that they were stationed in the province and he could send money to his impoverished family. The last thing he needed was a corrupt decurion.

"Is there a problem decurion?"

"It is this trooper Decurion Princeps. Most of them are only half-trained but he seems to have had no training at all."

"I agree decurion it seems Decurion Decius Flavius is not doing a good job over at Derventio. Your replacement in my turma Numerius Galeo is as bad. I think we will send them both back to Derventio for more training." He looked around and saw Decurion Metellus who was still injured and unable to take an active role in the daily life of the ala. "Decurion Metellus over here."

"Yes sir, "said Metellus warily. I want you to return Troopers Galeo and Cilo back to Derventio. They need to go through basic training again."

Metellus was almost going to say something when he saw that the two troopers looked relieved and he realised that it would be good to be away from Morbium and be with Marcus and Decius once more. "Yes, sir right away! Er, what should I say the problem was?"

"Tell Decurion Flavius that his training has not worked with these two and he needs to use his vine staff more." Metellus looked at the incredibly young man. When he gave Decius that information he would expect to see a volcanic eruption of Vesuvian proportions.

As the three of them set off across the cold and hard winter landscape they were all remarkably cheerful. It seemed that the moment they crossed the bridge and headed south-east their spirits rose. The two recruits couldn't wait to find out what it was like to be in combat. Many of their fellow recruits told them how much better it was in the turmae of the other decurions rather than their own and they had been told of the actions of the two bloodied turmae.

"What is it like sir fighting the Brigante?"

"When we first fought them, they were wilder than they are now. They have learned from us. They have better weapons for one thing and they had begun to adopt our tactics. They have not the foot soldiers to defeat the legions but their cavalry; I hate to say are almost the equal of us. Still, when we ride against them we will be behind Decurion Princeps Marcus Aurelius Maximunius and believe me he is a mighty warrior."

"We met him at Derventio. He looks young and yet we were told by Decurion Decius that he was with the turma who rescued Queen Cartimandua."

"That he was. I was not there but if you speak to Gaius or Lentius they will tell of that most glorious day. A single turma and a few bodyguards held off a Brigante warband led by their king. Before that day we had never achieved anything noteworthy after that day we became the stuff of legends. It is where Ulpius Felix was given the Sword of Cartimandua. Did you see the sword?"

"Yes, sir we all wanted to touch it but were afraid to ask."

"That sword is the Sword of Cartimandua and it is said to be magical. It has helped us more than once. I will ask the Decurion Princeps to show you the sword for it is the stuff of dreams and legends. Holding it must be like being in one of the tales of the old kings and warriors."

They rode in silence across the wide vale that led to Eboracum and Derventio. "It isn't fair sir."

"What isn't fair Trooper Cilo?"

"Us being sent back. I mean we don't mind going back there. You work hard but the officers actually praise you when you do something well. We were just criticised and beaten all the time. We had to give up pay to the decurions. We are from Britannia and we joined because we believe in the peace Rome can bring but if the peace is to be bought by serving corrupt men like Modius then we would be better off fighting against the Romans. At least we would die with honour. We are treated dishonourably. Why is that?" He looked hard at the decurion who looked equally uncomfortable. "Your turma don't get beaten and they had the same training we had."

Metellus shifted uncomfortably. "We all have our different ways I am sure there are things I do which annoy my men and not all decurions are like Modius. He is newly promoted after all."

"So is Decurion Julius Demetrius and he is fair."

"Actually, sir Trooper Cilo is right and your men all say they are glad that they were drafted into your turma and not eleven or thirteen."

"Well after you have been retrained we will see. Now let's get a move on I'd like to get past Tresche while there is still a little warmth in the air. The path up the cliff can be a little dangerous."

"We didn't come that way, sir. We came up the coast and along the river."

"I know and it takes almost two days. This is a little shortcut and means we sleep in a heated barracks tonight and not on the ground."

With that incentive, the two recruits kicked their mounts on and they soon found themselves at the top of an escarpment which, on a clear day would have afforded them a view all the way across to Stanwyck however the day was overcast and all they saw was scudding clouds. "That's the last climb so we can take it a little easier on our mounts. We will make the fort just after dark."

Derventio

"What in Hades name are you doing here Decurion Metellus? "Decius greeted his comrade warmly and then looked curiously at the two men with him. "And I thought we were well rid of you two pieces of dog's tail!"

"Nice to see you as well Decius. Decurion Metellus reporting with two troopers who need more training," he paused and added significantly, "that is according to Decurion Princeps Fabius Demetrius."

"I can see that this tale needs some wine and a warm fire. You two find Macro and tell him I said to put you up in his barracks with my lads. Metellus leave your horse here and we can go and find Marcus and the others." After a pleasantly rich hare and hedgehog stew and a beaker of wine with the other decurions, Metellus felt more human. Marcus gestured at his still bandaged arm. "That looks like you have been in action."

His face became very serious. "By all that is right, I should be dead. We were on patrol and ambushed by over a hundred Brigante. They had good armour and they had long lances. They killed my scout and came over a blind ridge if young Julius hadn't been on patrol as well we would be dead meat. As it was I lost half my turma."

"What was Julius doing out? We only ever had one patrol out."

"I know Gaius but he pissed his brother off and he punished him with an extra patrol. In hindsight, I am glad for it saved my skin."

"And what about the recruits. I know they weren't the sharpest swords we ever produced but they could have improved with a bit of effort at Morbium. We just do basic here. Everyone knows the real training starts when you are on patrol with your own decurion."

"You are right Decius but unfortunately they weren't put with one of the turma Decurion Princeps Maximunius trained they were put with Fabius and that bastard Modius."

"Modius is a decurion? In that case, any bugger can attain promotion. Decurion Princeps you can have my vine staff back."

Metellus gave a half-smile, "He said to tell you decurion that you hadn't done a very good job and he hoped you would do better this time."

"I'll stuff my vine stick up that little shit's arse!"

Marcus spoke for the first time. "I think you should keep it, Decius. And what did the prefect say?"

"Well he's been missing a lot but he seems to back his son up at every turn. All the rest of the turma are lickspittles, they are like Fabius' little gang. I think he is bent on promoting as many as possible." He paused. "Sir it is serious. Turma thirteen is demoralised and if more decurions like Modius were promoted it would spread."

"I tell you boss as much as I don't want to go back to Morbium the sooner you are there the better."

Marcus ignored Decius' comment. "So Metellus how is the arm?"

"Healing."

"Do you think it would benefit from a few days here? The weather looks to be closing in and we are a little short of decurions. Do you think you could help out?"

His face lit up. "Well, sir if it is for the good of the ala I could be persuaded!"

The rest of the night was spent consuming a couple of amphorae of fine wine and frequent revisits to the game stew. The decurions all went to their barracks replete and content unlike their counterparts at Morbium. Before the wine kicked in too much Agrippa pulled Metellus over to one side. "So why was it shit for brains decided they weren't well enough trained?"

"They had difficulty manoeuvring their horses in line while holding their weapons."

"But that's not the way we fight. We need space between each rider."

"I know it. You know it. Everyone else in the ala knows it but the prefect and his son think that is the way we fight. But apparently, the hero of Rome doesn't."

"Thanks for that Metellus. I will send him back two troopers who will make his jaw drop or rather Macro will."

Metellus looked curiously at Agrippa. "He's that good?"

"Trust me he's that good. He actually enjoys working out and training them. Me? I'd rather be a decurion but that young lad has something about him. He thinks and plans the training to suit the trooper. You mark my words he is a future leader, he's more like Marcus than even Gaius. Tell you what, come out tomorrow and watch him work. I guarantee you will be entertained and I am certain you will not have seen his methods used before."

The next day Macro and Agrippa walked out onto the gyrus. Decius had reluctantly bequeathed it to them for the day while he took the rest on a cross country march with full packs wielding training gladii. The two turmae who were about to be trained sat nervously awaiting their trainers. The two who had been rejected by Fabius looked uncomfortable and embarrassed. Agrippa spoke quietly with Macro. His final words were, "You take the two lads and I'll handle the rest."

Agrippa sent the other troopers off the far side of the gyrus. "So the Decurion Princeps sent you back to us eh?"

"Yes Sergeant Agrippa." The two men chorused.

"You will be the last lot I train as a sergeant. I am to be a decurion so perhaps Sergeant Macro will be able to use his new wonder techniques on you two and turn you into mighty warriors. What do you think?"

"Yes, decurion." They both added uncertainly. They were thinking if Agrippa couldn't train them to a high enough standard how could someone as young as Macro succeed?

Macro sidled over to Agrippa and said sotto voce. "I didn't know the promotion had come through."

"Listen, son. You have learned all you can from me. You fight as well as me and to be truthful it won't be long before you are beating me and the weapon trainer should not be beaten by his assistant. Besides I am looking forward to having my own turma. I know we haven't had the tournament yet but I think that the men we have just trained will easily beat the last lot. They are certainly stronger. You have three days to make these two as good. I would love to ride into Morbium with two rejects that are better than anything they have. You are doing what you want and I am doing what I want."

Rising almost a hand-span above his normal height Macro bellowed. "You are on sir! Prepare to have the two finest troopers, present company excepted, in the ala."

As Agrippa jogged towards the eighty recruits waiting expectantly Macro turned to the two troopers. "Right dismount and get rid of the armour I only want you in your tunic."

"But sergeant it is as cold as a witch's tit out here. We'll freeze."

"I tell you what, Cilo, if you are still cold an hour from now I will walk around the gyrus naked." The two men looked bemused. "You see those stones over there? Go and pick up one each." Macro had chosen the stones so that although they had weight they could easily be picked up. "Are we happy now?"

"Yes, sergeant but still cold."

"We have an hour to go before you judge that. Put the weight above your head. Now lower your body to the ground and up, and up and up. Repeat." The two men easily began to rise and then lower their bodies. "There that's not so bad."

"I can cope with this," puffed Galeo although his red face belied the statement.

"Good because I want fifty now start counting and I want to hear you counting." The other recruits actually smiled, their training seemed much simpler with Agrippa. By the time the fifty had been completed the two men were almost out of breath. "Put down your stones. Pick up those two piles of javelins and raise them above your head. Follow me." Macro took them at an easy jog around the gyrus. "Right stand still and open your legs but keep your javelins above your head." The two men looked at each other; was the sergeant mocking them?

"Sergeant?"

"Trust me, lads. I know what I am doing and anyway I am big enough to beat the shit out of both of you with one hand tied behind my back so do as I say eh?" The grin on his face took any venom out of his words and the two men complied. The sergeant then brought out two water skins and put them between their knees. "Now squeeze your knees together." The men did as instructed. "Right squats again." Fifty squats later Macro said, "Rest. I know it has only been half an hour but are we warm?"

The two men laughed. "Yes, sergeant."

An hour later and they were sweating as though they were serving in the desert having repeated the activities ten times. "Right drop the javelins and the water skins. Have a good drink of water and then grab your scuta and training spathae."

Even though they had only been exercising for a little over an hour the two men were sweating, panting and struggling to coordinate. They stood with their weapons in their hands. Macro walked around them adjusting their stance and grip until he was satisfied. "Right. Attack me both at once." They looked at each other. This would be easy. They split up and Cilo went towards Macro's wooden spatha whilst Galeo went towards his scutum. Before they could attack Macro leapt towards Galeo. He turned his shield to deflect the sword and then wrapped him hard on the buttocks with the flat of his sword. In combat with real weapons it would have been at least a disabling blow and, with a sharp sword, possibly a death blow. Without pausing he spun around and smashed his sword at Cilo's shield; he then punched him in the face with his own shield and the recruit crashed to the ground. When he opened his stunned eyes, he was facing the tip of a wooden sword. Not very good eh? Let's try to do better."

Marcus had left the office at Agrippa's behest to watch the contest. Agrippa stood next to him as the two turmae continued to slog around the gyrus in full packs. "He is good sir. These lads are no mugs but he makes them look as though they are. You look at his size and think this giant will be so slow. Not a bit of it he moves like a snake. I wouldn't want to face him in the tournament. "Marcus looked in surprise at the weapon trainer. "No sir I am good but that lad he has something special. You can't predict what he will do."

They both watched him spar for an hour and when he was satisfied he nodded at the two recruits. "Right get your horses."

Agrippa grinned. "Now watch this. I bet you a week's salary you have never seen training like this."

When the two men returned with their horses Macro signalled for them to close up. When they did so he took a piece of rope from his tunic and tied Cilo's right foot to Galeo's left. The two men looked as bemused as the Decurion Princeps. "Now your Decurion Princeps, not the gentleman watching us right now but the one you reluctantly left at Morbium, wants you to ride close together and still fight. Well now you have to fight close together or you will fall off and look extremely stupid in front of all the decurions and sergeants watching you." Marcus wondered how Macro had seen Decius, Metellus, Lentius, Cato and Gaius arrive to watch him work. "If you are going to beat me, and remember I am a slippery bastard, you will have to work together and use both your sword and shield at the same time. How will you do that?"

"It's impossible sergeant."

"It was difficult when I gave you all those exercises before. Let's see if they have made a difference. Give me your shields. Now hold your swords above your heads with two hands. When I give the command begin to trot and then listen to my directions and follow them precisely. That's all you need to do, follow my instructions, no fighting no one trying to knock you off just you two working together." The two men looked nervously at each other. "Trot." To their surprise, they found that by kicking their heels their mounts moved forwards. "Good. That wasn't hard, was it? Hard left." This proved a little trickier and Galeo started to slip sideways. He almost dropped his arm.

Suddenly Decius' voice boomed out. "Don't you dare drop your arm until the sergeant tells you, boy!" He paused and nodded to Macro. "Carry on sergeant."

"Thank you decurion. Use your knees and thighs, grip the horse. Hard right. Straight on. Hard right. Hard left. Gallop. Hard left. Hard right." After another ten minutes when they had not fallen off he shouted," Halt!" This proved to be their downfall. Galeo grabbed the reins and pulled hard. His horse stopped, Cilo's didn't and he flew majestically over his horse's head. For a heartbeat, Galeo grinned and then realised he was tied to Cilo. With an "Oh no!" he sailed over his horse's head as well. The decurions and sergeants could not stand for laughing so hard. "Better than the circus, Sergeant Macro."

Macro smiled, "Sorry lads forgot to say you could use your hands. Nice initiative Trooper Galeo. Get yourselves cleaned up, grab your shields and we'll start again." They bent down to untie their ankles. "Didn't tell you to untie, did I?"

He wandered over to his audience. "Very inventive sergeant. Have you used this method before?"

"No sir but hearing why they were sent here I thought I would improvise a training method which suited the purpose."

"Good I can see that decurion Agrippa is quite right you are ready to be the new weapon training officer sergeant."

The sun was dipping towards the skyline and the afternoon becoming even colder when Macro called a halt to the training. His two charges had improved beyond recognition. Even without being tied together they could fight tightly turn, halt and even manage to put Macro in difficulty. "That's enough for today but I am afraid tomorrow is more of the same."

"No problem, sergeant," Galeo was in high spirits. "I actually feel I have learned something today."

"Me too but I am beginning to ache a little."

"A little tip, rub oil on the inside of your thighs and do some squats, without weights, before you turn in. Build those muscles up and you will be able to control your horses. You might also ask Sergeant Cato for tips on controlling horses. He has forgotten more than I will ever know."

"Yes, sergeant!"

Four weeks later and Saturnalia was nearly upon them. Marcus held a short meeting with his decurions. "We have nearly finished the training and I would like to celebrate Saturnalia not with the normal alcoholic stupor but with a tournament. Find the champion amongst the men here."

Decius snorted, "That's easy, Macro."

"Maybe," interjected the recently promoted Agrippa, "but there may be someone out there better and he may get a little cocky.

"What do you mean, get? He is cocky already."

"The other reason is that it will keep their focus and they are returning to Morbium soon, well at least some of them. It will not be long before we all gather at Morbium for the invasion. I don't mind the men having a drink to celebrate but not to get out and out falling over drunk."

"Don't forget that around here they celebrate the shortest day with a daylong drinking festival," added Lentius.

"All the more reason for us to be on our mettle."

Decius shrugged, "I don't mind It is your decision Decurion Princeps but I will drink the same as I do every other night." The others looked at him. "Helps me sleep."

The tournament was an open entry. There were a number of categories: man on man on foot, man on man on a horse, javelin mounted and bow mounted. Marcus was pleased that almost every trooper took part. He had had another reason he did not divulge to the others. He wanted to know who were the best with javelins and the best with bows. He had yet to allocate those troopers who would be in his turma and he had it in his mind to make one of the effective elite archers and one of the effective elite javelins. If Metellus was right then these mailed Brigante needed to be stopped or at least broken up at distance. His two specialist turmae might just turn the tables.

The day of the tournament soon came around and the excitement was palpable. There was a good deal of betting on the outcomes. The first event was the archery and even the grumpy Decius was impressed by the standard. "They've all come on a bit when they started the only thing most of them could hit was their foot. "The standard was so high that it ran on longer than was anticipated.

145

The javelins were equally good and, as more men had entered, there was more competition but there were four who clearly outshone the rest and made it through to an exciting final. Agrippa and Macro had decided not to enter the man to man on horseback and Marcus found himself in the final against Gaius. Although Gaius was good he was not the horseman that Marcus was and his mount, Argentium, seemed almost to read his master's thoughts. The end came when Gaius made a clever move jinking at the last minute. He would have had a clear and killing stroke to Marcus' back had not Argentium stepped quickly back and Marcus managed the killing blow. "Well done Decurion Princeps although I think you owed much to your horse."

"I don't deny it. I have the finest sword and the finest mount in the ala. Think about that Gaius next time to choose the best weapon and the very best horse you can. In that critical moment on a battlefield, they can be the difference between victory and defeat."

The draw for the man to man on foot had been seeded and the final four were Decius, Agrippa, Macro and a powerfully built trooper called Postumius. They were the best in the whole fort. There was a hiatus however before the eagerly anticipated combat took place. It was late afternoon and the sentries suddenly announced the arrival of the prefect. "Sneaky bastard. I bet he hoped to catch us all pissed out of our heads."

Marcus gave Decius a knowing look. "In that case, it is a good job we are not pissed but engaged in a worthwhile activity then eh?"

"So you are a sneaky bastard too, sir." He smiled as Marcus tapped the side of his nose knowingly.

"Sorry to visit you unawares, Decurion Princeps. I just thought as I hadn't been here for a while this might be a good opportunity to see how the training is coming along." The calm manner belied the fact that he had expected a Bacchanalian orgy of drunken men, "Have I interrupted something?"

"No sir. Just the culmination of our tournament to find the best warriors. The training is largely finished and I thought this would be a good way to test the skills of each man and make more balanced turmae." The prefect looked at Marcus realising once again what a sound military man he was. "If you would care to join us?"

"I would love to."

Marcus glanced at the prefect as they sat down. If he was disappointed with what he had seen he did not show it. The first pair f troopers to step out were Decius and Agrippa. Marcus was not certain which way this bout would go. Agrippa was the better fighter but Decius was stockier and more cunning a better dirtier fighter. If there were any sneaky tricks he would use them. As he shifted his attention to Agrippa he could see that the weapon trainer knew this. Decius began cautiously feeling out his opponent. They exchanged blows sword on shield and moved apart. Decius feinted low but Agrippa merely stepped back.

The prefect leaned over to Marcus. "This is all very well but what about the combat we do as cavalrymen? Man on horse against man on horse?"

Marcus looked calmly at the prefect. "We already had that, sir."

Looking a little nonplussed Rufius said, "Oh and who was that champion?"

"Actually sir I was." Just at that moment Decius threw a handful of soil at Agrippa and darted in when he believed his opponent was blinded. Agrippa had seen the move coming, ducked and the soil went over his head. Decius stabbed into space as Agrippa whacked him in the back sending him sprawling with his momentum into the dirt.

"Nice move Decius."

"Ah well, you are too good for me. Luckily I had a bet on you to reach the final so I win either way."

Postumius and Macro came out together. After Decius, they looked like giants. "What are you feeding your men decurion, elephants? I have never seen men as big."

"We eat well here, sir lots of fish and game to augment our rations."

This time the combat was so quick that if you glanced away you missed six or seven blows. They were both very fit men but Macro just had that edge. He had the confidence to work his opponent. He recognised quite early on that Postumius like to follow up a shield punch with a hack down rather than the stab up taught by the legions and he used this to great effect. As the shield was thrust into his face he spun around and Postumius was hitting fresh air. Macro hit him in the back with his shield and then put the point of his sword in his back.

Around the gyrus, Marcus could see money being exchanged. Postumius' size had marked him out as the dark horse. Even though he had just fought, Macro was ready for the final and bounced up and down on the balls of his feet. Agrippa came out and nodded to the one-time apprentice. This bout had a beauty to it as both men used every stroke and blow that was available to them. Neither held back and the blows, even though they came from wooden swords, smashed down on shields and helmets. The end, when it came, was due to an accident. Even though he was a bigger man, Macro had great balance. The two men came together and as they twisted away from each other Agrippa fell and Macro wasted no time in putting the sword to his throat. As Macro helped Agrippa to his feet the crowd roared and the two men embraced knowing that they were as closely matched as it was possible to be.

"I see I was right to leave the training to you Sergeant Macro."

"I don't know sir; if you hadn't slipped we might have been out there all night."

Agrippa glanced over to where the prefect was talking with Marcus. "I have a feeling that our prefect would have ended it. He doesn't look particularly comfortable, does he?" Laughing the two men left for the Saturnalia celebrations.

"And now Decurion Princeps if we could go to somewhere a little warmer perhaps?"

"I have some wine and food waiting in my quarters, sir. I assume you are staying a while?" The prefect nodded. "Well in that case I will move my things into the decurion barracks. As we only have five decurions at the moment there is plenty of room."

"That is one of the things I wished to discuss with you. Have you trained all the men?"

"Yes sir. We are still training rather than have them idle and they get to patrol but, yes they could take part in any action immediately."

"Good. I had expected Decurion Metellus to return before now." There was more than a hint of reproach in the patrician's voice.

"Sorry about that sir but as I said we had the men more or less trained and with a shortage of decurions it was handy to have an extra one around. My fault sir. Of course, he will be able to return with you with a turma. You have eight turmae now at Morbium?"

The prefect thought for a moment and said, "Yes I think so."

As they entered Marcus' quarters he glanced at the prefect. Details were never the prefect's strong point. Marcus knew exactly how many men there were. "And with the recruits, you have received from us all the turmae are complete? Again, the prefect nodded but the vague look showed Marcus that he didn't actually know.

"So how many trained men have you now?"

"Including the two you sent back to us? Two hundred and fifty." He could see the prefect trying to do the mental calculations. "That is six turma. Morbium was built for ten so might I suggest you take Metellus and two turmae back with you?"

"Good idea." He stood with his back to the brazier warming his hands as Marcus poured a beaker of warmed spiced wine already prepared by his servant. "At my last conference, the Governor outlined his plans to me. We are to protect his flanks when he advances." The sneer in his voice clearly told Marcus of his opinion. This means that we will need to divide the ala. I have already spoken to Decurion Princeps Fabius Demetrius." Mentally irritated Marcus wondered why he could not have said, '*my son*'. "And he will command one wing. You will, of course, command the other wing."

"And you sir will you be with the Governor or one of the wings?"

He snorted in a derisory fashion, "With the Governor! I think not. No, I shall be with the other wing." He looked keenly at Marcus. "I don't think you need me looking over your shoulder eh?"

There was a discreet knock at the door, "Come in." The servant brought in a steaming bowl of game stew and some warm bread. "Thank you Semias. Could you just move my things over to the decurion barracks, the prefect is staying here?"

"That certainly smells good. I can see that you do well for yourselves here."

Marcus laughed, "One of the things I realised is that a good quartermaster is worth ten fighting men. Porcius Verres was a good trooper but he loves food more. He ensures that we don't pay a lot but we get high quality and he makes sure the cooks are the best we can get if only to satisfy his own appetite."

"Now about decurions." Marcus looked up expectantly." Have you sufficient experienced men here? If not I am sure that Fabius has some men he could promote."

Marcus was thankful that Metellus had warned him of this plot and had his answer rehearsed. "Well sir the majority of the more experienced troopers are here and if we are to campaign against the Brigante we will need officers who have battle experience. I don't doubt that the newer men will soon learn but they will learn better from those who have fought before." The prefect munched on some bread soaked in game stew and Marcus added quickly, "As you know sir it is a sad fact of life that we always lose decurions once we get into battle. Those men in turma eleven who have potential will soon get their chance. While we are talking of replacements, Cilo and Galeo? The ones who were sent here for retraining?" The prefect looked confused and then nodded absently. "Rather than send them back to, perhaps, cause problems in their own turmae we would like to place them with the recruits of this training batch."

"Fine. Fine. "Wiping his mouth Rufius leaned back on his couch and finished off his wine. As Marcus topped his beaker up he said, "It may be more efficient for the ala if you stay here until spring; it would be a little crowded with the whole ala together. You can hone your ala here and make it the cutting edge. We are mustering at Stanwyck but I suspect the general will call a meeting at Eboracum. He likes meetings. I will let you know when by messenger and you will then have a week to get there. I will send some of those Batavians to watch your fort while you are away although it may well be, "he said tapping the side of his nose, "that you don't actually get back here."

Marcus looked thoughtful, "The invasion then?"

"Our Governor is ambitious. If he could conquer the wild tribes of the north it would pacify the rest of the province, and now… I have had a hard day."

"Quite sir. I'll see you in the morning."

"And Marcus it was good to see troopers working purposefully and not overindulging Saturnalia." The look which he flashed him told Marcus that he had been right to hold the tournament and his information had been correct; the prefect was trying to catching him unawares.

Chapter 15

The West Coast of Britannia on the edge of Brigante territory.

Fainch and her sisters had chosen this midwinter festival for their meeting for a host of reasons; few travellers were abroad; the long nights suited their purpose; they were within sight of their objective.

"The Deceangli and Ordovices will retake Mona on the feast of Eostre."

Fainch looked in surprise, "You are certain?"

"The Roman garrisons have pulled back to Deva for they believe they have destroyed our order and our holy place will be a stronghold once more."

All the priestesses showed their delight. "That is great news sister. And the Silures?"

One of the younger priestesses spoke for the first time, her small voice belying the power of her magic. "They are keen to go to war and it was all I could do to stop them attacking immediately."

"The Belgae and the southwestern tribes are also eager to fight."

"Sisters this is wonderful news." She saw that the other priestesses did not look as pleased or comfortable. "And you sisters?"

"The elder of the four spoke. "They are too comfortable, too Romanised. Many of the young warriors have joined Roman auxilia."

"None will fight?"

"Some will fight but it will not be as here in the north or the west. They are happy with the Roman presence. Some bands will fight and will cause disruption but the legions will not be drawn off as we had hoped."

If they expected to be reproached they were disappointed. "You have done well sisters. Any rebellion, no matter how small will be like a stone thrown into a pond. It may be a small splash but the ripples travel a long way. Here in the north some of the northern tribes from Caledonia will join with the Brigante. In the north and west, we are a mighty boulder. It will not be a ripple but a tidal wave that will sweep the Romans away and cleanse the land of their foul civilisation. Go back, sisters. Our work will soon be complete. When Mona is free again we will meet there again."

Eboracum

It was early spring and the first snowdrops had already erupted, sprinkled the landscape a sparkling white and now started to die. Daffodils, bluebells and hyacinths struggled to splash a hint of green in the grey and white landscape. Eboracum had grown considerably since Marcus had last been there. There was far more stonework and the ninth slept in heated brick-built barracks. Best of all there was a bathhouse. Even though the three Pannonian commanders had not travelled far they were eager to partake of a bath, massage and oiling. When the three of them finally emerged, they felt much cleaner and, somehow healthier.

The Governor had arranged a feast to celebrate the start of the campaign. The feast would follow a sacrifice of a bullock and, hopefully, the auspices would be good but as Rufius confided to Fabius and Marcus in the bathhouse. "A good leader leaves nothing to chance. I would expect nothing less than good omens."

In this he was correct and the legionaries of the ninth roared their delight when the omens were pronounced to be good, and they would get to eat beef. They adored their Governor who had been their tribune and this was another sign that the gods were with them. He still led them, even though he commanded other troops, and they would have crossed the Alps barefoot if he had asked them.

The feast was a magnificent affair with delicacies sent from Rome and even further afield. The wines were the best available although Rufius found them a little rough for his taste. That may have been because the auxiliary officers were placed well away from the Governor and the legionary officers. He and Fabius rudely ignored the two prefects of Batavian infantry and their prima pilae. This suited Marcus for he enjoyed the company of Cominius Sura and Furius Strabo. For their part, they were happier to discuss real campaigning with someone who had actually taken part in many campaigns and was fast becoming a legend.

"My men still revere you for the way you saved them at Stanwyck."

"Do not worry Cominius there will come a time when your men will save us I doubt it not."

"How do the Brigante fight? We did not really see them fight at Stanwyck."

"They fight better now because they have adapted their style of fighting. They have seen how we fought. Remember that Queen Cartimandua was an ally of Claudius. They only fought us when her husband Venutius took over."

"The Governor maintains that Venutius is still alive and he will defeat him."

"He may say that but I knew Venutius and I saw him slain and burned. I think the Governor wants a big name as a trophy and King Maeve is barely known in his own lands let alone elsewhere."

"Yes," added Cominius, "my men captured a Brigante scout near Isurium he said much the same, under torture of course. The real power is held by a woman."

"That makes sense," agreed Marcus remembering the respect given not only to Cartimandua but also Lenta and Macha. "Unlike Rome, they do not ignore their women."

"I'd like to see them ignore my mother," went on Furius whose red face had become even redder as he consumed vast quantities of both beer and wine. "She would have scared even my first spear." They all laughed at the unconnected comment delivered by a huge man who was half asleep.

"Who is this woman then, the one who wields the power behind the scenes?"

"They say it is a witch."

The hairs on the back of Marcus' neck stood up and he suddenly became stone-cold sober. "A witch you say? Did you hear a name?"

Cominius was less drunk than his companion who was now gently snoring into his cheese and bread and he too became more alert. "Why Marcus do you know of one?"

"There is a witch I seek who murdered Queen Cartimandua and tried to kill my commander and the Queen's sisters. I swore an oath to my commander as he lay dying to bring her to justice."

"Well this witch, I wish I could recall the name but it will come. This witch guides King Maeve and his right-hand man Aed. It is said that it was her plan which resulted in the taking of Stanwyck and the trap that nearly ensnared my men."

"Then I have another two reasons to wish her death."

"Two?"

"Yes, she caused the deaths of my wife and son."

"I am sorry, Marcus. That is a heavy load you bear." He took another swallow of wine and then said, "Fainch! That was her name Fainch."

Marcus nodded. "That confirms it then for the name I was given was Fainch." He drew Cominius closer. "You can pay your debt to me if you give me information about her, should you hear anything."

"Marcus we will do this for you but we do it as friends. We will still repay the debt." They clasped arms as a symbolic bond. "Furius is a good fellow and I am sure he will help us. When he is sober."

"Does that happen often?"

"Not very" and they both laughed so hard that Fabius and Rufius looked around in shock. Cominius laughed so hard he broke wind and the sound echoed around the room making the two men laugh even more.

Fabius said, in a voice loud enough to be heard, "Barbarians! How uncivilized."

Cominius started to get up but Marcus restrained him and said in a voice only Cominius could hear. "Ignore him he's all piss and wind, and not much of that either." They both laughed again and Fabius reddened like a ripe water melon.

The next day there were more than a few sore heads although, surprisingly, Furius was not amongst that number. He ate more breakfast than anyone and consumed a flagon of ale before going into the briefing. He turned to Cominius and Marcus, "I tell you they might not have any wine worth more than horse's piss but they brew the best ale I have supped since I came to this forsaken rock."

"Sit down gentlemen. I hope you all enjoyed the feast." He looked pointedly at Furius who just smiled beatifically and mouthed an "I did." Shaking his head, the Governor continued. "Today is the first day of the campaign. I want all units to muster at Stanwyck. I assume that the auxiliaries will be there first?" The three prefects nodded. "The legions will take longer to arrive. I would like three large camps built North West of Stanwyck; one for the auxiliaries and one each for the legions. I intend to begin the invasion before the local feast of Eostre." They all looked at each other. "It is my belief that they will expect us to wait until after Eostre but I do not want to dilly dally. We strike hard and we strike quickly. No delays gentlemen. Our men are well fed, well trained and well prepared. We will be supplied throughout whereas the Brigante will not. I have my spies out and they talk of huge armies coming from the north. If we defeat these it may well put them off. Frontinus has not yet managed to subdue the west of the province. When we have defeated this barbarian army then Julius Agricola will take the twentieth to the west to help him. I intend to bring the new legion the second Adiutrix up from Lindum as a mobile reserve hence the presence of their prefect. Any questions?" For once even Rufius could think of no further questions. "Good. Rejoin your units and we meet at Stanwyck."

Derventio

As soon as Marcus entered the fort he shouted his orders, "Officers and sergeants to the Praetorium."

By the time he had dismounted and given Semias the goods he had purchased in Eboracum, the room was beginning to fill up. He did not feel guilty about buying a few luxuries for if they were to campaign for any period then some small pleasures would make the harsh life more bearable. He looked around at their faces; they were eager and they were keen. "We leave the fort tomorrow." He saw Decius collecting money from Macro and Lentius; he was incorrigible, you would never stop him gambling. "And I don't think we will be returning here soon." The last statement was important for all of the officers and men who had secreted money and precious objects. They were safe in the fort for no soldier would steal from another but if they were away for any time then it would not be safe. "Tell the men after this briefing. Porcius make sure we have plenty of wagons and mules. Take all of the supplies; our relief will be bringing their own."

"Relief sir?" asked Porcius.

"Yes, quartermaster, a century of Batavians. Don't worry I have seen their commander they will look after the fort and they will dismantle the gyrus." He saw Agrippa and Macro exchange sad looks. "Do not worry gentlemen it served its purpose for have we not the best-trained ala in the whole of

Britannia? Now on to more serious matters. We will be operating as an ala of ten turmae. Decurion Princeps Fabius Demetrius will command the other ten turmae as a separate ala. This gives the general two cavalry units instead of one." There was a pause and an intake of breath. Marcus milked the moment taking a drink from the beaker of wine on the table. "The prefect will accompany Demetrius." The grins told him more than a chorus of whoops would have done. "It does, however, leave us with a problem. We have five turmae without decurions. I assume Decius that we have a couple we can promote?"

"Well, I don't know about that. There aren't that many experienced troopers left. There are a bunch of recruits who might turn out to be officer material but…"

He left the sentence hanging in the air and the nods of the others showed that they concurred. "I agree so here is my plan. The two sergeants Macro and Cato will each take on the role of acting decurion." He silenced their protests with the flat of his hand. "The recruits are used to taking orders from you and I have made my decision. Quartermaster I would like you to act as a decurion for a while you too are used to giving orders and that is more important than anything else. These are temporary arrangements until we get to Stanwyck. I will say however that the prefect wished me to appoint some troopers from turma eleven; I told him we could cope."

Metellus said, "We would be better off with recruits than that criminal rabble!"

"Quite. So I would like you to watch the men in your turmae on the journey and while we are packing and setting up camp. Identify possible decurions and we will make more decisions at Stanwyck." He looked at them weighing up his next words carefully. "I also found out some interesting news. The witch Fainch who was responsible for the death of the Queen was also involved in the murders of Lenta, Macha and, "there was a catch in his voice as he added, "my son. She is also advising the Brigante and appears to be behind this latest rebellion." There was a stunned silence. "Just thought you ought to know."

"Sort of makes it personal doesn't it?" The others murmured their agreement with Decius.

"One last thing when we reach Stanwyck we also have to build the legionaries a fort." They all groaned and began moaning. "Governor's orders."

There was a silence and as they left Decius just grunted, "Screw the Governor."

Before he could be reprimanded Macro said, "No thank you sir there is a mule outside that will do."

Stanwyck

155

"The auxiliaries have done a fine job with the forts eh Julius?"

"I don't think it has endeared us to them, Governor."

"What do you mean?"

"I think they feel as though they are being treated as lesser soldiers than the legions."

Cerialis looked thunderstruck. "But they are. They are only there to support the legions. Without the legions, there is no need for auxiliaries."

Agricola sighed, the Governor was ever the military man, blunt and to the point, "I might agree sir but you might have phrased it differently."

The Governor thought for a moment. "Would the result have been the same?"

"Well yes."

"There you are then I have saved time. Now then where do we think the Brigante army is?"

Agricola was on firmer ground here. "The major Brigante settlement is Brocavum. I fought them there last time."

"It would be very accommodating if they obliged again."

"It would be perfect but I can't see them cooperating. They seem to have a better plan this time. I expected them to hit us piecemeal as they did last time but they appear to be waiting."

"Waiting? I wonder, waiting for what? I am not going to fall into the trap of letting them make the first move. Where is your best guess for where they will be?"

Agricola pointed to the west of the map. "What I would want is for them to have mustered in the land of the lakes. If they did that the legions could stop them like a cork in a wineskin. But I can't see that happening and all our scouts say the land is empty. North of East of Brocavum as I recall, the land is unsuited to moving large numbers of men; there are woods, cliffs and rivers. They would not be able to use their superiority in number count. Which leaves here as the place." He pointed to the far west. "The ships you sent around got as far as here which is why the rest of the map is vague. There is a wide river, the Taus. The land to the south is flat gentle plains with another river. If you want me to pick a place where they will fight it would be there between the two rivers. It is flat enough and their flanks are secure. It also means their allies; the Pictii and Caledonii can join them easily and yet be close enough to their own lands. There."

Cerialis walked around the map to see it from every direction. "It is a pity the Classis Britannica isn't here. With those moored in the Taus, we could use their artillery to flank them."

"Yes, I had thought of that."

"How far is it?"

"We have never been that far, any of us but if the map is accurate then I would say it would take us a week. Of course the other problem we would have would be our supply lines. The further we travel into their country the further our supplies have to come and of course we would be in a hostile country all the way. This might not be a good country to manoeuvre a large army but it is perfect for an ambush."

"That's where these auxiliaries will earn their salary. I want one Batavian legion in front and one behind the legions. Half the cavalry on our right flank and the other on the left. We'll be like a box with the legions in the middle. The auxiliaries may lose some of their men but we will reach the enemy with the two legions intact. Send for the prefects."

Shaking his head Agricola went to find a messenger. The auxiliaries would be used again; the Governor just couldn't see a problem with his attitude but Julius Agricola knew that the whole of the army needed to feel valued. Should the day ever come when he commanded an army he would see to it that they were all valued.

"So gentlemen once again we protect the precious legions." He turned to Marcus, "Didn't some of the ala serve in this area a couple of years ago?" He pointed to the area north of Glanibanta.

"Yes sir, we spent a winter and part of the spring there."

"Good, then your ala can have the southern flank. We'll take the northern flank. That's where they should be coming from anyway. The Governor wants a daily report. Use your scouts well and remember, Decurion Princeps Maximunius, I need a daily report as well as the Governor. Clear?"

"Yes sir."

When Marcus told the decurions about the plan there were mixed reactions. Those who did not know the area were excited whereas Decius, Lentius and Gaius were more cautious. "There are more places to ambush there than there are brothels in Rome."

Gaius looked at his one-time mentor, "Well you should be right at home then."

Decius sniffed, "The trouble was I didn't use my vine staff enough on you young Gaius!"

Brocavum

King Maeve was angry and King Maeve was confused. The first reports had just come in telling him of the movements of large numbers of Roman soldiers. Fainch had told him they would begin this war at Eostre when the whole of the island would rise. He was never the most strategic of leaders even though he had native cunning. He shouted to one of his guards, "Send for Aed. I need to see him." Over the winter Aed had become a far more trustworthy lieutenant. When he first arrived Maeve worried that he might be a usurper but since the early days, he had been the most loyal and obedient of

157

all his chiefs. The one person he could trust was Aed and of course Fainch but, as King Maeve peered across to the east and the invisible army making its inexorable way to him, he wondered about Fainch. She had spent less time with him of late. Did she have another lover? Was she plotting against him? Having been a plotter and a schemer Maeve had paranoia about others plotting to take his throne from him.

"Yes my lord, you sent for me?"

"Yes, Aed."

Even as he spoke Fainch swept into the room. "You will need my counsel will you not?"

"Yes, yes, I was about to send for you. The Romans…"

"The Romans have begun their invasion."

King Maeve looked in surprise at Fainch. "How did you know? I have just had a secret message."

"Remember oh king that while you rule these lands I serve Mother Earth and I know far more than you for I am a priestess of Mona." Maeve seemed to shrink a little in fear. Little did he know that the spy had reported to Fainch first.

"Well, what are we to do? The plan was of a rising at Eostre."

"The rising will still take place. This helps us."

"How?"

"They have committed their northern forces. They have moved a legion to Lindum to act as a reserve. The rest of the country is ripe for a rebellion. This just means that we must delay them a little longer."

"Aed what do you say?"

"I agree. It does not change our basic strategy. We still withdraw west. Most of our people have already moved, taking their animals with them. The army is standing by. All we wait for are our allies. Might I suggest we summon them?"

"Yes, yes see to it. And then we stick to our plan?"

Fainch came behind him and placed her hands on either side of his head gently massaging him as she spoke. "The plan is a good one. We move North-West towards Luguvalium. Aed takes his men to the land of the lakes and attacks the men on the flanks and the rear. When we get to the Taus we form our battle lines and wait for the Romans to attack us then the eastern tribes and the northern tribes attack the right flank of the Roman army while Aed attacks the left. They will have three attacks to deal with and only two legions."

"And the auxiliaries."

"Aed has shown oh king that the auxiliaries can be beaten."

Maeve nodded. Even he had been impressed when Aed had returned from his raid with Roman heads, horses and armour. His men had further added to his stature with the tales of the fight and many men had joined Aed's elite on the basis of it. "And if the other tribes do not join us?"

"They will but even so it does not need all of them as long as some do it will cause concern for the Romans. By then it will be Eostre and I expect the Roman leader to be receiving messages of rebellion throughout the whole land. Even if we have not totally defeated him I would hope he would retreat to help those in the rest of the province and then we can destroy his army piecemeal as he retreats."

Whether it was the words, the tone or the message, the effect was achieved; Maeve was calm and committed. "Order the stronghold to be abandoned we march west."

East of Brocavum

The prefect scanned the skyline which seemed to stretch as far as the eye could see. The only feature was in the distance; rising a little way above a fold in the land was part of a wooden tower. He turned to Fabius, "Take your turma and that of Modius. Scout that stronghold; I assume the wooden tower would indicate that it is a fortification of some description. Do not approach within arrow shot for I do not want to lose a single man uselessly. "

Without another word but gesturing the decurion Fabius galloped off the eighty men strung out in column of twos behind him. As he rode he relished the freedom. He eagerly anticipated finding some of the enemy. He had a buccina with him and, should he encounter odds too great for glory and success he could summon the other three hundred and thirty men to support him. The land before him had trees dotted to the north and south but ahead it rose and fell in gentle folds. Even someone as inexperienced as Fabius could see that there was little likelihood of ambush and they were able to make good time. He halted the men at the top of a rise about a mile from the stronghold. Although the gates facing him were shut there did not seem to be any sentries. He noticed that there was a wooden bridge leading northwards from the northern entrance. The bridge was not well made but it spanned the confluence of two rivers. From the muddy banks, he assumed that the inhabitants had fled that way. It looked empty. Ignoring the prefect's orders, he turned to the two troopers behind him, "Fanius, Marius. Ride up to the gates be careful and check if there are any sentries. If not then split up and ride around the stronghold. Then report back to me."

Modius drew his horse up next to that of Fabius. "Looks empty to me."

"And to me. I am just making sure."

"And then what back to the prefect?"

Fabius grinned and it was not a pleasant grin for it seemed to make his young face both older and more menacing. "We will send a message back but if they have abandoned it then who knows what we may find on the road beyond?"

159

Modius laughed, "Or even inside the stronghold. We will have time for plunder before the Batavians arrive."

They both watched as the two riders emerged from the circumnavigation of the fort. They drew up next to Fabius. "No sign of life sir and the northwest gate is open. Popped my head around and could see no sign of life."

"Thank you, Marius. Ride back and report to the prefect we will rest on the other side of the fort." As they watched Marius ride east Fabius signalled for the turmae to move off east. The Decurion Princeps glanced over as they passed the west gate, it was as reported; they would plunder after a short patrol. The trail taken by the refugees was clear; they had gone north across the bridge and then north-west although for the first mile or so they saw no one just discarded objects which showed them they were on the right track. As they crested a rise however they saw a knot of people heading southwest towards the land of the lakes. "In fours, two turmae." The training of the winter had paid off and soon there were two columns of men four abreast and ten deep. "Trot!" As soon as they began to move some of the refugees saw them and panicked soon the mob was racing in every direction. As he drew his sword and roared, "Charge!" Fabius could see that there was but a handful of poorly armed warriors protecting them.

The two columns swept over the warriors in heartbeats leaving bodies riven with wounds. "Kill them all, no prisoners!" His men needed no further urging and the neat lines were dissipated into a melee as every man chased down and killed the nearest refugee. Men, women, children, animals all were slaughtered. Some of his men went back to the warriors and adorned their horses with the decapitated heads. Although there was little plunder his men took all that the pitiful band had to offer. "Back to Brocavum!"

Approaching the emptied stronghold, they could just make out the standards of the Batavians and the rest of the cavalry. Modius bellowed, "Right lads make it quick. Get what you can and we share later on."

By the time the prefect reached the fortress, the scavengers had plundered anything that was left. Believing they would be back sooner rather than later many had trusted their precious objects to the ground to be dug up later on. However, in the cold hard earth freshly turned soil was a good sign and the two turmae had a good haul.

Fabius left the plundering to his subordinates and went to open the west gate with a couple of men. Whilst they struggled with the bar Fabius climbed to the tower. He could see a gaggle of staff officers heading his way. The Governor was coming. Turning Fabius said as loudly as he could, "Hurry it is the Governor!" Unfortunately, it came out rather squeaky.

The haste was not because looting was frowned upon rather it was encouraged to discourage opposition but the practice was to share with the whole unit. This went against the grain for Modius and his like; Fabius was not concerned with the lot but it bought him the loyalty of the eighty most cunning men in the ala. By the time he had descended to the gate Quintus Cerialis, Julius Agricola and the prefects had arrived. "Well done it is young Demetrius isn't it?" Fabius nodded. "Good. Any fighting?"

"None in the fort sir but we caught up with some warriors." He gestured behind to where two of his men waved the decapitated remains of the warriors.

"Gruesome but I dare say effective. Which way were they headed?"

"Northwest sir. There is a well-worn wagonway and there was clear evidence that a large number of people had travelled that way."

"Carry on." Ignoring the decurion, who stood in the narrow gateway feeling like a spare part, the Governor turned to his commanders. "It is as you said Julius they are heading North West rather than west. So we will move accordingly. We will rest here tonight and then strike early in the morning. They can move faster than we can so we might as well let them carry out their plan eh? No point disturbing a man when he is making a mistake." They all laughed dutifully at the old joke. "Prefect, keep this ala where it is but the one to the south is too far away to be effective draw them in."

Far to the south Marcus had his ala in four columns to two turmae. As he had said at the briefing, "I want the flexibility to send one south and one north and yet keep a large force as a reserve." They were travelling over the low hills of the eastern land of the lakes. There were no people to be seen and even fewer animals. The leaves had just started to emerge after a harsh winter but the icy wind which hurtled from the east behind them discouraged any young plants from growing just yet. The troopers new to the province, those from the southern tribes were finding it hard; they were cold to the bone and the wind seemed to find a way through the thick weave of their cloaks.

Decius shouted over to Marcus, "The last time we were here we were sneaking around trying to avoid finding anybody and here we are actually seeking for the enemy."

"We have not seen any sign for quite some time. I doubt that they are in front of us. We'll camp tonight at the head of that long lake in the lonely valley then decide if we go southwest, west or northwest."

Mona and the southern half of the province

The small garrisons dotted around the island had been lulled into a false sense of security by the peaceful winter. Many never awoke on the tribes' festival of Eostre for their camps had been infiltrated and sentries had had their throats cut. The whole of the border to the west of Britannia awoke to chaos and mayhem. Nearer to the civilised centres of Roman civilisation small groups of warriors murdered officials and wiped out small garrisons used to peace. Within a matter of hours, the Pax Romana had ended and Britannia was on the edge of rebellion.

Chapter 16

As the Roman army ponderously headed North West the group of warriors hidden in the trees to the south-west conferred. "It is as Fainch said, they are following the army. Find Aed and tell him where the army is." The rider took off, keeping low in the saddle to avoid observation.

Aed and his men were camped well to the west; had the Romans come his way it would have meant that Fainch's plans had gone seriously awry. He was eager for combat. He was certain that when they met the auxiliary infantry they would prove no match for him and his well-trained warriors.

His guards alerted him to the messenger's presence long before he arrived. "General Aed the Romans have taken the bait. Their cavalry is to the north. They have one auxiliary unit at the rear and one in the vanguard."

"Excellent that means there are no cavalrymen between me and the rear guard. When did they leave Brocavum?"

"This morning."

"Mount. Today we take Batavian heads." It took a very short time for the fifteen hundred strong warband to ride north. They would wait until they were making camp in the evening just when they were tired and looking forward to a rest. He would halt in time to rest and feed his horses. His men would be fresher. They would be ready to fight and the Romans would have no idea they had an enemy at their rear, they would just be thinking about food and sleep.

Marcus' ala woke refreshed having camped close to a lake and sheltered by two enormous mountains. Marcus had remembered this rocky valley from their escape from Glanibanta. It offered them security for an attacker would either have to travel from the north to attack them or the south. It made it much easier to defend. "Gaius your turma is to scout. Take Gaelwyn with you. I know he will moan but that can't be helped. The dispatch rider who arrived yesterday told me that the army is moving North West. Fortunately, they are so slow with the artillery that we will easily be able to catch them. Let me know when you sight the Batavians."

As it was Gaius who was in the vanguard Marcus felt very secure. All of the decurions were trustworthy but Gaius was extra careful. His caution would ensure that there were no surprises. His mind drifted back to the murder of Queen Cartimandua it seemed a long time ago and, in another way, only like yesterday. He had hunted her down in mind many times but now he was within touching distance. He was getting closer to his prey. When they met the Brigante in battle there would be more incentive for him to be victorious for when the battle was over he would find the witch and kill her. He would avenge his wife and child and fulfil his oath to Ulpius. An oath to a dying man was the most sacred oath a warrior could swear.

He was suddenly aware of Decius at his shoulder. "You alright boss?"

Marcus looked at him curiously, "Yes. Why do you ask?"

"You've been a bit quiet. The lads are concerned. You're not, you know, brooding about what happened at Stanwyck."

"You mean when my wife and child were murdered? There's not a minute that goes by when they are not in my thoughts. Before I go to sleep I speak with my dear wife and say goodnight to my tiny son. When I close my eyes at night I see them as clearly as if they were in the room with me. But when I am a warrior, when I lead this ala I think of one thing and one thing only. How can we defeat this enemy and find the people who destroyed my life? Does that answer your question?"

Decius looked sadly at his friend realising, at last, the depth of grief and the intensity of the man's need for revenge. "Yes, boss I understand."

All of a sudden, a rider burst over the skyline. It was a trooper from Gaius' turma. "Sir the decurion sent me."

"Report."

"The decurion has crossed the trail of a large number of horsemen travelling north towards Brocavum. He is trailing them."

"Could he identify them?"

"That Brigante scout, Gaelwyn, thought that the tracks were made by mailed Brigante warriors." He looked bemused. "I don't know how he knows that."

"Because he is a scout and a bloody good one at that. You useless excuse for a donkey's dick!"

"Right. Lead us to them. Single column." The four columns suddenly became one and they headed after the trooper now lathering his mount as he raced back to his turma.

They met up with Gaius southwest of Brocavum. "Sir come and look at this." The decurion took his leader to the site of the slaughter two days previously.

"Did the Brigante do this?"

"No sir," Gaius paused for effect, "we did."

"You mean your men…"

"No sir I mean Pannonians. There are bits of our weapons left in some of the bodies. It was the other ala, has to be and look at what they did to the children and women."

Marcus pulled Gaius over to one side. "Keep this to yourself. We will deal with it later. Where are the Brigante?"

"They are about five miles away and they look to be trailing the Batavians."

Marcus looked up at the sun which was dipping low in the sky. "We'll have to hurry. If they catch the Batavians they will be almost invisible until the last minute." He pointed to the reddening sky to the west. He shouted, "Decurions." When they arrived he outlined his plan. "I want the turma fourteen; the good javelin throwers as a single line with turma seventeen the archers behind them. I will be behind them. Decius, you take the left and Lentius the right. I intend to try to get the high ground and charge immediately. Agrippa and Cato I want one volley from each of you and then Agrippa form up behind me. Cato, form up behind Agrippa. Keep your archers working as long as you can." He looked at each of them in turn. "Gaius thinks they outnumber us but we have the advantage of surprise. I want us to surprise them before they slaughter Furius and his Batavians. Let's ride."

Furius was a heavy drinker and he loved his food but he was first and foremost a soldier. The Batavian auxiliaries were his life and he would spend his last drop of blood for them. He recognised that his men were tired and, as his first spear had said, "Eating the dirt and dust from two legions would make anyone want to join the enemy."

The prefect was well aware of what would happen if they did not put up a fortified camp. Because they had arrived first he could already see, in the distance, the other Batavian camp and the two legionary camps were well underway. His demoralised and weary men just wanted to sleep. "Come on ladies let's get this camp sorted and then we eat." Already his engineers had laid out the outline of the camp and some of the first century were digging their section of ditch. Furius turned to see if the others had started when his heart missed a beat. There, less than a thousand paces away thundered a mass of mailed men. "Alarm! Cavalry attack!" The buccina sounded and men threw down their shovels and grabbed spears and shields. Hastily they formed lines but there was no cohesion. Hurriedly the centurions chivvied and jostled the men into position. The Brigante, for now, they could see their enemy, were less than five hundred paces.

"Prepare javelins!" Furius placed himself at the right flank of the nearest century. He turned to them and said, "Just like in training. On the command throw your javelin then place the butt of your spear in the ground."

"One voice from the darkening gloom of twilight said, "But sir they have long spears and armour."

"I know lad but you can hold. Wait for the command, wait for the command!" The horses were snorting and thundering towards the thin line and the riders were leaning forward with their spears thrust out. "Throw!"

The first volley hit home and was as accurate as the prefect could have hoped for but the mail deflected some javelins whilst others merely wounded the horses. The two lines met in a crash of metal on metal and metal on wood. Horses screamed in pain as javelins disembowelled them but the cohesion of the line was not there. "Keep it tight, men! Keep it tight!" Out of the corner of his eye, the prefect could see his lightly armoured men being speared and crushed to the ground by heavy horses and mailed men. The young trooper next to him gave a silent scream as his throat was ripped by a razor-sharp blade. Furius slashed at the neck of the warrior's horse and it reared up throwing its rider. Before he could rise Furius stepped over the horse and stabbed the warrior in the throat. He risked a glance over his shoulder. His only hope was that the legionaries would come and find some of them alive or at least stop the carrion birds despoiling their corpses...

Suddenly he saw that the Brigante were looking over their shoulders and not pressing quite so hard. Then he heard a buccina and it was coming from behind the Brigante. It was the cavalry. "Come on lads hold! Help is at hand. Fight you bastards fight!" His men tightened their lines and his second line pressed hard against the first making an impenetrable barrier. The hope of the cavalry had put steel into their backbones and, for the first time, Furius began to believe that they would survive.

The Brigante commander realised his predicament he was between the rock of the Batavians and the hard place that was the auxiliaries. He made his decision quickly. Aed despatched the two Batavians grappling for his reins and shouted, "Retreat!"

In an instant, the Brigante broke away and headed south. There were many empty saddles and little knots of dismounted warriors still fought but in effect, the battle was over. Furius heard a familiar voice shout out an order, "Decius, Gaius take Agrippa and Lentius and see if you can catch them but come back when it is dark! I don't want to lose men in an ambush!"

Argentium pulled up next to the red-faced and heaving Furius. "Well, Marcus it looks like the second Batavians owe you as much as the first."

"Glad to be of service. Couldn't let those Brigante deprive us of the best drinker in the province."

Furius laughed, "When we have the camp up come and join us I have some fine ale."

Just then a gaggle of mounted officers arrived with a cohort of legionaries in close pursuit. "Well done Decurion Princeps it looks as though you arrived in the very nick of time."

"Thank you, Governor. Lucky really, we crossed their trail and chased them as hard as we could. We arrived just too late to stop them attacking but they have lost at least two hundred and fifty of their best men."

Furius looked around him sadly, "We have lost at least that and more."

The Governor pondered this. "Tomorrow morning we will have a meeting we can't go on losing men like this before we even fight the battle. Carry on." As the Governor rode off the rest of Marcus' ala arrived.

Decius shook his head, "We caught and killed a few but they split up and I didn't want to risk ambush."

"You did right. Let's get a camp built next to our friends here. Metellus despatch any wounded and collect our wounded."

Fabius and Rufius made their way from their camp in the hills to the north of the main camp. "I hear that Maximunius is the Governor's golden boy again. That man has more luck than is good for him."

"Fabius, you impressed the Governor with the capture of Brocavum."

"Yes, an empty stronghold. He saves a legion, again!"

"Our time will come. At least this means the threat from the south is gone and we are more likely to be in combat. You and your men will show their bravery then."

"I hope so," replied a sulky son.

As they entered the Governor's tent Fabius saw, to his chagrin, the Batavians thanking Marcus and patting him on the back. From the looks on the faces of Agricola and Cerialis they too had been praising him. "Ah prefect, you arrived a little too late to hear the praises heaped upon your cavalry unit. Once again they have saved this army from disaster." He held up his hand for silence. "In honour of this Decurion Princeps, Marcus Aurelius Maximunius and his ala are to be presented with the Crown of the Preserver for their actions in saving the Batavians. The Decurion Princeps is also to have a separate decoration as commander of that unit."

Fabius felt his father bridle when he heard this. Technically he was the commander but he had been nowhere near the action and it would have appeared churlish to bring it up. It galled both the patrician father and son that a barbarian was receiving such a high honour.

"And now on to other matters. We have done well so far but we have yet to bring the enemy to battle. I need to know where they are. Prefect your cavalry will now form the forward screen. Prefect Sura your Batavians will protect the right flank and the rear. Prefect Strabo you have suffered many casualties you will take the left flank. The land before us is less hilly and the legions can march abreast. The Brigante appear to be fond of ambush we will be ready to counter such moves. I want the army less strung out. Prefect Demetrius I want your cavalry to form a protective circle while the infantry camps are built each night then you may build yours." Rufius felt Fabius begin to rise and he restrained him shaking his head to silence him. "If there are no questions rejoin your men."

Keeping Ituna Fluvius to their right the army moved up the steep-sided valley which led North West towards the sea. The Batavians on the flanks looked up fearfully at the steep sides. If the Brigante had had any sense they would have hurled boulders down which would have decimated the auxiliaries but Fainch's plan was being adhered to; the Romans were being drawn to a battlefield of their choosing. Some way ahead the twenty turmae gingerly moved forward. The territory through which they were travelling was unknown to all of them; even their native scouts like Gaelwyn knew little of the land. At first, the turma were close together but as the almost dry valley bottom opened out they spread out from columns of two to columns of fours and gradually drew apart.

Gaelwyn was with Marcus' ala on the left. Periodically he left the main force and scouted ahead. In the early afternoon of the first day of the march, he returned with news. "Decurion Princeps. There is a large town ahead and a river. It looks like there is a ford not far ahead, we can cross the river. I can see the enemy; they are camped between the two rivers."

"Halt! Go and tell the prefect he may want you to report to the Governor or," he smiled sardonically, "he may wish to deliver the news himself."

His men rested and took the opportunity to feed themselves and their mounts. Marcus was right and Gaelwyn arrived back, "You must be a druid decurion! The prefect and the Decurion Princeps rode back with the news. He said to halt here and await orders."

The orders were soon incoming and were delivered not by the prefect but by Fabius Demetrius. "Our orders are to form a secure perimeter one mile from the enemy lines and when the legions and auxiliaries have built their camps we are to build ours."

The orders were delivered in a high-pitched squeak but with much pomposity. It took all of Marcus' self-control not to burst out laughing. "I assume the prefect wishes us to build two camps side by side?"

It was obvious that neither the prefect nor his son had thought of the logistics and Fabius just blustered, "Of course! What else would you do?" And then he rode off.

Decius had arrived and heard the orders. "Do you know I am certain that young Julius had to be fathered by the man who tended his mother's garden for those two are the biggest...?"

"Decius, "he said looking around, "the men are listening." Turning to the ala he added, "Forward."

Quintus Petilius Cerialis was in his tent eating with Julius Agricola and studying the map when the sentry put his head through the entrance and said, "Imperial messenger sir. I think it is urgent."

"Send him in."

The messenger who entered was filthy, dishevelled and obviously exhausted. "Sir despatches from Eboracum, urgent." His face spoke of terror and fear. He handed over the reports and as Cerialis read them Agricola indicated that the messenger should sit. He poured the man a beaker of wine which he gratefully drank in one swallow. Recognising that the man must be starving and aware that the Governor was still reading he put some food on a plate which the messenger began to devour voraciously.

"Been on the road long son?"

"Hastily swallowing the messenger said, "I left Eboracum yesterday with three horses. Two of them are dead." He paused, "There were five messengers sent. If the others haven't arrived…"

"Quite. They could be dead or even captured. This could be disastrous Julius." Looking at the sentry and the messenger the Governor asked the messenger, "I take it you know what is in this report?"

"Yes sir."

"Sentry wait outside but ask the prefect of cavalry to join me." The sentry left. "It looks like there was an uprising at Eostre."

"Where?"

"Everywhere but the south-east. The prefect at Deva said he has not heard from any garrison south of the river. Lindum and Eboracum suffered assaults and many casualties but they held. We still have the second Adiutrix as a reserve. Thank Mithras."

"Do we abandon this attack then and march south?"

Quintus stroked his chin reflectively as he thought it through. A naturally aggressive commander, some would say reckless it was not in his nature to pull back; on the other hand, if he did not pull back then he might lose the whole province. "We are too close to the enemy. We will attack tomorrow."

"Tomorrow? But sir will the men be ready? What about the artillery?"

"Julius they will be ready. We have camped early we can rise before dawn. Ensure that the artillery is unpacked tonight and we will take it with us ready to use. I don't care what their formation is we will attack come what may."

"They may outnumber us…"

"Let us be quite clear they will outnumber us." He looked up at the messenger, forgotten in all of this. "You are to return to Eboracum with despatches I will write now. Go and rest while you can for you will ride tonight." Grimacing with exhaustion the man left.

As he did so the sentry reappeared. "Prefect of cavalry sir."

Rufius entered. "By rights, I should have the two Batavian prefects as well but I don't have time. While I write the despatches I want you Julius to brief them. Sorry about this but you will not get much sleep tonight. Prefect, there are pockets of rebellion in the south and when we have finished with this tribe we will head south to deal with them However I need two of your men and their horses. I need messengers to go to Deva and Lindum."

"Yes, sir I will see to it." He started to leave.

"Sit down man I haven't finished."

"Sorry, sir."

"We are going to attack tomorrow. I want the camp broken by the middle watch." He looked up sharply, "Have the Brigante shown any sign of attacking whilst you were building camp?"

"Surprisingly no. We kept pickets out to warn us but they seemed content to let us build our normal camp."

"Your cavalry will move forward until you can ascertain the enemy dispositions. Leave your Decurion Princeps in charge, I think they are both sound men certainly Maximunius is and report back to me. I need a precise assessment of their battle deployment. No exaggeration understand? I need facts. We have one chance to win, defeat and slaughter these bastards and then sort out the rest of the province. Is that clear?"

"Yes sir."

"Good man. Well about your duties I have much to write tonight. Send in my clerk for he will have to make duplicate copies."

Brigante camp

King Maeve sat with his ally kings, Aed, his trusted lieutenant and Fainch. They were all looking very pleased with themselves. The captured, tortured and deceased messengers had told them of the rebellion in the rest of the province. Although not as widespread as Fainch had hoped it would still work in their favour. The end of Roman rule in Britannia was nigh. If Maeve noticed the looks exchanged between Aed and Fainch it failed to register. Indeed, he was looking ahead to the day when he would become High King of Britannia. The nearest they had had was Caractacus, famously betrayed by a Brigante Queen. His ally kings were also plotting for the best way to use this victory in their own lands. That they would win was never in doubt. There were but two legions and a few auxiliaries. The two rivers prevented flanking and, even now warbands were gathering to the east, to fall upon their rear and others making their way to the north bank of the mighty Taus. They would outnumber the Romans by ten to one.

"We must wait for the Romans to commit before we launch our flank attack and our attack on the rear. Those attacks will only have auxiliaries to contend with. Watch for the legions to engage and then strike." King Maeve looked directly at the Caledonian war chiefs and the Novontae leaders. He had been well briefed by Fainch for she knew these warlords would not take orders from a woman. She did not mind. King Maeve could have his temporary glory. At the feast following the victory, he would suffer a mysterious death; a death almost identical to that suffered years earlier by Queen Cartimandua.

It was still almost dark when the prefect, red-eyed and tired from a sleepless night reported. "At the moment the enemy looks to be camped between the two rivers. They have horses to the south where the land is flatter. From their fires and what our Brigante scouts reported, having crept closer to their lines, they look to outnumber us ten to one. They are the usual barbarian rabble."

Cerialis thumped the table. "Excellent!" He turned to the other prefects and commanders in the room. Here is our plan of attack." He looked at Prefect Strabo. "The second Batavians have suffered the most casualties and I have a special role for them. Do not dismantle the camps. Strabo your men will occupy those camps and use them as forts."

"But sir any enemy attacking the rear could roll right over them."

"I know which is why you will dig a ditch between each one and put stakes behind. The ones closest to the rivers can be connected. It won't be a complete line but it will break up any attack. Anything which slows them down will work in our favour. The legions need time. The auxiliaries will buy them that time, with their lives if necessary. I am gambling gentlemen on breaking through their lines. To do that I need to use every man I have. Our weak spot is our rear. The ford we crossed is to the east and the other river looks like it cannot be forded. Prefect Strabo; even if you lose every man you must stop any enemy attacking the rear. Understood?"

Furius stiffened, "Yes sir. We will hold."

"Good man."

"Prefect Sura your men will form a skirmish line in front of the legions. You have to buy the artillery time to get close enough to do damage."

"Yes sir."

"Prefect Demetrius, one ala will support the Batavians. I would suggest Decurion Princeps Maximunius; he seems to work well with the infantry." The prefect was about to object when the general continued, "I would like the other ala to charge and despatch their cavalry, if our legions have an Achilles heel it is cavalry. You can eliminate them. Right?"

The chance to charge enemy cavalry appealed to the equestrian Patrician and he snapped out a, "Yes sir. We will don't worry."

"Julius I will manoeuvre the legions you get the artillery as close to their front lines as possible."

"Yes sir. I think that is all. "He looked at them all one by one. "It is no exaggeration when I say that the fate of the province lies in our hands. Every legionary, every trooper must perform at a higher standard than ever before if we are to succeed. When we do it I will see that every man is rewarded and each of you will receive honours."

Dawn had broken sometime earlier but still, the enemy remained in their serried ranks. On their right, the mailed horsemen looked magnificent. Marcus had tried to persuade the prefect to use archers to break them up but he was convinced he could rout them with a charge. Marcus was not too certain but he had his own problems. The ground in front of him was a little

171

boggy. Not enough to slow his horses down but sticky enough to make wheeling difficult. The warbands in front of him were a riot of both colour and weapons. He could see very long spears, swords and shields, double-handed axes, and even war hammers. There looked to be an eclectic mixture of tribes with Carvetii mixed in with Brigante and Caledonii. Whoever had formed the tribes up had done a sound job.

What Marcus did not know was that there was a huge warband approaching the rear of their lines and they were just awaiting the Roman command to attack. "When they going to give the order sir? We've been up for hours. The lads'll start to get tired and hungry soon."

"Tell them to chew on their dried meat," Decius nodded and rode down the line. Since the days of Ulpius, the ala had cured and dried meat to use in just such a situation. Marcus too wanted the battle started but the longer the delay the more the ground would dry out. He realised he was becoming nervous and he wiped his hands on the cloak protecting his groin. He drew his sword from its sheath. Whether it was a conscious or unconscious gesture one could not tell but the effect on the men was instantaneous. Even the new recruits had heard of the Sword of Cartimandua and its magical qualities. As he rode down the line Marcus could feel the men standing taller. Some braver voices called out, "We'll have them, sir, let's get at them, and we'll avenge your lady." They were silenced by decurions and sergeants but Marcus smiled, pleased with the spirit and he raised the sword. He could not have anticipated the reaction. There was a huge cheer not only from his ala but from most of the troopers in the other ala.

Cerialis heard it and said to his aide, "Well the Pannonians seem in good spirits. I hope the rest of the army is, if they are then it bodes well for us."

The prefect and his son were less happy for it showed to whom the men owed the most loyalty. "Do not worry Fabius. At the end of today, there will be a new hero who will be cheered. We will scatter these barbarians before us like a seed in the wind."

By the time Marcus and Decius met again at the centre of the line the men were like greyhounds straining at the leash. Marcus turned to Agrippa and Cato behind him. "Remember your turmae are crucial. Cato, keep your men pouring arrows into them. We have to create a weak spot. Agrippa, make sure your men have plenty of javelins; if they run out then get them from the other turmae."

The two men chorused," Yes sir," just as the buccina sounded.

Marcus looked briefly at Cominius who nodded and he shouted, "Move forwards!"

To his left, he heard the prefect shout, "Trot!" This part of the battle would be at a walk for Marcus and Cominius. As they moved forward Marcus watched the enemy line. If they charged it would change his plans but they seemed immovable. Behind him, he could hear the bolt throwers and ballistae moving into position. He and Cominius had agreed that they would halt together even though the Pannonians had a greater range because of their horses. The ranks of auxiliaries all stopped at the same time. The archers drew back their bows, their chests heaving with the exertion. Those with javelins pulled them back almost behind their right ear. The command "Loose" saw the sky blacken as the air filled with arrows and javelins. Away to the left, he could hear the shout of, Charge" and then a roar as the prefect and his son led his men to what they hoped would be glory and perhaps, a civic crown.

The tribes had learned from previous encounters with the auxiliaries and shields came up to ward off the missiles. They had developed shields more like the Romans with metal strips to give strength. Some missiles struck home but not as many as might have been expected. As they lowered their shields the barbarians hurled insults at the Romans. There were remarkably few corpses lying on the field of battle. Decius shouted over to Marcus, "That could have gone better!"

"Don't worry our job is just to fix them while the artillery gets into position." As he said that he glanced over his shoulder. The artillery was just twenty paces behind him and the deadly bolts, iron tipped and lethal to files of men, were already being loaded.

Agricola rode up to him. "A couple more volleys and then retreat to the left to cover that flank. Your comrades look to be in the thick of it." He looked to where the general pointed. The two cavalry forces were engaged in a furious battle. It was difficult to see who was winning but the prefect was doing his job and keeping the cavalry from flanking them and for that both Marcus and Agricola were grateful. A cavalry charge as they were setting up the artillery would have been a disaster...

Suddenly they heard a buccina sound from the rear. Agricola's face became a mask of fear. "The Batavians, they are being attacked." Just then there was an almighty shout from the enemy and the barbarian horde moved forward. "Better give one volley and then retreat. Cornicen, sound the signal for the Batavians." The pre-arranged signal was given and the Batavians moved back through the artillery to give the crews some protection.

Marcus shouted, "One volley then follow me!"

Even as his men moved away from the field he heard the twang of bolt throwers. The heavy tipped missiles tore through the ranks of the enemy. Their last volleys also took down many more men who could not be protected by shields. The Batavians also hurled their javelins and the charge of the tribes' front line faltered as the bodies became a barrier to the men following behind. Whoever was in command of the barbarian army had anticipated this for slingers and archers began to pelt the artillery crews and

173

Batavians with missiles. As the crews took hits their speed diminished allowing the horde to move inexorably closer. Marcus shouted to Cato, "Target their archers."

Just then Gaius, who was on the far left of the line, galloped up. "Sir, the prefect, he has gone off chasing the enemy cavalry."

"What's the problem?"

"Most of them are still there and they are charging," he looked back with an apprehensive look, "us! It looks like he has dropped us right in it."

"As usual, "muttered Decius.

"Form line! Cato! Agrippa! Stay here and keep pounding them. The rest of you, we have some cavalry the prefect kindly left for us to deal with." He waited until the men had dressed their ranks and drawing his sword, yelled, "Charge!"

The advantage the Pannonians had was that they were rested having just been stood. The Brigante had been fighting for some time; even so, they were closely matched. The prefect had charged off with almost eight hundred men chasing a small force of only two hundred. The one thousand warriors remaining outnumbered Marcus and his men. Still, they gave no thought to that. They were the Pannonian cavalry and they would emerge victorious.

Behind the legions, the General was cursing. "That damn fool of a prefect. He had one job to do; take out the cavalry and all he has done is to deprive me of half my cavalry and leave me wide open for a flank attack."

Just then an aide sent to investigate the rear returned. "Sir. There are thousands of barbarians in the rear and they have rafts in the river. They are trying to flank the Batavians."

"Prefect Demetrius, again! He has destroyed my reserve. Return to Prefect Strabo and ask him to hold for as long as possible, I will try to get some help." As the man rode off he turned to another aide, "You find Decurion Princeps Maximunius ask him to send some of his men to relieve Strabo." He saw the man's expression and said, "I know he is already engaged but he is all we have." He turned to the tribunes. "The prefect of cavalry has decided it for us; we attack." The buccina sounded and the general shouted above the din, "Men of the Ninth and Twentieth today we end this rebellion. Today we show these barbarians that it is not the number of men that win battles but quality and I have with me the best that Rome has to offer. Are you with me?" The roar could be heard across the battlefield and the two legions marched forward led by their general on a horse and the tribunes and centurions. The gambler had thrown the dice.

Chapter 17

Marcus heard the roar and the buccina from his right as his men thundered into the Brigante lines. He had no time to turn but he knew that the legions were committed. If he could not deflect this cavalry charge then the legions would be attacked on two sides. He had the advantage of the slope and the fact that his men still had two javelins. They had been trained well and they knew the perfect time to throw their missiles. They thundered over the open ground the short distance to the enemy. Marcus lowered his sword. Even as the first javelins left their hands they were preparing to use the second as a spear.

The first line of the Brigante crumpled under the impact of the missiles some hit horses which careered into others or crashed to the ground. Many hit warriors their iron tips taking them through the mail shirts they word. Once the Romans hit them it became a melee with every man for himself. Marcus had thrown both javelins preferring to use his long sword. He saw a war chief and headed for him roaring his challenge. The war chief saw the Decurion Princeps and recognised not only the soldier and his rank but, more importantly, the weapon. Every Brigante knew of the sword and longed to own the mystical weapon. Drawing the sword and waving it acted as a magnet for every warrior. They were all drawn to the Decurion Princeps who found himself surrounded by an avalanche of enemies. The war chief, a lieutenant of Aed's called Fachnan; saw this as an opportunity for greatness and glory. Aed would be watching with King Maeve and Fainch from behind the lines; he would kill this Roman, retrieve the sword and the battle would be theirs. It would become a song long sung! He lowered his spear and charged at Marcus who turned Argentium at the last minute to take the spear on his shield. He struck down with his sword and the blow was so hard it penetrated the mail and sliced into the war chief's shoulder. He roared in pain and anger and turned his own smaller mount to attack again. As he wheeled and hacked at his enemies, Argentium did his part kicking out and snapping with his teeth. Fachnan saw that Marcus was occupied with two foes and he thrust his spear at his unprotected back. Some sixth sense made the Decurion Princeps jerk Argentium's reins around and the spear sliced through the soft flesh of his upper left arm ripping away a piece of ragged flesh. Fachnan was committed to the thrust and as he came past the Roman, the sword of Cartimandua took his head off as cleanly as a knife through an apple. He had no time to rest for three more men came to claim the sword as their own. As the best warriors were attacking Marcus the rest of the turmae found that their enemies were not as strong and soon superior skill told.

Even as the enemy started to fall back Decius shouted, "Macro, Metellus help Marcus. Gaius, Lentius keep after them." The three decurions rushed to aid their beleaguered commander and not before time. Despite his best efforts his shield was almost splintered and was so useless as a defensive weapon that he threw it at one of his enemies and drew the gladius he carried instead of a knife. Ducking beneath the spear thrust at his head Marcus stabbed upwards catching the warrior beneath his jaw and penetrating his brain. Even as he withdrew his sword he deflected a second spear with his gladius. He was now surrounded and things would have gone badly but for the arrival of his chosen man, and the three decurions. Artorius saved Marcus' life but at the cost of his own. The sword which would have sliced through his neck found instead his chosen man's. Macro killed that warrior and a second as his blade continued its arc it seemed to sing in the air and the song it sang was death. Decius and Metellus also fought with a fury that few men could live with and soon the four of them sat on their heaving panting mounts in a sea of bodies. Their frenetic and frantic charge had broken the back of the barbarian cavalry. That added to the fact that their leader lay dead demoralized them completely. Before they could even draw breath the general's aide found them.

"Sir. The Governor has asked if you can relieve Prefect Strabo. He is being attacked."

Marcus looked at Decius who said despondently, "He can't expect you to go, sir. Look you are wounded." The blood was flowing freely from his leg and his arm but Marcus could tell they were neither fatal nor incapacitating.

"We can't let the Batavians down." He looked at his tired and exhausted men and then at the Batavians fighting for their very existence. "Macro, bring Agrippa and Cato. Metellus and Decius gather your turmae, Macro's and mine. We will have to manage with six turmae." As they rode off to carry out his commands Marcus looked at the main battle line. The two legions were almost at the enemy line. Much of the artillery was in pieces and the Batavians looked to be spent as a force. As he waited for the men to reform he glanced at the left flank. Gaius and Lentius were doing well but there was no sign of the other ala.

"Right men. It looks like we are doing the Batavians another favour. Two lines. Walk. "The two hundred troopers rode back through the deserted part of the battlefield towards the frantic conflict around the four camps. He could see men still fighting but there appeared to be a flood of barbarians. He turned to his Cornicen, "Give three blasts on your buccina to let them know we are coming." As the horn sounded Marcus noticed some of the Batavians turn around. It was little enough that they had done but it might give the prefect hope if he was still alive. His arm and his leg felt numb and in his body, he felt weary. He had had little sleep the previous night and the battle had taken much out of him. The thought came to him, however, that he would have to find an inner strength if he was to succeed and relieve Strabo. Even then it might not be enough. If the legions failed then all was lost.

The legions hit the barbarians as a solid block. Each man was touching the man next to him and the man behind held his scutum tight against his back. When they were close enough the centurions ordered them to throw their last javelin then they drew their killing weapon the gladius. There was no speed in their attack just sheet weight of men and armour. The front lines of the barbarians crumbled under the onslaught of javelins followed by men and swords. They could not reach the legionaries for they faced a solid line of shields. The gladii came under the shield to hamstring the warrior or over the shield to be thrust through face and brain or they were thrust between shields into the unarmoured midriff. They were a killing machine. The barbarians had thought to deny the Romans the opportunity to outflank them but they had merely played to the Roman strength and provided a battlefield with no exit. They were a relentless machine. When the centurions felt that the front rank was tiring they would order the passage of ranks and the second rank would come forward to become the front rank, the third the second and the first rank would rest a while as the third rank. The barbarians had no answer to this and they constantly faced fresh soldiers and the savage, slicing swords.

In the centre were the first centuries of the Ninth and Twentieth fighting side by side. Not only were these the biggest centuries in each legion they had the best men and the best centurions. They began to force their way through the battle line. They became the arrowhead and the flanks were pushed out. As the other centuries gained ground more and more of the barbarians found themselves at the edge of the river; whilst looking over their shoulders many of them were slain whilst others fell into the wide and icy cold river. If death was not instantaneous it was inevitable.

Above it all, the legionaries could hear the voices of Quintus Cerialis and Julius Agricola encouraging and leading. It made it easier to fight knowing your general was just as much in harm's way as you were. "Come on the Ninth one more push and these savages are in the sea. Heave!" Heartened by their commander and eager to be the ones to secure victory, they pushed and stabbed forward again and another rank of northern tribesmen fell slain at their feet.

Maeve, Fainch and Aed stood on a small knoll overlooking the field. There were two kings from the Caledonii with them and they were all unhappy about the battle. "Aed, your men where are they?"

"They obeyed orders sire. The first cavalrymen were led off by my men who appeared to retreat then Fachnan did as we ordered he charged the lines. It is just unfortunate that he did not manage to break through."

"It does not matter for the Novontae and Pictii will soon overwhelm their men at the back and nothing can stand in their way. They will attack those legions in the rear."

"Those legions are killing my men like reapers in a cornfield. Can nothing stop them?" The two kings of the Caledonii looked at each other. This was the first time they had seen the Roman war machine. When they had first seen the pitifully small numbers of Romans and the huge army of tribesmen they thought the battle would be over in the blink of an eye and then they had to watch the warriors slaughtered by artillery and missiles. Whatever the outcome of this battle, and both men were already planning their escape and that of their men, they would have to find some other way to defeat the Romans.

Furius Strabo looked around at his depleted command. His men had done well but all their javelins had been thrown and the ditches were now filled with barbarian bodies. The weight of the enemy had been upon the centre camps and it was here that the most casualties had fallen. Having begun the day with two hundred men in each camp, the two centre ones had less than one hundred and fifty. It mattered not if the two outer ones held, if the centre fell then it would be as a dam breaking and the flood would be a bloody and vengeful wall of weapons wielded by wild warriors. "Hold. We cannot let our brothers down. If we fall it means the end of the legions and the end of our Batavian comrades!" The appeal to their loyalty lifted their spirits and they fought with renewed energy forcing those who were next to the palisade back.

Marcus saw the parlous state the defences were in. The camps in the middle were almost over-run. The problem was that the ditches made it hard for his men to use their horses. He made a decision; Metellus, Agrippa and Cato keep your turmae harassing them with missile fire. The rest of you dismount. Horse holders take the horses away from the fight. Follow me."

Shouting for the Batavians to open the west gate Marcus led his men into the centre camps closer to the river. The other beleaguered camp was looking stronger and Marcus could see why, Furius Strabo was laying about him with an axe to great effect, obviously taken from a barbarian. "Macro take your turma. Kill any who are in the camp; I want it emptied of Brigante. The rest of you to the walls and stop any more warriors coming over!"

His men need no urging. All the training on foot with Macro and Agrippa in the gyrus at Derventio had paid dividends. They were just as confident on foot as mounted. They had muscles more powerful than their opponents and the tricks given to them gave them an edge over men who only fought for half the year and farmed the rest. The auxilia were professionals. Macro, especially, was in his element and none could stand before him. He used his shield as an extension of his mighty fist and he knocked unconscious the first warrior he met. He did not even pause and took a second in the throat. Around him, the troopers of his turma were inspired and began chanting Macro as they fell upon the hapless warriors caught in the middle of the camp. In the time it took for the rest of the ala to stand behind the palisade all those who had managed to get inside the fence were dead. The reinforcements brought dismay to the attackers who went from almost certain victory to ejection from the camp they had so nearly captured. Marcus turned to the nearest centurion who was heavily bandaged about the head. "How many men have you left?"

"Couldn't say exactly but no more than thirty."

"Then we have doubled your defenders." He shouted above the clash of arms. "Pannonians find any javelins and spears you can let us take the fight to them." His men looked around and quickly found missile weapons either thrown by the barbarians or dropped from the dead hands of defenders. The barbarians faltered in face of the renewed attack. Soon Cato's archers began to rain arrows down on them. Marcus shouted to his men, "Drive them from the palisade!" His troopers pushed with their shields and hacked down with their swords. Many of their enemies lacked shield and their fresh energy drove them back as they could not face the relentless wall of blades. As soon as they moved from the walls they became a target for the archers and so a gap of forty paces was cleared around the camp. For the moment the attack was stalled as the war chiefs rallied men and brought in fresh troops.

Marcus turned to his Cornicen. "Sound recall." The man looked at him as though deranged. "Just do it."

The three turmae who had been harassing the warriors suddenly rode into the camp. "Sir?"

"I know Agrippa you think me mad. But listen we cannot charge across ditches but in front of this gate and palisade, there is no ditch for it is filled with bodies. All we need to do is to get a little breathing space and hope the legions can win this battle quickly." The horse holders arrived. "Pannonians, mount!" The Batavian centurion looked aghast. "Do not worry. We are not deserting you; we are going to charge them." He pointed at the barbarians. "Open the gate!"

Superbly trained the column of twos following Marcus leapt the ditch and formed swiftly into two lines. The barbarians stood shocked. They had gone from attack to defence. What was worse was that they were in open formation. To the auxiliaries, it was almost like target practice. "Charge!"

Furius Strabo looked on in admiration as the pitifully small group of cavalry charged forward at what seemed to be a fast walk. His friend was doing all he could to stop the enemy from turning the tide of battle and Strabo was in no doubt, if they held, then the legions would win. The cavalry struck and stalled, the prefect could see that the enemy had surrounded the

179

cavalry who had turned their mounts outward to create a defensive circle. The Pannonians were going to die buying their comrades the time they needed to win the battle. He made a decision, turning to his Cornicen he shouted, "Sound form up!" The man looked confused. "Just do it!" he had seen that the attacks on the camps had stopped as the barbarians took their revenge on the cavalry who had thwarted their attack. "Sound the charge!" The five hundred men moved forward at double time which still enabled them to keep their cohesion. They were not pristine, smart legionaries for most were wounded and many had lost shields and pieces of armour but the prefect was proud of them nonetheless. They might not survive the battle but their sacrifice could win the battle for the Romans.

The barbarians whose backs were to the Batavians knew nothing of their impending doom. They were so engrossed in getting to these horse warriors that they assumed the movement behind was that of comrades. They were soon disillusioned as the Batavians carved their way through the vulnerable backs of warriors. In the press, in the middle, Marcus and his decurions were frantically moving around the shrinking circle of death to plug the gaps as men and horses fell.

Out of the blue, Decius shouted, "The Batavians they are attacking! Push forward." Marcus and the other decurions took heart and repeated the order. It was like a stone beginning an avalanche. The barbarians suddenly found enemies all around them and they began to fall back. Some of the Novontae looked at the Pannonians and remembered the stories of the slaughter they had inflicted last year on a raiding war band. For many, it was enough and they began to trickle away. As comrades saw them the trickle became a flood and soon the spent horsemen and weary infantry found themselves left with the dead and dying. The enemy had fled. Decius turned to Marcus, "There's still more of them than us. Why did they run?"

"Because we wouldn't give in and we wanted this more than they did. We were fighting for each other; they were fighting for someone they didn't know. That is why we will conquer this province Decius; they may have more men but we have better men. Had they been Carvetii or Brigante they might have stood longer but these warriors will just go home. We'll have to beat these another day." A heaving Prefect Furius Strabo, bleeding from minor wounds pushed his way towards Marcus, his arm outstretched. "Well, Prefect Strabo I think honours are even."

Strabo shook his head, "No my friend we are still very much in your debt. I thought we were insane but that was the maddest charge I have ever seen!" He turned to look towards the sea where the battle still raged. "I wonder how our friends are doing."

Over at the main battle, the solid line of legionaries was grinding forward. "Come on men we are nearly there. "Cerialis was actually enjoying himself.

He had dismounted from his wounded horse and was just behind the front rank. He turned to the nervous aide who felt that they should be much further back. "Ask Prefect Sura to move the remaining bolt throwers to our right flank and see if we can discourage them a little more." Gratefully the aide ran off eager to be away from the barbarians. Looking over at his fellow general the Governor saw that Agricola's men were doing just as well as his. They were not moving at a fast speed but the two legions were inexorably driving the barbarians back and the further back they went the nearer they were to a hostile sea and a wide, deep river. The tribes still outnumbered the Romans but the battlefield meant they could not bring all those numbers to bear.

On the knoll, the two Caledonii had left. Only Fainch had noted their departure. She glanced over her shoulder to the small fishing boat pulled up on the beach; should things go awry she had her escape already planned. When Maeve and Aed did notice the missing warriors it was because the Caledonii warriors were funnelling and fleeing through a small gap on their left flank. Had they been more aggressive they might have tried to turn the Romans but they knew the battle was over and were bent on escaping across the river on the crude rafts moored on the south bank by the Novontae who had used them. Those same Novontae were now fleeing east to find the nearest ford. They could have walked for Marcus and his men were in no state to pursue.

Quintus Cerialis saw the departing tribesmen and knew the battle would soon be over. He had two cohorts in reserve and now was the time to use them. He turned to his aide who was already out of breath having delivered his message to Marcus. "I want the reserves to attack the right flank immediately. Let us end this battle now." The man sped off his horse already flecked with sweat and saliva. Julius, push harder they are breaking." Without lifting his head Agricola nodded and continued to hack at the enemy warriors who were being slaughtered with ease.

Many miles to the south the prefect finally ordered the recall. He was exhilarated. He had chased, harried and killed many of the mailed cavalry spoken about in such reverential terms. They had proved to be an insignificant and unworthy foe. He could not believe they had run so easily. If all the enemy were like this in Britannia then his ala alone could destroy them and conquer all of the province. He would only need legions for forts! As his turmae returned he noticed with some pleasure but a stoic face, that both his sons had survived; indeed he could not see any casualties amongst his decurions. They had lost minimal numbers of troopers and that was mainly because they had tripped in the woods or fallen in the difficult terrain. He made a mental note to increase the riding training. It had been the most successful day of the Demetrius family. They had won honour at last; he would be bound to receive a crown. He had his route right back to Rome, he would return a conquering hero.

"Well, boys how was your first battle?"

"Wonderful! It is a pity there were not more of them," Fabius had a grin from ear to ear.

"They seemed very eager to flee father, perhaps we should have returned to the battle. They were running not fighting."

"Nonsense Julius. Our task was to eliminate their cavalry and we did. And they only ran because we were so good. You must learn to be like your brother, be less modest. You have done well, you have both done well. You should be proud."

Quintus Saenius rode up, "Not all of them ran sir. There seemed to me to be more left on the battlefield than ran."

"Ridiculous decurion. There may have been a few isolated groups left on the field but I am sure the other ala dealt with them. Right, let us go back and celebrate our victory." He turned to Fabius. "I will stay with the ala you ride on and inform the Governor of our great victory."

Aed was becoming nervous. The Romans were on the point of breaking through. He turned to Fainch. "All is lost."

If he expected her to disagree with him he was wrong, she took him to one side, the King still viewing with increasing dismay his diminishing forces. "Take your bodyguard and return to the land of the lakes. Your men can act as a magnet for the survivors of this battle. You are right the battle is lost but we have not lost the war. Leave the king now for he will die on this field and that will leave you as the only legitimate ruler of the Brigante. There will be other survivors and they will come to you"

"And you?"

"I will return to Mona and join my sisters. Now that the rebellion has started we can cause more mischief from there."

"But how will you get there?"

She pointed to the waiting fishing boat bobbing in the surf. "Now go!" She turned to the king. "There is one more chance oh mighty king. If you and your bodyguard attack now it will give the men hope and you still have enough men to defeat them. Your men have killed many Romans and you still outnumber them."

He did not look convinced. "Do you really think we can still win?"

"I know so and I can see it; it is written in the earth."

He looked around anxiously and saw Aed and his men heading south. "Where is Aed going?"

"I have sent him to attack the Romans on this side. He will die so that you and your bodyguard can gain a glorious victory."

"I will reward him when we are victorious. Come, men. The King goes to war." With a roar, the bodyguard and oathsworn charged forward. His men heard the roar and took heart, perhaps they could still win. Men who had been on the brink of surrender or flight stood their ground and faced these relentless Romans.

For the Romans, the gesture was like taking a beaker to put out a forest fire. They were not going to be stopped. The first centuries of the two legions were determined they would have the victory. They saw the standard of the King of the Brigante and the two centuries renewed their efforts. The men they were fighting were exhausted and in no condition to fight the ruthless killing machine. They fell even faster until the legionaries came face to face with the bodyguard of the King. These men were fresh and these men were oathsworn. They would never run.

Pontius Glabrio, the first spear of the Twentieth picked out the biggest warrior he could see. He was a huge man with a conical helmet, a war axe and a round shield. His upper body was naked but for the torque and the spirals of silver hanging from his braids. His body was painted and tattooed. Shouting in bad Latin he roared at the centurion, "You die today, Roman!" The men behind, pushing to get into the battle looked on in eager anticipation. Craiftin was, as his name suggested, like a fox and very cunning. The contest was an anti-climax but it sucked the heart out of the others for Glabrio punched the man in the stomach with the boss of his scutum and as he reeled forward, winded he sliced across the big warrior's throat with his razor-sharp sword. Until he fought this warrior he had only used the point and the edge was not dulled. The warrior was dead before he hit the ground. The legionaries charged forward and the Brigante fell further back.

Not to be outdone Rufius Vetus, the First Spear of the Ninth, began to hack his way towards the king. By now the bodyguards were losing heart; Craiftin was the best that they had and he had been dispatched so easily that they knew they could not win. They were still fighting but they did not believe they could win; they were fighting because they had sworn to do so. The last few before the king fell quickly until Rufius stood facing the king. He looked every bit a king; he was totally encased in polished and silvered armour with a fine helmet embossed with gold. His breastplate gleamed with gold and silver and the sword he wielded was decorated with jewels. The King kept his shield up and smashed his blade down on Rufius' scutum. The blow was hard but all the training over the years had made the centurion's arm like an oaken branch. Heaving forward on his shield the centurion pushed hard and the king toppled over like a tortoise. Had it not been a battle, had it not been momentous, had it not been a pivotal moment it might have been laughable. He did not have any time to get back up nor the strength. The centurion sliced into the abdomen of the king and then moved on to the next man.

Fainch was on the boat when the king received his wound. Her plan had not totally succeeded but she had achieved her aim; Mona was free and the Romans had been driven from the west. The bigger plan and the bigger picture were more important than one battle. She cared nothing that the north was now firmly under the Roman heel; for her, it was all about the mother and all about her beliefs. Mona and the sisterhood were worth more than any man or any kingdom.

When the king fell and the bodyguards were slaughtered, the Brigante, the Carvetii and the Novontae who remained threw down their weapons.

Quintus Petilius Cerialis shouted, "Cease!" to prevent further slaughter. This was not altruism but pragmatism; legionaries might die and he needed every legionary to rescue Britannia. He also knew that as slaves they would help to pay for this expensive war. He turned to an aide, "Send for the two Batavian prefects and the Decurion princeps, Marcus Aurelius Maximunius." He paused, "Oh and when the prefect of cavalry returns have him placed under arrest."

Chapter 18

Aed had barely three hundred men as he sped south. He counted on the fact that some of his diversionary force would have survived and he would find them but he had survived that was the important matter. He had also helped eliminate any other contenders for the succession of the Brigante throne. This was a setback, nothing more. He rested his men in a glade through which the path passed. It provided good shelter from prying eyes and he wanted his men rested. They were far enough from the battlefield to be safe. His only worry was the cavalry unit who had pursued his men. Some of them could be quite close. "Feed your horses but no talking. We need silence."

He stiffened as his scout returned. "Sir Roman cavalry."

"How many?"

"Thirty, thirty-five. Hard to say they are moving quickly."

"Have they scouts out?"

"No lord."

Aed quickly made a decision. The path he would take led from this main path. He could not allow a turma to be in his rear and he did not know where the rest of the ala were. This turma would die. All of them. "Half that side of the path; the other half with me. Wait for my signal. No one leaves the glade alive."

Fabius was elated. He had fought in his first battle and emerged triumphantly. True, most of the enemies he had killed had had their backs to him but he had killed two in the initial charge. He was not certain how but the man tumbled from his horse with a wound so he was truly a warrior and soon when the Governor lavished decorations and honours upon them he would be a hero as well. His men behind him were just looking forward to looting the bodies on the battlefield. They were unhappy at the speed with which he was taking them through these woods but that speed meant they would get to the battlefield before their comrades some miles behind them and with luck, the dead would still lie where they fell.

The first they knew of the ambush was when their decurion's body flew from his horse run through by three spears. Before the last pair could turn around they were unceremoniously stabbed and hacked from their mounts. After that, it was when and not if they died. Mercifully for these butchers of women and children they did not suffer long. Not a single Brigante suffered a wound. Although he was short of time Aed could not resist a cruel gesture. "Strip the bodies and mount their heads on spears." Less than five minutes later every living thing had left the glade and all that remained was thirty-six naked and despoiled bodies and thirty-six heads adorning spears and marking the path.

Aed and his men disappeared south to surface in the land of the lakes as the only survivors of the Brigante army. They would become the nucleus for the next army to fight the Romans.

The Governor had had a small tent erected by the time his guests arrived. As each man arrived he clasped them by the forearm. When Strabo and Maximunius arrived the whole of the staff, including the Governor applauded. Strabo looked bemused whilst Marcus looked embarrassed. They both looked in a sorry state; Marcus had a heavily bandaged arm and leg while Strabo looked comical with a huge bandage around his head and another, seeping blood from his middle. "I am forever in your debt. Prefect Strabo had you not held the line my legions might not have had the complete victory which now lies in our hands. I intend to nominate you for a gold crown." They all looked in amazement for such an honour was rarely awarded. "No, you deserve it. Never let it be said that auxiliaries are inferior to legionaries. You have proved the valour beyond any doubt."

Strabo looked at the general, "I for one would never have said that. Sir."

There was an embarrassed silence and the Cerialis let out the loudest laugh anyone had heard him utter.

"Quite right too! Decurion Princeps what can I say to you? You did everything I asked and then more. Three charges! Gentlemen, have you ever seen three charges by auxiliary cavalry? Sorry three successful charges?" They all laughed. "If only your prefect had had the same sense of duty. Your wounds speak well of your honour. I am, especially in your debt. Is there anything you need? My surgeon perhaps?"

"No sir, I am fine but there is one thing you could do for me."

The governor and the whole assembly looked at the Decurion Princeps for they all knew it was not in his nature to ask for things." Yes, what is it?"

"There was a witch advising the King. Did she survive? Or have you found her body?"

Cerialis looked around at his aides. "No sir no women but the king still lives. He will die but he lives for the moment."

"Could I be permitted...?"

"Of course. You take him to the man."

Clasping arms with Strabo and Sura, Marcus bowed to the Governor and then left with the aide." I think I shall request more auxiliaries they are so useful." A cheeky smile played over his face. "And cheaper."

Everyone laughed and then Furius added, "Until you have to buy a round!"

Marcus smiled as he heard the laughs. It could have all ended so differently; he and Strabo and all of his decurions could be corpses but they had had the Allfather supporting them and they had survived. Now if the Allfather willed it he would find out what happened to Fainch.

The King was grey and ashen. As he entered the legionaries recognised him and saluted, respect apparent in every fibre of their being. One of them shook his head. "King Maeve."

The king opened his eyes. "You are the one. I saw you. You killed my cavalry."

"Yes, king I did."

"You are the one with the sword, the sword of Cartimandua." Marcus nodded. "You are a warrior and I salute you."

"King Maeve, what happened to Fainch the witch?"

His face became infused with anger. "That bitch tricked me."

"Where is she?"

"She escaped. I think she had a boat."

"Where will she go?"

"To Mona." Suddenly the eyes became clear. "You will find her?" Marcus nodded. The king took off his torque; the pain was obvious. "I give you this. Kill her and I will be revenged. Kill her and you will be revenged for she ordered the deaths of your wife, sister and son. Swear it. Swear it on the sword."

Gripping the sword in both hands he intoned. "I swear she will die."

"Good," he relaxed, now I can go to the Allfather. Please, let me have your sword for my journey..."

The legionaries' hands went to their gladii but Marcus shook his head and placed the sword of Cartimandua in the king's hand. He held it, sighed and then King Maeve of the Brigante died.

As Marcus took the sword from the dead man's hand one of the legionaries said, "You took a chance, sir. He could have gutted you."

"No, for he worships the same god I do. He believes that if he dies with a sword in his hand he will be reunited with his comrades in the next world. Do you really think he would have slain me?"

Neither legionaries nor aide had an answer to that but the aide said, "Sir Will you kill that woman, Fainch?"

"Fainch the witch? Oh yes, she will die the next time I see her. Believe me, she will die and die at my hands."

The ice in his voice and the intensity in his eyes convinced the three men that Decurion Princeps Marcus Aurelius Maximunius would carry out the sentence of death.

As the men saluted and Marcus left he suddenly realised that he had sworn an oath to another dying man. He shook his head and smiled the grim smile of the ultimate reaper. He had sworn the same oath to Ulpius Felix and over the graves of his family. This was no new oath this was his purpose this was his life.

187

The object of the oath was even now sailing serenely south planning her next campaign against the Romans. The fact that her plan had not totally succeeded did not worry her at all. The main part had and that was the important matter. She had her own tame putative king in Aed and when the time was ripe she would use him as a thorn in the Roman's side. He was still bewitched, still entrapped. Once the west was back in Druid hands she would turn her attention to the far north. They had been even more in awe of her than the Brigante. She would bewitch them too. Her laugh carried over the empty bay and echoed like the crying of the gulls. The sailors clutched at their amulets. The sooner the witch was delivered the better.

The irony was that it was the prefect who first chanced upon the scene of the massacre and the first head he saw was that of his son. The shock silenced him and the blood drained from his face. He had placed all his hopes and all his efforts on his eldest son and his life had been snuffed out like a candle. He sat on his horse with his head drooped, silent tears coursing down his cheeks. The troopers looked around for command and it was a Demetrius who took command, Julius Demetrius. "Septimus, Vettius, Marcus get those heads from the spears. You men find their bodies." The young man seemed to grow in that instant and change from the youth to the man. "Father." He put his arm around his father's shoulder and held him as the prefect sobbed out his grief.

By the time the bodies were laid out his father had straightened up. "I'm fine now." Looking at his only son he said simply, "Thank you, son."

"I think it best, father if we burn the bodies here. It would not be right for them to be seen this way by others." As his father nodded Julius again gave orders, "Quintus build a pyre. We will honour our fallen comrades."

As the afternoon drifted into the evening the battlefield was cleared. Bodies were piled up; the Brigante into one mass grave and the Romans into pyres of their dead comrades. A pen was built to contain the prisoners and the surgeons worked long and hard to save men, legionaries and auxiliaries. Gaius was with Marcus who was being stitched up when he saw the smoke. "Marcus in the woods to the far south, smoke."

Wincing with the pain Marcus said, "I wonder what that can be. Gaius take your turma out and investigate." He saw the tiredness in his friend's eyes. "I know you are tired and so are your horses but yours is the only turma with anywhere near a full complement of men and horses."

Smiling Gaius said, "Yes sir."

Decius who was in the next cot having a wound to his ribs being bandaged looked up. "That lad has grown up."

"We all have Decius."

188

When the orderlies had left them Decius spoke in a quiet voice to the Decurion Princeps. "Those bodies we found close to Brocavum?"

"Yes, Decius I know. I had put it from my mind. The only units who could have committed such an act were the turmae of Fabius and Modius. I will speak to the prefect when he arrives. I would like to keep this in house if possible."

"I know but it isn't right that all the good lads, the lads who lie out there dead, should be tarred with the same brush as those…"

"Even so. We keep this in house. Understood?"

"Understood."

When Gaius found them his comrades from the other ala were preparing to leave. He was surprised at just how many had survived. As he glanced around he could see that only Fabius was missing and the prefect looked like a man who has suddenly added twenty years to his life. He edged his mount towards the prefect but Julius intercepted him and placed his hand on his reins. "Not now Gaius."

"What happened?"

"Here?" Gaius nodded. "Fabius was ambushed and killed along with his whole turma. Their heads placed on spears. My father found them."

"Aed."

"What?"

"It was Aed who did this, we saw him escape with some of his men from the battle. The spears were the long Brigante ones." Julius nodded. "Then it was Aed. We have a score to settle with him."

"Then the battle…"

"We won. It was a close-run thing." He lowered his voice, "The Governor is not happy that the prefect took half his cavalry chasing a few Brigante all over the countryside. I fear he is in for a hard time when we return."

"I too felt it wrong to follow them but my father and brother… They wanted the glory."

"Now that they have it do you think they will feel it was worth it?" As the two decurions looked at the shell of the man who had been prefect their views were obvious.

By the time that the Pannonian cavalry returned to camp, it was almost dark. The pyres were still burning but the legions and auxiliaries were safely in their camps. The barbarians might have been defeated but the general was taking no chances. He did not want to lose a single more man. One of his aides rushed in, "Sir. The Pannonians. They have been sighted."

Cerialis' eyes hardened. "I want to see the prefect as soon as he arrives."

The Governor and Julius Agricola were studying maps when the prefect reported. They were keen to find a way to get down to Mona and put down all traces of the rebellion there for it was obvious from King Maeve's dying words and the intelligence from prisoners that the priests and priestess from that corrupt cult had been instrumental in the uprising.

"You sent for me sir."

The dull flat tones alerted the Governor that something had happened. When he looked up he had to look twice to make sure he was looking at the same arrogant, cocksure patrician who had left the briefing that morning with such confidence. "Gods man what has happened?"

Before he could answer there was a slight commotion outside and then a heavily bandaged Marcus burst in. "Sorry to interrupt sir but it is important."

The general waved away the sentries. "It had better be young man. If you had not been so brave today you would be enduring a flogging now."

"Sir I have just heard that the prefect's son was killed in an ambush on their way back to the camp. He and his whole turma wiped out. I thought you should know before you er, interviewed the prefect who is obviously distressed."

"Ah. Yes, I see." He looked thoughtfully at the Decurion Princeps. "There is more to you than meets the eye. I will see you tomorrow when you have rested. You can leave the prefect with me." The look on his face showed that he would brook no further comments. "Go back to the sick bay man before you fall over." Glancing at the prefect Marcus left. The prefect had the same dull look on his face as though he had not heard a word. "Perfect, I sympathise with your loss and I will make this as brief as possible so that you may grieve properly with Decurion Demetrius however I would be failing in my duty if I did not tell you that you are facing serious charges of dereliction of duty. Today we almost lost a battle because of your vanity and were it not for that young man who just left we would have done so. Now go and I will see you in the morning."

Marcus had disobeyed the general again and was waiting for the prefect outside of the tent. "I am sorry to hear of your loss sir. I know what it is to lose a son and to lose one in such a cruel manner."

The prefect looked up almost seeing Marcus for the first time. "I did not know such pain could exist. How did, how do you cope?"

"You don't sir. It never goes away. It is always that empty part of you that can never be filled. The only thoughts which bring relief are those of the happy times and you sir, well you still have a son and if I might make so bold a good son." He paused, "Perhaps sir a better son than you know."

The old Rufius appeared for a moment in the prefect's eyes and then subsided. "You are probably correct. Impertinent but correct thank you Decurion Princeps."

The Pannonian camp was a little quieter than it had been. With their losses, it had been deemed more effective to build one camp. There were two tents for the decurions of the two alae and Marcus made for that of his own decurions. As he entered a very flushed and half-drunk Decius waved a wineskin at him. "Result sir. Furius sent over some lovely wine, said he preferred ale."

"Do you know, Decius, I might just join you."

There was a small roar as he sat down amongst his comrades. They all looked around when the tent flap opened and Julius put his head through. "Sorry sir I will see you later I don't want to…"

"Come in Julius. You are amongst friends here. Join us." The tone in Gaius' voice was reassuring and inviting and the young decurion sat down.

After toasting the ala Julius said to Marcus, "I just wanted to thank you for what you did for the pre… for my father neither he nor my brother treated you well and it shows your nobility."

Marcus shook his head. "I would do the same for any man in this ala for we are all brothers. We might not like each other but we are brothers. You know that. You did not always see eye to eye with your brother but you would have defended him with your life and you grieve for him do you not?" Julius' eyes began to well up and he nodded unable to speak. "So you understand eh? You are one of us now. We are your family."

They all drank and ate and talked of the day Macro relived every blow thrust jink of his horse in excruciating detail. This would normally have annoyed or irritated the others but his heroics of the day had meant that they forgave him his idiosyncrasies and treated him as a rambunctious little brother. When there was a silence Lentius spoke. "Have you mentioned to the prefect about the incident near Brocavum?"

As soon as the other decurions looked at him Julius spoke. "What incident?" They all looked down. "From your looks, I fear it concerns my brother but the Decurion Princeps said I am one of you. Will you not share?"

As they all shuffled around looking embarrassed there was a movement outside. Modius had come looking for Julius. He had already found himself isolated amongst the others now that Fabius was dead and he was clinging to the idea that Julius might become his brother. When there was silence he halted unsure of what to do. So it was that he heard the revelation.

Metellus spoke, "We found women and children murdered and mutilated just outside of Brocavum. It had to have been Pannonians and …"

"And the only units that were there were my brother's and that of Modius. Yes, I remember they were sent ahead to scout the stronghold but they returned with a few warrior's heads."

"Aye well, those few warriors were protecting almost fifty woman children and old men."

Outside Modius froze with fear but he stayed to hear more. "What will you do, Decurion Princeps?"

There was a silence and then Modius heard Marcus reply to Julius' question. "It did not seem right to burden the prefect with the accusation today but when he is over his grieving, or as much over as one can be, I will tell him for Modius must be questioned and, if necessary punished."

The drunken voice of Decius rose loudly, "And this time I will flog him and I won't hold back this time."

Modius waited to hear no more. He would be punished and that he could bear, just, but he could now return to the ranks as a trooper. He had made too many enemies and he would suffer. There was but one answer he would flee. He had seen the direction the Brigante cavalry had taken. He would join them. He was certain he would have information which would be to their advantage and he would leave a rich man for he knew where Fabius and the turma had hidden their loot after all he had been one of them. Added to his own it would enable him to buy allies if the Brigante chose not to enlist him. Without a further look, he gathered his loot and belongings and slipped out of the camp for the sentries were too tired to notice the shadow leaving; they were too focussed on barbarians arriving, uninvited.

Epilogue

The next day Rufius Demetrius stood in front of the general. He looked less ashen but still shocked. Marcus stood behind him as next in line. The two Batavian prefects and Julius Agricola, who looked decidedly uncomfortable, sat next to Cerialis.

The Governor's voice was quiet and measured as though he was controlling his emotions out of respect for a grieving father. "Prefect we have laid serious charges at your door. You were ordered to drive the enemy from the field and protect the left flank. You chose to disobey your orders. Why?"

The prefect stood tall and straight. "I believed I had followed my orders and I believed that we were doing what auxiliary cavalry do best pursuing the enemy from the field."

The general became irritable in his tone. "I might accept your explanation if you had halted when they left the immediate battlefield but you pursued them long after they ceased to pose a threat."

"I have no answer for that. I suppose I believed that we would not be needed. I know now that that was not true."

"You place me in a difficult position."

"Perhaps I can make amends, sir?"

"Go on."

"I will tender my resignation and retire from public life. To be truthful, sir, my heart is no longer in soldiering."

Cerialis looked at the other prefects and Agricola all of whom nodded gratefully for the prefect had given them all an honourable and clean way out. "In that case, I accept your resignation."

"There is one more thing, sir."

"Yes?"

"I have to report that one of my decurions has deserted. Modius Varro."

"That's all we needed. Right, you had better send out men to look for him but don't spend too long." The Governor realised he had addressed his words to the prefect. "Sorry Decurion Princeps. Would you send out men to look for him for the prefect will be gathering his belongings? I take it you will run the alae until I can appoint another prefect?"

"Yes sir."

The prefect turned to leave and grasped Marcus' hand. "Thank you. The alae are in good hands."

"And Decurion Princeps we will soon need all your men if we are to end this rebellion."

Mona

The small fishing boat edged its way around the headland to the tiny bay that was Porthdafarch. Glad to be rid of the witch they worked the boat to the pebbly beach under the low cliffs. As soon as she saw the shallows Fainch leapt into the icy, salty waters. Even as the boat was working its way offshore the gaggle of women raced down to embrace their sister. "At last my sisters we are free. Now we will make the whole of Britannia free."

Land of the lakes

Modius sat on his horse before Aed and the warriors who had surrounded him as he watered his horse. "Were you so confident Roman that we would not kill you out of hand?"

"As you had followed me for some time to make sure I was alone I knew that you could have killed me anytime you wished. I was confident you would want to know what I had to offer."

"And what could I possibly want from you Roman?"

"My sword and my knowledge for I know the Pannonians and I know that you have never beaten them. With my knowledge and your men I can show you how to beat them."

Aed looked at the powerful warrior. He needed to build up his war band again and the man's knowledge might prove the difference. "Very well but if you are a traitor…" leaving the threat hanging the war band headed back into the hills and forests of this natural stronghold.

Brocavum

"So gentlemen we will leave the first Batavians here where they will fortify the stronghold. The second will return to Morbium and the Ninth back to Eboracum. The Pannonians, the twentieth and the Second Adiutrix will go to Mona to crush this rebellion." He paused for questions; there were none. "I know that we had a little luck in this campaign but I would like to believe that we had more courage and military skill. Remember that as General Agricola leads you to a final victory."

As the Pannonian cavalry led off the column south Decius turned to the acting prefect. "Do you think we will find her?"

"Find who?"

"Don't give me that vague look. You know who I mean. As soon as the general said Mona your face lit up. You know that's where you will find your witch."

"I still don't know what she looks like and there is no one alive who knows what she looks like."

"There is Aed."

"There is Aed."

"And we will have to travel through the land of the lakes who knows you may find him but don't you worry about that witch. You might not know her she knows you and something in these old bones tells me that she has not finished with you yet."

"Then that suits us both for I can only fulfil my oaths to the dead when she dies, at my hands."

Author's note

This is a work of fiction. I have however used certain places from Roman Britain as the places they would inhabit. Derventio and Morbium were two cavalry forts, Malton and Piercebridge respectively. I have used other places which would have existed, such as Streonshal (Whitby) to flesh out the local aspect of the novel. Where possible I have used the Roman names for places. Although Colonia came later on as the Romans had been in the province for over thirty years I have used Isurium Brigantium as an early, informal Colonia. When Stanwyck was destroyed by Cerialis the local administrative capital was moved to what is now Aldborough St. John, which is less than two miles from Stanwyck and has extensive Roman remains. Stanwyck itself still exists and is a magnificent Iron Age fort and well worth a visit.

Quintus Petilius Cerialis was a real figure and a very aggressive general. He gambled during battles but his men loved him. He used oratory to inspire them much as Henry V at Agincourt. He had been prefect of the ninth when Boudicca rebelled. Agricola returned to Britannia many times and eventually conquered, albeit briefly, the whole of the island. Mona was recaptured by the locals sometime in the early seventies; the actual event is not recorded but Agricola had to recapture the island in the mid-seventies. The priests and priestesses of Mona were feared by the Romans as was the far west of the country. Roman legions threatened to mutiny rather than venture that far. Eostre was the goddess of rebirth and fertility although she had a number of names. She was celebrated in the spring and the Christians hijacked this festival to coincide with Easter. It would have been a significant event in Iron Age Britain for the winters were very harsh and the goddess would need to be appeased to ensure bounty for the coming year. There was a great deal of unrest on the borders of the province towards the end of the 1st century although the southeast had largely been civilised or quite possibly ethnically cleansed after the Iceni revolt. The Classis Britannica was the Roman fleet based in the south of Britannia. It was used by Julius Agricola in his campaign in Scotland to circumnavigate and prove that Britain was an island and to support his legions.

Although we know for certain which legions fought in Northern Britain we are less certain about the auxiliary units. The Pannonians and the Batavians were both stationed in Britannia during the first and second centuries AD. I have used artistic licence to base my story around these units. The foot units were organised on the basis of the legion with centuries and centurions. The nominal commander was the prefect but as in the legions, the real leader was Prima Pila or First Spear. The cavalry was organised in turmae (singular – turma) - a unit of between 32 and 40 troopers under the command of a decurion. In each ala, or wing, there would have been a Decurion Princeps, the equivalent of a prima pilum. The whole unit would have been commanded by a prefect. There were also sergeants in both the legions and auxiliary who carried out training etc and had specific roles. The Cornicens were the men who signalled with the buccina. They tended to be as with the signifiers a brave set of men who fought and acted as the focus of the enemy's attack.

This is the second book set in Britannia and telling the tale of the Pannonian cavalry. The third will tell of the invasion of Scotland under Julius Agricola.

Other books by Griff Hosker

If you enjoyed reading this book, then why not read another one by the author?

Ancient History

The Sword of Cartimandua Series
(Germania and Britannia 50 A.D. – 128 A.D.)
Ulpius Felix- Roman Warrior (prequel)
The Sword of Cartimandua
The Horse Warriors
Invasion Caledonia
Roman Retreat
Revolt of the Red Witch
Druid's Gold
Trajan's Hunters
The Last Frontier
Hero of Rome
Roman Hawk
Roman Treachery
Roman Wall
Roman Courage

The Wolf Warrior series
(Britain in the late 6th Century)
Saxon Dawn
Saxon Revenge
Saxon England
Saxon Blood
Saxon Slayer
Saxon Slaughter
Saxon Bane
Saxon Fall: Rise of the Warlord
Saxon Throne
Saxon Sword

Medieval History

The Dragon Heart Series
Viking Slave

Viking Warrior
Viking Jarl
Viking Kingdom
Viking Wolf
Viking War
Viking Sword
Viking Wrath
Viking Raid
Viking Legend
Viking Vengeance
Viking Dragon
Viking Treasure
Viking Enemy
Viking Witch
Viking Blood
Viking Weregeld
Viking Storm
Viking Warband
Viking Shadow
Viking Legacy
Viking Clan
Viking Bravery

The Norman Genesis Series
Hrolf the Viking
Horseman
The Battle for a Home
Revenge of the Franks
The Land of the Northmen
Ragnvald Hrolfsson
Brothers in Blood
Lord of Rouen
Drekar in the Seine
Duke of Normandy
The Duke and the King

New World Series
Blood on the Blade
Across the Seas
The Savage Wilderness
The Bear and the Wolf
Erik the Navigator

The Vengeance Trail

The Danelaw Saga
The Dragon Sword

The Reconquista Chronicles
Castilian Knight
El Campeador
The Lord of Valencia

The Aelfraed Series
(Britain and Byzantium 1050 A.D. - 1085 A.D.)
Housecarl
Outlaw
Varangian

The Anarchy Series England
1120-1180
English Knight
Knight of the Empress
Northern Knight
Baron of the North
Earl
King Henry's Champion
The King is Dead
Warlord of the North
Enemy at the Gate
The Fallen Crown
Warlord's War
Kingmaker
Henry II
Crusader
The Welsh Marches
Irish War
Poisonous Plots
The Princes' Revolt
Earl Marshal

Border Knight
1182-1300
Sword for Hire

Return of the Knight
Baron's War
Magna Carta
Welsh Wars
Henry III
The Bloody Border
Baron's Crusade
Sentinel of the North
War in the West
Debt of Honour (May 2021)

Sir John Hawkwood Series
France and Italy 1339- 1387
Crécy: The Age of the Archer
Man at Arms
The White Company (July 2021)

Lord Edward's Archer
Lord Edward's Archer
King in Waiting
An Archer's Crusade
Targets of Treachery (Due out August 2021)

Struggle for a Crown
1360- 1485
Blood on the Crown
To Murder A King
The Throne
King Henry IV
The Road to Agincourt
St Crispin's Day
The Battle for France

Tales from the Sword I

Conquistador
England and America in the 16th Century
Conquistador (Coming in 2021)

Modern History

The Napoleonic Horseman Series
Chasseur à Cheval
Napoleon's Guard
British Light Dragoon
Soldier Spy
1808: The Road to Coruña
Talavera
The Lines of Torres Vedras
Bloody Badajoz
The Road to France
Waterloo (June 2021)

The Lucky Jack American Civil War series
Rebel Raiders
Confederate Rangers
The Road to Gettysburg

The British Ace Series
1914
1915 Fokker Scourge
1916 Angels over the Somme
1917 Eagles Fall
1918 We will remember them
From Arctic Snow to Desert Sand
Wings over Persia

Combined Operations series
1940-1945
Commando
Raider
Behind Enemy Lines
Dieppe
Toehold in Europe
Sword Beach
Breakout
The Battle for Antwerp
King Tiger
Beyond the Rhine
Korea
Korean Winter

Tales from the Sword Book 2

Other Books

Great Granny's Ghost (Aimed at 9-14-year-old young people)

For more information on all of the books then please visit the author's website at www.griffhosker.com where there is a link to contact him or visit his Facebook page: GriffHosker at Sword Books

Made in United States
Orlando, FL
14 October 2022

23401181R00121